Death underfoot

Brash, provocative, scarred, but undeniably sensual, and thus a threat to many wives, Diana Farwell exuded a powerful aura of mystery and danger.

So when her first excursion on her return to Africa after a few years' absence ended in her hideous death at a game-viewing lodge in Kenya, questions were immediately posed about her past and her evident familiarity with not a few of the males at the lodge party that fatal night.

To Inspector James Odhiambo of the Nairobi CID Diana's death stank strongly of murder. A jealous husband or lover from the modern Happy Valley set? Or someone who fears resurrection of the past?

The authorities need an instant scapegoat and a quick solution to an embarrassing incident which could harm Kenya's flourishing tourist trade.

A hasty arrest leads to another fatality, and soon the political pressures threaten to overcome the highly competent and incorruptible Odhiambo, putting his marriage, future career and even safety at risk.

A savage panga attack on a respected white lawyer and a mysterious boat trip to Entebbe, revealing the extent of Mrs Farwell's shadowy past, lead Odhiambo to the solution and a final dramatic encounter with a horrifying conclusion.

With his extensive knowledge of Africa and his deep sympathy with its people, Dennis Casley has written an impressive first crime novel about corruption, blackmail, revenge and murder.

DEATH UNDERFOOT

Dennis Casley

Constable · London

First published in Great Britain 1993
by Constable & Company Ltd
3 The Lanchesters, 162 Fulham Palace Road
London W6 9ER
Copyright © 1993 by Dennis Casley
The right of Dennis Casley to be
identified as the author of this work
has been asserted by him in accordance
with the Copyright, Designs and Patents Act 1988
ISBN 0 09 472190 4
Set in Linotron Palatino 10 pt by
CentraCet Limited, Cambridge
Printed in Great Britain by
St Edmundsbury Press Limited
Bury St Edmunds, Suffolk

A CIP catalogue record for this book
is available from the British Library

1

The verandah provided a splendid view of the Ngong Hills, poised like a giant's knuckle behind the well-watered lawn, the flamboyant trees and flowering bushes that provided such colour to the suburban homes of the prosperous residents of Nairobi: of whom, even some twenty years after Kenya's independence, a substantial proportion remained white.

Peter Shropshire reached into the small refrigerator situated under the verandah bar. He was of above average height, and his girth, at the age of forty-nine, reflected all the years of sundowners and other excuses for alcoholic consumption that are a common feature of expatriate life in the tropics. However, as he moved with the drinks towards his guests, his step was still light, befitting a winner of the seniors' tennis championship, open to those past their forty-fifth birthday.

'Haven't drowned the gin, but I'll leave the bottles in case you want a little more tonic.'

Diana and Morgan Farwell accepted the proffered glasses and waited while their host retrieved the remaining glasses from the bar. Shropshire handed a vermouth and soda to his wife without a word, clutched his own glass and turned back to the Farwells.

'Cheers. Good to see you again, Morgan, after all these years. And to meet your . . . er . . . to meet Diana.'

He had nearly said 'your new wife', but stopped himself in time. Helen Shropshire smiled to herself at her husband's verbal stumble and then muttered her accentuation of the toast. She had not met the Farwells before: although Diana was the newer wife, Helen was by far the younger of the two. Diana, she thought, must be forty. Although at first sight she seemed older, owing to a deeply lined but still attractive face, she retained a young woman's body. Helen had noticed her husband's reaction when he returned from the airport with his guests: he seemed confused, fussing over their entrance into the bungalow and stuttering over the introductions. Helen knew the look in the older woman's eyes – mischievous or worse. Christ, at twenty-eight you shouldn't have to worry about women more than ten years older, but Helen's defences were aroused.

Morgan Farwell responded to the toast but then addressed Helen directly. 'If ever there was an argument for avoiding matrimony as long as Peter did, you're it. If you wait long enough a veritable Helen will arrive.'

The smile he gave her over his glass showed clearly enough his intent, but he didn't phrase his compliments very adroitly, thought Helen. He seemed the sort of retiring mild-mannered man that took it for granted people would know he meant well. He reminded Helen of a family solicitor – size, plumpness, facial features all medium, neutral and unremarkable.

Diana looked at Helen speculatively.

'I expect you've found, like me, there's a lot to be said in favour of older men. Men are so callow and clumsy when young.'

Helen flushed.

'Oh, Peter is young enough for me.'

As she spoke she realized it sounded silly and coquettish. Diana raised her eyebrows.

'Yes, he looks up to it. Perhaps there's something to be said for hanging around with his bulls.'

Helen noticed that Morgan seemed uncomfortable at his wife's crudity, but Shropshire himself quickly changed the subject.

'Now, we must think about your plans. There's a lot you should see up here before you go to the coast next week. You're free to come and go as you please, of course – we don't want to act like those bloody tourist guides, do we, Helen? You will haf your case outside your door by six a.m. and you vill be in ze dining-room for breakfast by six fifteen. Is that understood, ja?'

His guest nodded. 'Yes, we wanted to relax as much as anything. In these beautiful surroundings. But, of course, we must get about a bit.'

The empty glass he waved vaguely at the garden and hills

beyond was removed by his host, who spoke with his back to his guests as he returned to the bar.

'I've made one booking already, which I trust is convenient. A trip to Hawk's Nest.' He turned back from the bar with the replenished glass. 'It's one of the game-viewing lodges – built in the trees. There's several of them now, but I understand this is the best these days in terms of the chance of seeing elephant and such. Few years more and there'll be precious little game left.'

Morgan duly expressed his pleasure at the trip in store while Diana looked superciliously amused. Helen made the offer her role of hostess required.

'Peter will be at work most days, of course, but I'll be happy to drive you about.'

Her husband expanded the hospitality. 'And if you want to go off to one of the parks, I have my own Landrover you can borrow.'

Morgan Farwell gestured again with his glass.

'You're too generous, Peter. But talking of your work, I haven't congratulated you in person on becoming head of the centre. You must show me around while I'm here.'

'Well, I was lucky. Right place at the right time and all that.'

But Diana was having none of that.

'I'm sure you're being too modest, Peter. Director of the African Livestock Disease Control Centre – I'm sure they don't give that job to anyone who hasn't done major research work.'

Oh, my God, thought Helen. The words were innocent enough but her eyes as they locked on Peter were anything but. Look at her staring at Peter. The bitch is actually licking her lips. And Peter looks guilty already. This is going to be a long fortnight unless I do something about it. Her unkind thoughts concerning Diana's future were interrupted by her steward.

'*Memsahib. Chakula tiari, tafadhali.*'

'Let us go in to dinner.' Helen rose to usher her guests inside. 'I arranged for it to be early tonight. After flying all last night you must be tired, Morgan. And I'm sure Diana is looking forward to her bed.'

The day following the arrival of the Shropshires' guests, another visitor to Kenya was also welcomed. The Safaris Hotel bar on the mezzanine floor, for residents and guests only, still had spare tables at this hour, John Mallow noted. Some months earlier it would have been crowded with local Kenyan and expatriate businessmen and the Grade 1 prostitutes who plied their trade with both. The hotel management had tackled the problem none too soon, Mallow thought, before the sleazy atmosphere became a deterrent to tourists.

'Ah, there you are, old boy.'

Mallow moved forward to greet the tall, elegant man emerging from the lift.

'Good evening, er . . . John. Good to see you.'

'Welcome to Nairobi. Your first trip back to East Africa for a long time, isn't it?'

Mallow shepherded his friend to a table. He had known Guy Fulton some twenty years ago in Kampala, when Fulton was the young novice and John Mallow the more senior of the two. Even in those days, Mallow thought, he had a touch of arrogance. When they met in London recently, after a gap of many years, it was soon obvious that Fulton's arrogance had developed over the years as, indeed, had his career. As a senior official of the International Bank for Investments in Development (IBID) he had, Mallow supposed, some basis for feeling superior to his old banking colleague who was still in East Africa as a manager of a local bank rather than in the power corridors of Washington. John Mallow was not jealous of the younger man's advance; he enjoyed his life-style in Nairobi and aspired to no greater things. He was a firm believer in the dangers of rising above one's level of competence – he wondered if his companion had reached this point in his career.

Mallow raised his hand to signal a waiter. He always executed this gesture with a certain diffidence. The call of 'boy' was no longer acceptable in independent Africa and alternatives such as 'steward' or 'waiter' had never caught on with either patrons or bar staff. Waving one's hand about seemed to Mallow a somewhat inelegant and rude way of calling for service. Unfortunately, unless summoned in some manner the waiters would not come; the colonial heritage of not intruding until requested died hard.

Over his beer and Fulton's gin, Mallow kept the conversation to the old days. After all, Fulton's return to East Africa was sufficient excuse for reminiscences and tomorrow, when they met at his office, would be time enough to talk of the loan IBID was preparing for a major urban development project. But Fulton seemed less ready to wallow in memories and started to probe the local man on the local situation and the investment climate. Mallow tried again to keep the conversation light.

'Letty is looking forward to seeing you again after all these years. You remember my wife Letty? She remembers you as the ladies' man of Kampala.'

'Yes, indeed, I remember your good wife. She was very kind to me when I was the new boy in town. Inviting me to dinner and introducing me to suitable young ladies, as I remember.'

The men laughed in genuine shared comradeship for the first time, but the unease between them did not dissipate.

'I didn't ask when we met in London last year – I suppose you've settled down with a family now?'

Fulton shifted in his chair and crossed his legs, taking care not to affect the sharp crease in his slacks.

'Afraid not. I've moved around so much and had so much on my plate that somehow one hasn't had the time.'

Their glasses were empty and Guy Fulton turned in his chair to search for a waiter. As his eyes passed across the stairs leading to the lobby he stiffened. Mallow followed his gaze. Descending the stairs was a group that included Peter Shropshire and his wife with a couple that Mallow didn't know, although there was something vaguely familiar about the woman.

Fulton turned back to the table. He looked startled. Mallow looked at him quizzically.

'Saw someone you recognized? Lot of you international agency people pass through Nairobi.'

'No, no, not exactly. We were talking about . . . Just for a moment I thought I saw . . . Tell me, who were the people going down the stairs just then? Did you see them?'

'Don't know two of them. But the big man is a chap called Shropshire. Head of one of the research centres here. ALDCC, it's called – livestock disease research. You might have run into him somewhere. He goes across to the States for meetings of the bodies that fund centres like his.'

Fulton gazed at the man across the table with his mind seemingly elsewhere.

'No, I wasn't – I mean, no, I don't think I do know him.'

His eyes seemed to regain their focus on to his companion.

'Trouble is, one meets so many people in this business one has difficulty keeping names and faces accessible in one's memory bank. Now, you'll have another? The same again, is it?'

Nick Causington drove his car up the drive and reversed it to a position that would ensure his exit was not blocked. One never knew when an evening might turn out to be an utter bore and an early departure was desirable. His arrival was twenty minutes past the invited hour, so, it being Nairobi, he was the first to arrive. He accepted the usual platitudes that he was lucky to have no wife to make him late and tucked into an opening drink and a bowl of salted nuts.

'The Shropshires are coming,' said his hostess chattily, 'and a couple who are staying with them. Helen rang to ask if that was all right. It makes us ten with the Purleys and Jean Sharpe, but we can manage ten around the table – just. I keep telling Paul we need a bigger table.'

She sighed at the dilatoriness of men in responding to reasonable requests while Causington winced inwardly at the name of Jean Sharpe. It was going to be a bore. Jean would talk tennis at him and coyly suggest he should take up games. Commotion outside heralded the arrival of the Shropshire party. They entered and introductions were made. Nick Causington heard little of the names; from the moment the woman entered the room his whole attention was focused on her. When he was able to digest what his eyes had devoured, he realized that she was far from young. Probably ten years older than me, he thought, but the attraction was immediate and total. He desired this woman – what was her name? Diana. Yes, that was it, Diana – he desired her more than any woman he had met. And, by God, he thought, she looks like a few good tunes have been played on that fiddle with more to come. They shared their first secret smile when Jean Sharpe bounced in apologizing for being late due to a long tennis match. Nick marshalled himself for an evening of establishing a relationship, whilst fending off the attempted incursions of Miss Sharpe.

2

Inspector James Odhiambo sank into one of the cane chairs on the verandah of the hotel that featured on so many tourist brochures. The outlook across the garden was pleasant enough – developed over many years by the couple who had built this small hotel, the range of shrubs and flowers bore ample testimony to their dedication. The flamboyant hydrangeas and hibiscuses intermingled with euphorbias and the delicate variegated blooms of the yesterday, today and tomorrow bush. Around the bushes, lilies of the Nile, gerbera daisies, busy lizzies and a host of other flowers provided a multi-coloured base. But it was the mountain in the distance that made the view breathtaking: Mount Kenya looked the way a mountain should, rising spectacularly from the forested land below – not just one peak amongst many, but a mountain with its own shape. Odhiambo had purchased his beer at the bar and carried it to the verandah, not to save a small tip, but because he felt in some peculiar way that it distinguished him from the tourists expecting waiters to be poised for their call. The fact that in doing so he deprived the staff of much-needed earnings bothered him, but there were many paradoxes in modern Kenya that bothered him.

He was not left to gaze at the view alone for long.

'Good time of evening to mountain-gaze, eh? Clouds usually clear just before sunrise and sunset. May I join you?'

Scarcely waiting for the hand gesture towards the second chair, George Albinger plumped himself into it. Portly, with shining pate, he reminded Odhiambo of the drawings of Pickwick in his copy of the *Papers*. The comparison was aided in his mind by the fact that he liked the little lawyer. Albinger had the genial qualities of a Pickwick: except when he was on his feet cross-examining a government witness who was perjuring himself – then the suppressed anger surfaced. Unfortunately this trigger to his anger was becoming increasingly common.

'This may sound ridiculous to you, George, but until I came

up for this case, do you know, I'd never seen Mount Kenya close up.'

'Never got posted to these parts, James, eh?'

The two men knew each other well enough and were sufficiently comfortable in each other's presence for Albinger's gentle sarcasm to be offered without risk of offence. Both of them knew policemen with names beginning with O could find life difficult in Nyeri, the heartland of the Kikuyu tribe, who viewed those coming from the west with suspicion.

'Well, you've read the book – now see the film,' continued Albinger.

Odhiambo smiled. *Facing Mount Kenya* was the famous statement of Kikuyu aspirations by the man who led Kenya into independence, written long before such independence was regarded as a serious proposition by either Africans themselves or the British settlers.

'Congratulations, by the way, on your performance today. You picked a lot of holes in that fellow from the Auditor-General's office.'

Albinger nodded to acknowledge the policeman's tribute.

'Can't bear to let sloppy witnesses get away with it. Won't make any difference, you and I know that, James.'

The bitterness was there, just below the surface of the jolly, pink face. It was the eyes that gave the game away, thought Odhiambo. He gazed around, but they were alone on this part of the verandah.

'You know your client deserves what he gets, George. I did a lot of investigation of Gatutu's little company.'

Albinger gazed at his companion. He was fond of this large, dark man. He felt sorry to see such talent unrewarded. 'God knows,' he had exclaimed, in the safety of his Nairobi club, 'this country needs all the talent it can get, yet it wastes some of what it has.'

'You did your homework, James, unlike our friend in the box today. But would it make any difference if you hadn't? Or if I had more talents to offer for the defence? Gatutu is in the way of the RA's land deals and when the learned judge and assessors assemble tomorrow he will pay for his crime of being an impediment – the fraud charge is a convenient proxy. You wouldn't have got within a mile of my client's operations if he kept on the right side of Aramgu.'

Odhiambo felt both embarrassment and annoyance: the lawyer was right, but he shouldn't state it so bluntly to an official. After all, Odhiambo was still a policeman.

'That's enough of your white man's golf course slanders, George. To return to your first point, I am going to remedy a life-time deficiency and spend the weekend walking in the foothills of the mountain. Take a little time off.'

Albinger smiled and leant forward to tap the policemen on the knee.

'Great. Because you've never been to Hawk's Nest either, I daresay. My niece from England is joining me tomorrow and we're spending a night there. But I booked for three as I expected someone else who now can't make it. I'd like you to join us as my guest.'

Odhiambo hesitated. Hawk's Nest was an expensive tourist trap built in a tree, which afforded a great view of the forest game as they paused at the salt-lick below. He would like to go once, more as a voyeur of his human companions than from a desire to see elephants. But should he accept an offer like this from a lawyer who was often on the opposing side of cases in which he had to give evidence?

Albinger detected the hesitation.

'Robert McGuiry, the warden who runs the place, owes me a favour. He is keeping three places for me. Compliments of the management. Pity to spurn his hospitality by leaving an empty spot.'

Odhiambo thrust aside his misgivings and smilingly accepted the offer before excusing himself to return to the police station in the centre of the town.

Albinger waited until the policeman, with his purposeful, slightly forward-leaning gait, strode from the verandah then he followed at a more leisurely pace and found his way to the manager's office. He knew the lawyer and assured him his request would be accommodated. 'I'm sure that will be all right, Mr Albinger. You want one more place at Hawk's Nest tomorrow night. I don't think it's full tomorrow. But in any case Mr McGuiry will fit your friend in.'

Albinger left, making a mental note to seek out McGuiry the next morning on his return for breakfast at Mountain View with last night's visitors to Hawk's Nest. He would have a quiet word so that Odhiambo was given no reason to suspect that Albinger was paying for the policeman's visit.

As he drove down the tree-lined road from the hotel to the police station, Odhiambo felt his depression returning. He had detoured via the hotel for a drink and a quiet half-hour, but with the court in session, the hotel was bound to be crawling with Nairobi lawyers, such as George Albinger. This trip to Nyeri brought him to question what he intended to do with his life. As a Luo, whose evidence was likely to send a prominent Kikuyu to prison, Odhiambo had been left in no doubt how he was regarded by many officials in this centre of Kikuyu influence, even though the prosecution had been brought by the government, with Odhiambo merely obeying the orders of his Kikuyu superiors. Albinger was right, of course – the defendant had been foolish enough to compete with the Regional Administrator, who, although not a Kikuyu himself, was intimately connected with the ruling family.

It had been made perfectly plain to Inspector James Odhiambo in recent years that, given his record and ability, the unfortunate fact that he was a Luo was not an irremovable impediment to advancement. One condition, however, was clear: criminal investigation by senior officers was to serve the interests of the government, and 'government' meant the powerful ruling families. Odhiambo had difficulty in accepting this message. Getting evidence that would stand up in court was not easy in Kenya: once he had obtained it, to be told that the subject of the investigation was off limits induced in Odhiambo a rage which more than once had led him to physical violence. All he asked was to be a policeman, an honest policeman. It was bad enough working in an environment contaminated by politics, but when he returned home to Nyanza, in the west of the country, the Luo elders assumed he was only lending himself to the government to prepare the way for the Luo resurgence. Thank God he had married a girl from a minor tribe that had no say in politics and wanted none. It also provided him with an excuse to make his trips back west fewer. His father was dead and a brother, who had prospered in business in Kisumu, took care of most of the family obligations, for which Odhiambo felt both gratitude and, in a perverse way, irritation. His minor role in such extended family affairs was a source of guilt felt deep in his soul. He was after all a Luo, only one generation removed from a long tradition of farming Luo land amongst his family and clan.

3

'Well, Inspector, what do ye think of our wee place here?' The manager of Hawk's Nest, Robert McGuiry, was a lean, rangy Scot with a somewhat forbidding countenance, but, relaxed with a whisky or two already inside him, his tone was light and amiable. Odhiambo thought that McGuiry looked a little like a hawk himself with his long nose and deep-set, piercing eyes, shadowed by heavy eyebrows.

'It's a comfortable nest you've got yourself up here, Mr McGuiry. I expected it to be well appointed to meet the needs of your foreign customers, but I didn't expect so much space.'

Indeed, Odhiambo had been surprised earlier that afternoon at his first sight of the tree-house from the mini-bus that brought the guests through the forest. It was not strictly a tree-house at all, but a substantial structure supported on large wood pilings, artfully incorporating branches of the surrounding trees into parts of the interior to create the impression that the whole edifice was perched in a tree. Access from under the building was via a wooden stair which could be raised at night, so ensuring security from the unlikely incursion of a stair-climbing wild animal, but, more importantly, heightening further the desired atmosphere of being marooned in a tree with dangerous wildlife below. The portable stairs ended in a platform used as an interim storage area for visitors' luggage prior to individual delivery to the bedrooms. These were reached by crossing a substantial lobby into the long arm of the L-shaped building. The viewing verandah, bar and dining areas formed the shorter arm alongside the salt-lick that served to attract the animals and provide the required spectacle. Access to these social areas from the bedrooms was via the lobby that formed the joint of the L.

'Och, call me Robert – and you'll be James, I'm told. It's good to see an honest black face here, if you ask me the truth. Get tired of looking at Germans and Americans night after night. Pity we don't get more Kenyans. Would help if the folk here took a wee interest in the animals.'

They were sitting at dinner together with George Albinger and his visiting niece. The niece was in her early twenties, pale, slim and quiet: she contributed little to the conversation, although Odhiambo noted that when she spoke it was because she had something pertinent to say. It was Albinger who took up the defence of the black citizens of Kenya.

'They may or may not have an interest, Robbie, but they don't have the requisite number of shillings to partake of your hospitality. And, come to think of it, their main interest in elephants is keeping them off their fields.'

'Ay, true enough, George. But I wasn't thinking of the lads on the local *shambas*. James here could name a few who wouldn't miss the shillingees if they had a mind to come.'

Odhiambo allowed his attention to divert to the table facing him and behind McGuiry. This was the largest party at one table and contained some locals, albeit white locals. Odhiambo knew one by name – Shropshire. They had met when Odhiambo was investigating a break-in at the Livestock Centre. Another he knew by sight as a local bank manager. Two of the women who had sun-tanned skins were probably the wives of the men he recognized. There were three other men and one woman in the group; it was this woman who interested the policeman.

He had noticed her when she arrived at the hotel in Nyeri. Her lined face seemed to Odhiambo's experienced eye to be the result of plastic surgery rather than age. She exhibited a quality that was almost sinister. She had a sensuality that made her the focal point of attention for the males around her, but she seemed not only to dominate them but to frighten them. She led the conversation at her table – in fact she was the only really animated member of her party of eight. The youngest of the men unknown to Odhiambo was holding his end up, but the others seemed to be watchful and, yes, nervous. The attitude of the other women was perhaps simpler to understand – Odhiambo thought they were sulking.

Odhiambo switched his gaze to his left. Albinger's niece, Jennifer, was looking at him, but she glanced down blushing when he met her gaze.

'I'm sorry, my thoughts drifted away for a moment. That lady over there, she's got quite a personality, don't you think?'

Jennifer glanced across to the other table and wrinkled her nose.

'Yes. Yes, she has. But . . . but it's as if she is playing a part. And the others aren't sure what the play is, or whether they want to be in it.'

Good for you, Jennifer, thought Odhiambo. You're more perceptive than I thought. Albinger, noticing their area of interest, looked towards the other table.

'They came in two different groups. I was nearby when they met over tea. Seemed to be a surprise for all concerned. One of those "Oh, isn't it a small world" coincidental meetings, I gather. Now Jennifer, are you going to have some of this excellent pudding? No? Trouble with you young girls these days, you all want to emulate some consumptive lass out of Trollope.'

One of the Kenyan staff, uniformed as a ranger, entered the dining-room and crossed to whisper in the ear of McGuiry.

'Good. Thank you, Daniel.' McGuiry leant forward to inform his table companions. 'We'll have some cheerful faces on the verandah anon. Daniel tells me a large herd of elephant is heading this way. Be here later. Must spread the good word. Can't always guarantee that the beasties will stop by these days. Not as many around, of course. The big herds are as scarce as heather on yon Mount Kenya.'

McGuiry pushed his chair back, rose and tinkled his wine glass with his spoon to attract attention. His promise of elephant to come produced a spattering of applause from the dozen tables around the wood-panelled dining-room and a buzz of cheerful anticipation. Antelope, buffalo and warthogs were well enough, but elephant and rhino were what everyone was hoping to see.

Odhiambo gazed idly at the happy faces of the tourists. How will we get their dollars when the elephants are gone, he thought. When those in charge, including those directly responsible for the game, had smuggled the last ivory tusk and rhinoceros horn to meet their insatiable greed, what then for the future of the tourist industry? His attention was captured again by a voice from the next table rising above the general hubbub.

'Ooh, I just know it's going to be a wonderful night. Just like the old days. Do you remember, John? Guy? The Murchison Park all those years ago? We had some nights there, didn't we?'

Whoever the named individuals were, there was no great joy of remembrance coming from any of her party – at least from those that Odhiambo could see. The words were innocent enough, but the impression was of a different meaning intended. His Luo elders would have cautioned her, he thought. It is not wise to awaken the spirits from the past.

At the table that was attracting Odhiambo's attention, Peter Shropshire suppressed a groan at McGuiry's announcement. He was hoping to get away reasonably early on the pretext of retiring to bed. It would look odd now though, if that fellow McGuiry was right: one could scarcely say I'm off to bed just as a large herd of elephant came trumpeting up. On the other hand, he wasn't sure he could stand Diana's chatter and gloating eyes much longer. He was just a little tipsy already with whisky and wine, but to put up with this lot much longer he would need to take a great deal more whisky on board.

He glanced around the table and grimaced to himself. Why Morgan Farwell had married Diana he could not imagine. It had taken but a few hours in his house for confirmation of his belief that she was a spiteful bitch. It had taken him scarcely longer to accept that there was to be no meeting of minds and intentions as far as Diana and he were concerned. Now, with the bizarre meeting with two men she had known in Uganda some twenty years earlier, she was in her element. John Mallow he knew. He was still reputed to be something of a ladies' man, so Shropshire thought it likely he had slept with the young Diana. The other banker, Fulton, seemed a pompous bore, but his obvious unease at Diana's references to the old days probably meant that he had been mixed up with her too. Although, as he was a bachelor then, as now, why not? Something odd there. Mallow concealed his embarrassment better, but his wife Letty did little to hide the fact that meeting Diana again was not high on her list of desirable encounters. Damn the woman! Even his own wife, Helen, couldn't stand her.

Then there was the young idiot Nick Causington. He was obviously moon-struck. His obsequious fawning at Diana's feet was positively disgusting. No wonder Morgan Farwell looked disconcerted and uncomfortable. Peter wondered if he'd known what she was like when he married her. Odd choice to make, from what he knew of Morgan from the old days. Anyway, altogether a bloody queer party to stay up all night watching elephants. What am I going to do, he thought, but at that point in his reverie Diana made clear her own ideas on the subject, at least for the short term.

4

McGuiry passed up and down the verandah, speaking to his guests, explaining facts about the animals in view and generally being the good host. Although he tended to speak caustically about his tourist visitors when in the company of fellow Kenyans, the truth was that he enjoyed his role as host at Hawk's Nest. Although many of the tourists were boors, many others were genuinely excited and interested, and McGuiry was still boy enough to enjoy the respect they accorded him. Tonight's tourists were giving him no trouble – of course, it helped when there was plenty to see and they were getting what they'd paid for. The elephants duly arrived, adding their particular star quality to the proceedings, relegating the cape buffalo, assorted deer, warthogs and others to the role of supporting players. The elephants were not likely to be upstaged unless a rhinoceros arrived and that was a rare event these days – no animal had suffered more from the deadly attention of poachers than the rhino, due to the extraordinary value placed on its horn in the Arab and Oriental worlds.

No, the tourists were fine tonight, not even a lone female making advances to him – something which occurred too frequently, genuinely embarrassing McGuiry with his Scottish reticence. The only cause of concern to McGuiry's practised eye was the group of local white residents. Although their drinking was heavy, McGuiry assumed they could be expected to hold their liquor well enough, but there was an air of strain about this group which worried him. Usually, this meant a sexual entanglement, a not uncommon feature of white Kenyan life in McGuiry's experience. He did not want an incident, particularly between drunken women.

One of the group detached himself and left the verandah for the bar. McGuiry followed him.

'Had enough of the elephants? No novelty to you, perhaps?'

Peter Shropshire looked up from his glass.

'Nothing wrong with the bloody elephants. It's the silly bastards watching them that depress me. Particularly some of my bloody group.'

McGuiry realized that the man at the bar was not far gone in drink. He sounded genuinely angry and upset.

'That's one wee snag of meeting friends unexpectedly in Hawk's Nest.' said McGuiry. 'You have difficulty getting awa'. Trapped with an extended dose of auld lang syne.'

'Some of them', Shropshire said, gesturing towards the verandah, 'would like to bury auld lang syne. I reckon there's a few reminiscences they'd sooner not hear. And they sit there frightened that the silly bitch is biding her time to recount them. How about a drink? You must need one after chatting up the Krauts and the Yanks.'

McGuiry smilingly declined and, relieved now that he wasn't dealing with the prospect of a fall-down drunk, said, 'I've one or two things awaiting doing in the office. Of course,' he added, 'you could always go to your room and get a little shut-eye.'

'Not while that lot's bubbling away. Might have to try to keep the lid on. But I do need a leak. I'll see you anon.'

Back on the verandah the subjects of Shropshire's criticism were observing each other more closely than the elephants. It was not Shropshire alone who was finding the evening long. His wife, Helen, was quiet and seemingly rapt in her own thoughts. John Mallow's wife Letty, on the other hand, had set herself into competition with Diana, but finding herself overmatched, took succour in her glass, becoming increasingly morose. Mallow occasionally managed a laugh but it was forced. Guy Fulton assayed a demeanour of aloofness, but was clearly ill at ease. Diana's husband, Morgan, alone seemed interested in the spectacle around the salt-lick. Diana, however, was clearly enjoying herself and the same could be said of the besotted Nick Causington.

'I must say, Nick,' said Diana, 'I could tell you some stories about these fellows. They may be respectable now but it wasn't always so.'

Nick Causington giggled but there was no merriment to be seen elsewhere in the group.

'Don't talk in riddles, darling.' This was Letty, gazing with a certain lack of focus over her glass. 'You're not quite old enough to be the Sphinx.'

'Oh, don't be a killjoy, Letty,' said Diana. 'You were such a sport in those days. We've had some experiences, you and I.'

The malice was close to the surface now. An uneasy silence was broken by the eager Causington.

'I prefer women who have experienced life. There's nothing attractive about a pretty face that has no story to tell.'

He stopped abruptly, seemingly conscious that inadvertently he might have drawn attention to the unduly lined face of Diana.

Morgan Farwell coughed gently and, turning his eyes away from the salt-lick below the slatted balcony, scanned the group seated in a semi-circle around a casual table.

'It's getting late,' he said. 'The elephants seem content to mill about all night. What's the time? Goodness, it's after one. I think I may avail myself of a few hours' sleep. Some of us are not so young any more for all-night vigils.'

'Oh, I don't know,' said Letty, now slurring her words quite badly. 'I think Diana still fancies herself up to an all-night session.'

Diana laughed, a mocking, triumphal sound. Letty looked at Morgan and suddenly seemed to crumple slightly.

'Yes, you're right, Morgan. I'm sorry. Morgan, I think I've had . . . I think I'll turn in.' She stood up somewhat unsteadily, shook off her husband's arm as he half rose to assist her, and said with the dignity of the drunk, 'If you're going, Morgan, perhaps you would acco . . . acop . . . go with me as far as the rooms.'

'My pleasure, Letty. Here take my arm, it's rather dark on this verandah. Good-night to you all, and see you for the early-morning tea they threatened us with. Letty and I will be as fresh as daisies, won't we, my dear?'

They left, Letty grateful for Morgan's arm. With the continuity of the semi-circle broken, the group seemed to lose its sense of identity. Diana and her young swain edged closer together, and something Nick was whispering caused Diana first to look at him as if he too was drunk and then to giggle in a schoolgirlish way. Helen Shropshire continued to be lost in her own thoughts, although they did not appear to be bringing her any pleasure, whilst the two bankers were left isolated, separated by the whispering couple. John Mallow finally broke the awkwardness by rising.

'I see George Albinger over there. Must ask him what brings him here. Seems to be half Nairobi here tonight.'

The departure of Mallow seemed to bring Nick Causington to a decision. He, too, rose and, taking Diana's hand, pulled the only slightly resisting woman to her feet and then shepherded her through the door leading back to the bar and the lobby.

Odhiambo, leaning against the verandah balustrade, was genuinely interested in the changing scene below him, finding it more impressive than he had anticipated. There were a lot of elephants; Odhiambo heard one tourist claim she had counted twenty-six, and their splashings, mud-bathing and the antics of the three very young members of the herd were giving the tourists their money's worth. He found the reactions of the supporting cast of interest. The cape buffaloes seemed wary of the presence of the larger and more outgoing animals; they drew closer together as if, Odhiambo thought, they were elderly matrons who disapproved of the noisy exuberance of a younger, larger generation. The deer kept their distance, edging patiently towards whatever part of the salt-lick and water the elephants seemed to relinquish at any given time, whilst the warthogs seemed more impervious to the giants around them, pushing in whilst exercising reasonable discretion. Odhiambo's thoughts returned to his own mid-career preoccupations – he saw himself as the warthog, pushing himself into the centre but always needing to watch that he didn't irritate those who could dash him against a tree or trample him underfoot with no need for great effort or thought of consequences. To shake off his concern with his own predicament, Odhiambo focused again on the group he had observed over dinner. They stood out from the other guests because they seemed largely oblivious to what was happening around the lodge: their attentions seemed to be focused inwards – there were clearly tensions there, thought Odhiambo, and, yes, he was now certain there was a tangible sense of fear.

George Albinger, further along the verandah, called Odhiambo over and introduced him to John Mallow. He had already introduced his niece, who had remained demurely by her uncle's side since dinner. Mallow, as if relieved to find a woman who did not have the commanding personality of the woman whose company he had just left, turned back to Jennifer and engaged her in friendly questions about her trip and reactions to Kenya.

'I suppose this is your first visit to Hawk's Nest?'

'Yes, it is and it's marvellous,' said the girl. 'But the funny thing is, it's Inspector Odhiambo's first time too, isn't it, Inspector?'

Odhiambo smiled an acknowledgement.

'Well,' Mallow continued, 'do you know there's a tunnel that passes from under here out to the salt-lick? You can get a closer look at the elephants from there.'

'Do you know, I'd forgotten about that,' Albinger interjected. 'Shows it's been a long time since I was here.'

'Oh, that would be fun,' said the girl and then she paused, obviously not wanting to seem pushy. But her new acquaintance was happy to extend an offer.

'Yes, it would, wouldn't it? Right, why don't you let me show you the way, while these tuskers are still about? OK with you, Albinger? Will you join us? And what about you, er, Inspector?'

Albinger and Odhiambo made their excuses, and watched as the banker and the girl headed back into the lobby. They then turned to lean on the balustrade. Albinger puffed at his pipe, the smoke from which was caught in the light from the beams directed from the roof of the lodge on to the salt-lick. He waved his pipe in the general direction of the area below.

'You know, James, those big buggers down there will be gone in a few more years. They're under threat because of their tusks, an asset which served them well through so many years, but now is the cause of their doom.'

Odhiambo looked at his friend. The lawyer seemed to have decided on a little homily and Odhiambo was not sure he wanted to hear it. While he hesitated, Albinger leaned closer.

'Kenya's a strange place today, James. Integrity, a highly valued attribute in most circumstances, can be like those tusks and be a serious threat. Especially if it's paraded and obvious. The bigger the tusk the greater the danger: the more obvious it is that one's principles are rigid the more likely one is to be cut down.'

'It's too late at night to get melodramatic, George,' said Odhiambo. 'And there's not much the elephant can do about his tusks, is there? He can't sheath them like a sword. And he wouldn't last long without them either. So it's – what did my old English master say at the Prince of Wales? – it's Hobson's choice.'

The lawyer was contemplating a reply when a change in the tempo of action at the salt-lick drew their, and the other watchers', attention. The elephants appeared restless: one trumpeted loudly which increased the agitation of the others. The seemingly purposeless milling about now took on a faster and more nervous appearance. Even Helen Shropshire and the visiting banker, Guy Fulton, were aroused out of what had become a lengthy silence and moved to the rail next to Odhiambo.

Albinger pointed once more with the stem of his pipe.

'Something's upset them,' he said. 'I can't see any new arrivals, can you? No rhinos to disturb them.'

Fulton turned to the woman next to him.

'I think I'll get my camera from the room. If they get into a state there might be a good picture. Will you be all right here?'

Helen nodded. She seemed to be reasonably sober.

'Yes, of course,' she said. 'In fact, I'll go and look for Peter. He's probably in the bar somewhere. He ought to come and see this.'

The two departed, leaving Odhiambo and his companion to watch the elephants. They seemed now to be settling down, as if they had decided that the alarm, whatever it may have been, was a false one. Albinger put his lighter to his pipe and puffed fresh smoke into the beams of light.

Odhiambo gazed past the elephants to the edge of the forest. Had he picked up some movement in the trees? He thought something had caught his eye. The sudden sharp explosion caused everyone to jump, so unexpected was it and so loud as it echoed now around the open area bouncing, it seemed, off the walls of trees. The effect on the animals was drastic. The deer literally left the ground in fright and then took off with the gleam of white on their backsides vanishing into the trees. The elephants tossed their heads, backed away from the source of the noise, ears extended, and seemed for a few moments to be uncertain what to do. Then, suddenly – and it was almost as shocking as the original noise – several of the herd trumpeted in unison, turned away from the perceived source of danger towards the lodge, with the row of riveted human eyes hidden by the glare of the spotlights, and slowly at first, but with fast-gathering momentum, charged towards the lights. The entire herd quickly bunched together and followed the leaders with the young squealing in their midst. Only one large tusker remained, slowly backing but still facing the source of the noise with ears extended and trunk flailing as he trumpeted his defiance to cover the retreat.

The stampede took the animals right under the tree-house. Their passage with the repeated concussive effect of their enormous feet on the ground was sufficient to make the verandah tremble, but some of the frightened herd caught some of the pilings supporting the building a glancing blow, creating a shaking that made Odhiambo in company with the others clutch the balustrade for support. Thank God it was built before the Gasungu brothers were active in the building trade, he thought. He was currently investigating why two buildings erected by them had collapsed.

But worse than the shaking was the noise. Odhiambo had read that after a major earthquake it was the memory of the accompanying noise that haunted many of those who experienced it. This was similar. The trumpeting, which had the sound of a scream to it, the crashing of the smaller bushes, and the pounding of multiple trip-hammers as the force of tons of flesh repeatedly hit the ground combined to make a truly fearsome cacophony.

One tourist started to scream and another let out a string of what Odhiambo took to be German curses. But as the noise of the elephants started to fade into the forest the voice of McGuiry penetrated through to the verandah as he approached from the bar.

'Keep calm, yon beasties are off and awa' and us none the worse, but a braw memory for ye all.' He arrived on the verandah, saw Odhiambo and gave him a wink and a whispered, 'Calm these good people down as best ye can, Inspector, if you'll be so good. I'll awa' and check the bedrooms in case some poor wretches think they fell asleep and woke in Bedlam.'

He hurried out, joined by two of his staff who seemed as unperturbed as the Scot.

Other people were spilling through on to the verandah and a hubbub of excited voices gained in confidence and strength by the minute. The scare was over and the memory of a thrill remained. The frightened woman had subsided and seemed to be in good hands among her companions, so Odhiambo followed McGuiry through into the bar. He was still there, presumably having dispatched the lodge staff to check on the bedrooms. He was talking to the Kenyan who had apprised them over dinner of the approach of the elephants. As Odhiambo approached, he realized that they were worried about the same incident that was concerning him.

'I think we'd better take a look about,' McGuiry was saying in Swahili, 'and get us a pair of guns from my locker in case our prowler is still about.'

'I'll meet you on the stairs,' said the ranger. 'But there was nobody about – I saw no one when I was out earlier.'

As the ranger turned and left with a nod to Odhiambo, McGuiry half turned to face him. Odhiambo realized he was under inspection – McGuiry was unsure of how far to bring Odhiambo into his confidence. To freeze him out, or ask for his assistance – both options carried risks for McGuiry. After all, Odhiambo was the law, although registered game rangers had legal powers inside a national park and McGuiry as manager of Hawk's Nest also had a status akin to the captain of a ship. On the other hand, if he involved Odhiambo in the affair it might cause him more bother in the long run, if indeed someone was popping off guns at night within earshot of a major tourist spot. McGuiry was wary of the complications of involving officialdom other than his hotel management and the parks authorities.

'Well, Inspector – er, James, isn't it?' McGuiry reverted to English, placing Odhiambo on a higher status level. 'Well, James, I'll warrant y'ken what's bothering me?' McGuiry had come to a decision – at least, an interim one.

'I do, Robert.' Odhiambo chose to match McGuiry's desire for informality. 'That was a rifle shot which scared those monsters, and if it wasn't one of your wardens tripping over his rifle, then who was it?'

'Ay, that's the question, laddie. Only yon Daniel who's gone to pick up the guns was abroad and that was a wee bit earlier. It's a puzzle, that it is. Would'na want ye to think we have the local laddies going around here with rifles on a normal evening.'

'And no poachers in this area either, I suppose?' asked Odhiambo. He was aware that this area of forest surrounded by habitation and with all the comings and goings of the tourists and their keepers would be the last place to find poachers, who preferred the big open and relatively unprotected parks in the plains.

'No. They'd no be so foolish as that,' answered the Scot rubbing his face with a large lined brown hand as if to wipe away the events of the last few minutes. 'Anyway, Daniel and I will have a bit of a ferret about. I suggest, unless you're used to the forest, you bide a while here. Will fill you in when we've had a look-see.'

It was said pleasantly and man-to-man, but there was uncertainty in the older man's eyes. Odhiambo smiled.

'Quite right, Robert. You don't want me blundering about and I don't want to ruin my new Bata safari boots in the mud. I left my police boots in Nyeri.'

The message and the manner of its delivery were received by a relieved McGuiry.

'Right y'are, James. Will be on my way or that hare-brained lad of a ranger will think I've gone without him.'

Odhiambo watched the Scot leave and then, policeman's instinct taking over, turned to survey the room. There was a considerable amount of coming and going through the bar. A few people who had retired to bed now reappeared from the direction of the bedrooms. Odhiambo noticed some members of what he had come to call the local group arriving amongst this trickle of people, including, as he watched, the young man who had left the verandah with the woman. He saw Albinger's niece arrive through another door. She was alone; there was no sign of her banker companion. Odhiambo allowed his feelings of unease to surface. He had a nasty suspicion that his weekend break could end with his becoming involved in a messy affair. Someone had fired a shot and, whatever the reason might be, Odhiambo could see a police enquiry resulting, one which was out of his jurisdiction, but in which he would be involved as a witness. Anyone going around with a gun, other than members of the army, the police and game wardens, was likely to mean a potentially sensitive situation, particularly in a famous tourist area. Odhiambo hoped he could fade out of the picture and leave it to the Nyeri police. Unless McGuiry found some simple expla5ation.

Any lingering hope Odhiambo was harbouring along these lines was dashed the next moment. One of the staff came into the bar and sought him out.

'The Bwana wants you,' he said. And unable to maintain the discretion that had probably been imposed on him, he continued in a rush. 'The memsahib, one of the guests, Bwana McGuiry find her down below, under the stairs. She is dead. The elephants they step on her.'

Odhiambo had a sense of almost total certainty as to the identity of the 'memsahib' concerned. The waiter spoke in Swahili, but there was at least one person close to Odhiambo who he assumed would understand it: and from the look on Nick Causington's face he shared Odhiambo's premonition. Odhiambo followed the waiter towards the stairs and the commencement of the complications he wished to avoid. Only now it was not a mere nuisance he was faced with. Odhiambo viewed the next hours and, probably, he thought, days with something approaching dread.

5

Odhiambo rose from his kneeling position in the mud beside the body. McGuiry stood beside him, framed in the rays of the spotlight that one of his men had adjusted from the platform above so as to provide a view of the body. Not that it was a view the tourists would appreciate and Daniel, the ranger, had been dispatched to keep them well away.

'Well, we'd better get the husband down to identify her formally,' said Odhiambo, 'and then cover the body and guard it until the Nyeri police get here.'

'Maybe we should cover the poor lassie's body,' said McGuiry. 'Bad enough asking him to look at her face without showing him the rest of her.'

Odhiambo nodded. The elephants had crushed the woman's body as well as her face which had taken on a twisted appearance. The jaw-bone seemed to have been displaced and the nose had been severed. Yet identification was a formality, with those deep lines around what, even in death, seemed young eyes. Eyes that had danced as those she watched squirmed. Well, they'd dance no more: Diana Farwell was as dead as it was possible to get. Certainly the terrible force of the trampling would have killed her – unless she was already dead.

One of the lodge staff left to get blankets for the body and Morgan Farwell in that order.

'You told me one of your men was radioing Nyeri?' Odhiambo asked McGuiry, knowing the question had already been answered.

'Ay. They'll get through to Mountain View, assuming the duty chappie is awake, get him to wake the manager and he'll phone the police. What do ye think, James? Is this', the warden gestured at the remains at their feet, 'connected with the shot, d'you suppose?'

'The only shot we heard was the other side of the pool, so she can hardly have been hit by it, unless by some freak chance.'

'Y'know,' said McGuiry, 'I've done a bit of tracking in my day. Looks to me she was lying or sitting here when the elephants ran over her. There's no sign she was running. And she's been trampled on, not gored or thrown about.'

Odhiambo stared at the warden. He was tempted to ask how the old man could tell, but he thought the conclusion was probably right.

'And why wouldn't she be running?' continued McGuiry, sucking air through his teeth as he followed his thoughts to their logical conclusion. 'Because, either she'd fallen off yon platform,' gesturing to the luggage deposit area at the head of the stairs, 'or she was hit by that bullet that some bugger fired. By chance, yes, but chance can be a funny thing, Inspector.'

Odhiambo returned to the facts. 'You're sure the stairs were up at the time we're talking about?'

'Och, I'm sure. I passed by meself some ten minutes earlier. And they were still up when Daniel spotted the body.'

'Then she must have fallen. There's no other way she could get down without sliding down one of the support poles. And if she fell she was incapacitated one way or another. Unconscious or unable to move when the elephants came through.'

The two men were silent for moment, both rendering up a

hope that the woman had indeed been unaware of the giant beasts bearing down upon her.

'Damn funny though.' McGuiry made the peculiar sucking noise again. 'You're asking me to believe that someone, a bit tipsy perhaps, leans over the rail and falls over more or less at the same time someone is firing a gun the other side. Weird sort of coincidence that, if there's no connection.'

Odhiambo did not reply. He saw Farwell coming down the stairs escorted by one of the other men in his group. They were preceded by the lodge staff man who, with a glance at McGuiry to seek confirmation of his action, draped blankets over the crushed body. McGuiry was right though, thought Odhiambo. The woman's fall and the shot could hardly be independent events. That was stretching coincidence too far. What was she doing alone on the platform? Where was the companion who was with her when she left the bar? As he turned to greet the bereaved husband, Odhiambo thought it was this companion he wished to speak to next. Then he pulled his thoughts back into control. It's not your business, he reminded himself. Just go through the motions until the locals arrive. He could cling to that, at least for now.

The identification was over quickly. The husband, identified formally to Odhiambo as Morgan Farwell, nodded almost imperceptibly in the artificial spotlight and turned his head away.

'Yes, she is my wife, Diana Farwell.'

Nothing more, no protestations, no questions. Farwell was exercising great self-control, but Odhiambo was sure that he was facing a very astute man. Behind the pale face, which the light threw into an odd relief of glare and shadow, Odhiambo sensed a mind racing ahead of the inevitable questions. He shepherded the man away from direct line of sight of the body.

'I have to ask. Can you tell me how your wife might have come to be down here?'

Farwell looked at the policeman and Odhiambo felt himself being assessed.

'Not from direct knowledge, no. I'd retired a few minutes earlier, leaving Diana with friends.' There was a pause and then a minute sigh. 'But surely, er . . . Inspector, is it? . . . She must have fallen and then, and then . . .'

The mask lifted momentarily as Morgan Farwell faced the thought of his wife's last moments.

A few minutes later Odhiambo climbed the stairs on to the platform from which, he supposed, the deceased had fallen. McGuiry was making arrangements for a makeshift stretcher to be used to move the body. Odhiambo wondered whether to ban the movement until the Nyeri police arrived; but what would be the point, and after all, there were other wild animals about although the rangers could stand guard. The point was simple, he answered his own thoughts. It was his own sense of unease. He gazed at the scene below and then looked around the platform. No good looking for evidence of how the accident occurred here, he thought. All the tramping about of the last few minutes had left plenty of mud on the steps and the area on which he stood. He examined the balustrade. Insubstantial, but then this was a luggage platform not a viewing stand. Insubstantial, but unbroken.

Odhiambo assessed his immediate surroundings more closely. The platform was open on two sides – where the steps were raised and lowered and the side from which the woman had fallen. In front of him was the door facing the steps and on his left the outside wooden wall of the lodge. And then he saw, to the left of the door, clamped to the wall, a small axe. At that moment, he knew what he would sooner or later discover.

'Mr McGuiry, could you come back a moment?'

The Scotsman, who had just passed through the door, returned to the platform, surprised at the urgency in the policeman's voice.

'That axe – no, don't touch it. It's always there, is it?'

'Och aye, Inspector. Although it's been put in the wrong way round.'

McGuiry peered at the offending instrument which was indeed precariously held: it had been placed with the axe head facing the door whereas the clamp was designed for the head to face in towards the wall.

'Wonder who had it out?' continued the warden. 'It's there in case the ropes around the pulley controlling the stairs get stuck. Fire chappies insist on it. Hack the rope and the stairs'll drop.'

Odhiambo, using a handkerchief, and grasping the axe near the head, gently removed it from the wall.

'Here, come under the light, your eyes may be better than mine.'

McGuiry looked mystified, but did as he was asked. He and the policeman stood by the spotlight attached to the wall. The blade shone brightly as it reflected the light, but as Odhiambo turned the axe over, they saw the dull patch on the blunt end of the head. Odhiambo bent closer: he could see the stain and, yes, he could see hairs stuck to it. He closed his eyes as if to remove the image on his retina and then straightened, thrusting the axe closer to the warden's eyes.

'Look closely, McGuiry. Do you see, man?' Odhiambo's tone was angry – resenting the situation both were now in. 'And now tell your men to leave the body undisturbed. It wasn't the bloody elephants that did her in, it was one of your guests!'

6

Dawn rose spectacularly over the Aberdares. The rising sun caught the clouds around Mount Kenya which seemed to catch fire in a glow of orange and yellow with tendrils from the blaze extending across the sky. Outside Hawk's Nest the early-morning chorus was a competition between the wide variety of birds awakening in the trees. The weavers were already about, darting in and out of the reeds that surrounded the salt-lick. At ground level the scene around the salt-lick was quiet. The smell of man and the noise he made discouraged the gazelles and the smaller animals from taking a morning drink. Only the monkeys gazed down with curiosity and interest from close range, while the cape buffaloes observed proceedings from the shelter of the trees with their usual impassive watchfulness which spoke of time to spare and patience to allow events to unfold.

A few of the guests at Hawk's Nest milled around the verandah and gazed blankly at the scene, revealing nervousness in their constant aimless shifting as if parroting the actions of the animals earlier in the night now passed. Inside, at the bar, others drank the tea and coffee and nibbled the biscuits provided by the staff, who proceeded about their duties with no trace of their usual ready smiles. This morning their sombre faces befitted a household in which a death has occurred.

Odhiambo, sitting in the warden's office, was oblivious to the light and colour show outside the window. He sipped a cup of hot sweet tea and mentally cursed his fate. The Nyeri police had yet to arrive, although word was they were finally on their way. The delay was not a surprise to Odhiambo. Provincial police stations were not amply provided with vehicles. Some broke down and the recurrent budget needed for repairs remained caught in the bureaucracy in Nairobi. Serviceable ones on a Saturday night were likely to be part of the support convoy of the Regional Administrator at whatever function or private party he and his entourage were attending. Receiving the message, relayed via the hotel back to the game lodge, that the police would come as soon as they obtained a vehicle, Odhiambo sighed and reluctantly set himself to the task of conducting the preliminary interviews. At least, he thought, the delay might improve the chances that someone competent would be in charge of the contingent when it arrived.

As he sipped his tea he recapitulated to himself the findings so far. His earlier statement to McGuiry involved jumping to a conclusion that was not necessarily indicated by the facts. Elephants do not wield axes but McGuiry's staff could, and McGuiry himself could not be automatically excluded. Nevertheless, Odhiambo was convinced he need look no further than the group associated with the dead woman. He had been accused many times, both by his tutors and by his superiors, of jumping to premature conclusions, but he trusted his instincts and believed he was a better detective because of them. The circumstances of this case put other possibilities beyond Odhiambo's credulity. The chance that a passing waiter or guest that she did not know had hit Diana Farwell on the head and tossed her to the elephants was so remote that Odhiambo wasted none of his thinking or interviewing time upon it. Despite his cursing of the fates that caused him to be a participating witness, he recognized his true hunter's instincts. He had proceeded with the interviewing of those in the dead woman's circle with a sense of urgency. He wanted his chance with them before the locals arrived and reduced him to more of a spectator's role. Odhiambo rationalized his actions as accepting the duties thrust upon him, but, in fact, he was exhibiting the passion for the chase that was his true identifying characteristic.

The statements he obtained would need time to digest and fit into an overall sequencing of events so that inconsistencies could be detected. And now would come the more laborious task of checking the location and movement of all others in the lodge. What, or rather whom, they had seen at vital moments would provide the means to pick out the lies amongst the stories already collected.

Odhiambo knew he had identified one liar. The question was whether the lies were intended to cover up murder or a lesser crime. Odhiambo reviewed the sequence of events as claimed by the participants, mentally preparing a summary for the Nyeri officers. He would need to keep his tale simple, he thought: he did not have a very high opinion of the intelligence of his Nyeri colleagues, based on his experience of them these last few days.

Diana Farwell's group on the verandah originally consisted of seven persons in addition to herself. Peter Shropshire left soon after the move to the verandah and spent most of the time thereafter at the bar, but claimed to have been 'paying a visit' to the lavatory at the outbreak of the disturbance. He hurried back through the bar to the verandah, but was too late to see the stampede. The lavatory was down a corridor leading to the bedrooms, so on his return he passed through the lobby that led not only to the bar and verandah but also to the platform where Diana met her fate. According to Shropshire, he did not see Diana or anyone he knew in the lobby; but by then people were milling about in excitement all over the place and he would scarcely have noticed anyone in particular, as he put it. However, he had seen his wife in the bedroom corridor.

Helen Shropshire had a similar tale to tell. She left the verandah to go in search of her husband assuming he was in their room. On her way back she saw him emerge from the men's toilets and thought she also saw one of the bankers, Guy Fulton, in the lobby. She also claimed to have seen the dead woman's husband and the younger man Causington in the bedroom corridor walking towards the lobby.

Fulton himself was vague. He claimed that he set off towards his room to fetch a camera but, realizing he would be too late to capture the action, turned back into the lobby. Odhiambo detected a hesitation when he asked the banker where he was then heading. Back to the verandah, came the stammered reply, but Odhiambo wondered if this was true. On the face of it, the luggage platform would be a logical place to go as the elephants rampaged through and past the lodge. But no one admitted doing so: although the dead woman and at least one other must have taken that option.

Morgan Farwell reported escorting Letty Mallow to her room and claimed to have been in bed and asleep when the noise of the stampede awoke him. Emerging from his room he encountered Nick Causington in the corridor and they returned to the bar together. He assumed Letty remained in her room as, he said with a delicate cough, she had probably 'drunk sufficient nightcaps to ensure sleeping through a stampede'. Indeed, Letty was found asleep in bed by her husband some time later. Alcohol was a relevant issue in all their statements, thought the policeman; the drinks they consumed in the hours preceding the murder affected their recollections of events and who was where at a given moment. Mallow remembered taking Albinger's niece through the tunnel to the ground-level viewing site and excusing himself to visit another set of toilets in the tunnel. He could not recollect why he did not return to escort the girl back to the main part of the lodge, excusing himself by saying the combination of the noise of the stampede and the alcohol must have confused him. Jennifer Harris confirmed the initial part of Mallow's statement, saying she found herself alone in the viewing chamber when the other tourists hurried back down the tunnel as the elephants headed for the lodge. She waited awhile and then made her way back alone.

And then we have Bwana Causington, thought Odhiambo, the obvious liar and a poor one at that. From the outset of the interview his nervousness was clear, a nervousness he tried to mask with bluster, evasion and, yes, a touch of old colonial arrogance. He, alone, demanded proof that Odhiambo was a police officer and suggested it would be better if McGuiry undertook the enquiries.

'After all, he's in charge here. Don't know where you come into it, actually.'

Odhiambo used shock tactics to short-cut this non-co-operation.

'Mr Causington, I have reason to believe that Mrs Farwell

was not alone on the luggage platform immediately prior to her fall. Were you with her when she met her death?'

Causington blanched and twisted in his chair, turning away from his inquisitor across McGuiry's desk. Turning back he maintained an aggressive attitude.

'What an outrageous suggestion! Are you mad, man? If I'd been with her when she fell, I'd have gone for help. You should be more careful what you say. I don't wish to complain to your superiors, but I may tell you I know Price-Allen and I don't expect you want me to go to him regarding your conduct.'

A weak man, thought Odhiambo, brought up to believe that even timid white men could intimidate Africans. Typically seeking to bolster his position by dropping the name of a white Kenyan involved in the intelligence arm of the Kenyan police, albeit in a role that was carefully unspecified.

Odhiambo leaned forward and sharpened his tone, aiming to cut through the bluster and reach the weakness under the skin.

'You may talk to anyone you wish, Mr Causington. Later. For now I must insist formally on an account of your movements. You must be aware that I was present when you left the table in the company of Mrs Farwell.'

'Can't say I noticed you. Should have done, I suppose. Rare to see a black face among the paying customers here. Most of you prefer the nightlife in the Black Bull to Hawk's Nest, as I hear it.'

Causington smirked at his reference to the nightclub-cum-brothel in Nyeri that, indeed, was well patronized by local officials and businessmen.

'Mr Causington, I must officially warn you that I am not satisfied as to the cause of Mrs Farwell's fall. Unless you are willing to provide me with an account of your movements, I shall request the Nyeri police to hold you in custody for further questioning.'

'Oh my! We have learned to speak properly, haven't we!'

But Odhiambo could see the bluster fading and the fear in the man's eyes. Causington fumbled for a cigarette from a silver cigarette case. An old-fashioned touch there, thought Odhiambo. Symbolic, probably, of Causington's preference for the past when white men ruled and black men knew their place. The hands trembled slightly as the cigarette was lit.

'Well, Mr Causington?'

'I did leave with Mrs Farwell, certainly. We walked together as far as my bedroom where I left her. Her room was a few doors further along. Her husband had already retired.'

'You and Mrs Farwell did not give the appearance of being about to part company when you left together. Hand-in-hand, you were.'

The cigarette trembled and ash fell on to the smart safari suit worn over a silk shirt and a cravat in the colours of a local sporting club. The club, as Odhiambo recalled, that remained nearly all white in membership. But Causington kept finding more resolve to battle with the inspector than the trembling hands indicated. Pointing his fingers that held the cigarette at the policeman, Causington simulated outrage.

'How dare you! I find your suggestions offensive. Impugning the reputation of a married woman, who, what is more, is now dead.'

The word 'dead' seemed to bring the woman's death home to the man. For the first time he sounded sincere as he muttered to himself rather than to Odhiambo.

'How could it have happened? Poor Diana. It's a terrible thing. She was so alive and enjoying herself. And it's not fair on me.'

'If you left Mrs Farwell at your door and she was heading for her room, can you explain how she came to end up on the ground outside?'

'Of course I can't. It's terrible.' Causington paused to inhale from his cigarette. 'She must have still been dressed when the rumpus started. When the elephants started to stampede. She must have rushed to the nearest vantage point to see them. And stumbled and fallen over into their path.' The man shuddered. 'It doesn't bear thinking about. It's too horrible.' He focused on Odhiambo, for the first time meeting him eye to eye. 'I've nothing more to say. I know nothing more. Good God, man, we're all badly shaken. Doesn't help to have to put up with your questions. I'm leaving now.'

Causington got up, a little uncertainly, as if expecting to be reprimanded. He opened the door, which was only a step away in the small office filled by McGuiry's large desk, three chairs, a filing cabinet and an arms rack.

As he went through the door, Odhiambo spoke. 'Tell me, Mr Causington, did you hear the shot?'

Causington looked back at the policeman. No words came in answer to the question, but his face gave all the answer Odhiambo needed. It was the face of a very frightened man.

Odhiambo expected nothing from Letty Mallow who was hungover, frightened and embarrassed. She seemed to think that a drink-assisted sleep while Diana met her end was a breach of good form. Because of this, Odhiambo treated with some scepticism her one contribution to his knowledge. She might, he thought, be so anxious to show she was not blind to the world that she was inventing a tale to tell him. For what it was worth, she claimed to have splashed water on her face when she was alone in her room and then to have sat looking out of the window prior to getting into bed.

'I saw someone moving through the poles holding this place up. He seemed to deliberately stay under the shelter of the building and disappeared more or less under me at the bedroom end of the lodge. I only caught a glimpse or two and I couldn't see very well. The glare of the spotlights blinded me but didn't fall on him.'

The woman stared anxiously at Odhiambo and bit her lip. Doesn't want me to think she couldn't tell if she saw one man or three gorillas, thought Odhiambo sardonically.

'And you don't know who it was?' Odhiambo prompted the woman. 'Was it someone who seemed familiar?'

'No, I don't know. I couldn't see, you see. I wouldn't have thought anything about it, really, except I'm sure it wasn't a . . . it wasn't an African . . . I mean, Inspector, I think it was a white man – and he was carrying a gun.'

'It wasn't the warden – McGuiry?'

'I don't know. You know, when I first got a glimpse I expected it to be one of the guards, rangers I mean, but then when I got another glimpse it was a white man – I'm sure of it.'

It was after this conversation that McGuiry brought him the news that one of the rifles belonging to McGuiry's staff had been found amongst the trees. The warden was embarrassed and cross.

'One of my rascals left a rifle where he shouldn't have, I've no doubt. And someone took his chance.'

'It could have been one of your men who fired the shot, couldn't it?' Odhiambo replied. 'Why are you so sure it wasn't?'

'They'd lose their job, man, and they know it. This is a soft number they've got here. Why would they risk that for a mad idea of frightening those beasties? They see them all the time. Nothing strange for them. No, you want my view, James, one of yon visitors with the drams sloshing through his brain decided it would be a wee joke to cause a stampede.'

'Or to cover a murder,' said the policeman.

But as he watched the befuddled expression on the warden's face, he didn't accept his own hypothesis. And he found himself anticipating the next embarrassed admission.

'I have to tell you, James. I'm sorry, but these damn fool fellows of mine, they – they picked the gun up. Handled it. Told them not to, but in the excitement of finding it . . .'

Thinking back over his conversations now, Odhiambo smiled to himself. He didn't have great faith in the Nyeri police handling the gun carefully either. As he drained his cup, one of the African rangers came to inform him that the long-awaited police vehicle was bumping its way down the approach track.

The next few hours passed as Odhiambo had predicted. The local inspector was a plodder who slowly went through the whole cast of characters at Hawk's Nest, both guests and staff, asking questions regarding their whereabouts at the significant time, but without any inspiration or visible sign that obvious anomalies registered with him. Odhiambo briefed him regarding his interviews and, after attending the first few of the new set of interviews, left with the excuse that he would type up his notes. As he passed through the main bar area on his way to a small office McGuiry indicated he could use, he and McGuiry were badgered by guests claiming important reasons for leaving Hawk's Nest on time – reasons that overrode any claims the police had on them as potential witnesses to a nasty death experienced by one of their fellow guests. Odhiambo had observed in previous encounters with tourists their wish to be regarded as spectators sealed from the realities of the lives and circumstances in which they found themselves. They were voyeurs wanting the sights and smells of Africa but not the pain or joy of participation. Particularly not when it threatened to interfere with their closely held triplicated schedules.

The constables who arrived with the inspector drew outlines of the body on the ground, then wrapped the body in plastic sheeting and moved it into the back of their Landrover. Charged with no other purposeful task they now milled about outside the lodge chatting desultorily with the staff. The local inspector clearly did not believe his men were up to a little discreet detective work; he intended to see every person himself and take copious notes of each encounter. His only concession to Odhiambo's account of the interviews already conducted was to leave those individuals till last. Odhiambo wondered how some of them would take to a repeat interview that followed a more pedantic pace than the first.

In the event, he was not there to witness their reactions. A radio message stated that the Regional Administrator, informed of Odhiambo's presence at Hawk's Nest, wished to see him immediately. With one of McGuiry's vehicles and a driver, Odhiambo was soon deposited outside the Administrator's office in the newly built and still clean three-storey building that housed the Regional Administration in Nyeri.

He waited for over thirty minutes before the door to the inner office opened and an aide to the Administrator gestured Odhiambo to enter. The aide was a slim man, dressed in a Western-style suit with shirt and tie. Of medium height, he was considerably shorter than Odhiambo, but both men were dwarfed by the huge figure behind the desk. Felix Aramgu, Regional Administrator and confidant of the President, was a very large man indeed, well over six feet in height with a wide body, long arms, enormous hands and a belly that bespoke of a large appetite for *ugali*, the local maizemeal dish, goat-meat and bottles of East African beer. He was dressed in a loosely fitted safari suit, which even so was strained around his middle regions. He was speaking on the telephone as Odhiambo approached and left him standing at the desk as he completed his conversation.

'I will come and brief the President myself. I'll drive down this afternoon after I've had a chance to get the facts straight.'

Aramgu now listened, interpolating brief interjections once or twice, but seeming to Odhiambo to be on the receiving end of the lecture. The telephone was a bulky old-fashioned one, which looked incongruous in the spacious office sumptuously equipped with modern Swedish furniture. Bulky though it was, it seemed about to be crushed in Aramgu's great hand and when finally he slammed it back on to its stand Odhiambo was surprised that it did not crack.

'So, Odhiambo, is it?' Aramgu half rose to greet his visitor, seemed to think better of it, subsided and stabbed a sausage-sized finger towards Odhiambo. 'I won't ask what you're doing at Hawk's Nest without anyone here knowing about it. I thought you'd gone back to Nairobi after the Gatutu case. I hear you did a good job on that, by the way. Bwana Gatutu won't be troubling us for a bit. But no, you're off partying with the *mzungus*, which is OK if you like Germans and all the rest. Personally, if we've got to have *mzungus* I prefer our *mzungus*, now that we've shown them how to behave as whites in black Africa. But if you're going to spend your time with these people you might stop them killing each other. It's you who's saying this woman was killed, right?'

Aramgu sat back, looking at Odhiambo as if at a lesser breed. The aide, seated to the side and slightly behind Odhiambo, intervened before the policeman could speak.

'Superintendent Kalavu has passed on a summary as given on the radio by the man in charge out there – the warden, what's his name?'

'McGuiry,' said Odhiambo, wondering if the unnamed aide was trying to warn him that Aramgu had McGuiry's version. And why hadn't Kalavu asked to speak to him? He focused on Aramgu, who was now kneading his belly with one hand as if he had an ulcer.

'Good morning, Mr Aramgu. I'm sorry we meet in these circumstances. My presence at Hawk's Nest was at the invitation of Albinger – the lawyer representing Mr Gatutu. He, that is Albinger, does not seem to be involved in this unfortunate incident: he was with me at the vital times. But, yes, the woman was murdered – almost certainly, that is. We'll have to wait for the post-mortem to be quite sure.'

Aramgu waved a hand, dismissing legalisms and post-mortems as an unnecessary constraint on action.

'If she was killed, the issue is how to get the matter settled fast. Let me remind you of some facts, Inspector.' Aramgu seemed to linger on Odhiambo's title as if wondering how long it would remain applicable. He leaned forward until his belly pressed against the desk. 'We've had enough problems of white women getting themselves killed here in Kenya. Remember the lion woman, what's her name? Adamson, yes, that was it.' Aramgu acknowledged the name as it was muttered *sotto voce* by his aide. 'You think the Big Man wants stories that no white woman can look at game here without getting herself killed by the *wananinchi*? Have you been to America, Inspector? You know how much their papers like to make big stories of white women killed by black men? And if it's in Kenya not New York, better still.'

Aramgu paused, contemplating, Odhiambo thought, his pending visit to the President's office in Nairobi. He was rehearsing on Odhiambo the charges that could be coming his way later in the day.

'You know what the tourist business is worth to Kenya, Odhiambo? What is it, Gachui? Well, whatever it is, it's about the biggest earner of dollars, bigger than coffee, isn't it?' Gachui lookd doubtful, but did not care to offer any figures. Aramgu continued. 'And now we've got another *mzungu* dead. And this one gets herself killed with a Kenyan police officer watching. I can see the headlines now. White woman killed as policeman watches elephants.'

The Administrator's reference to headlines was not, as all three men knew, a fear of reading them in tomorrow's local newspapers. Nothing would appear in them that would be likely to cause offence to the Big Man, as Aramgu had described the President. It was the international press which raised the blood pressure of senior Kenyan officials.

Aramgu snorted.

'You should join the Tourist Department if you like mixing with them. Let's see you sell holidays to white women. Two weeks, all costs included, if you survive that long.' The Administrator straightened up and adopted a more official voice as if passing judgement on a convicted felon. 'Well, now we have this mess in which you are involved, as Administrator I am requiring you to assist in sorting the matter out. You will return to Nairobi this afternoon and I'll speak to your boss. Who is it, by the way?'

'Chief Superintendent Masonga of the Nairobi CID.' Odhiambo considered for a moment before continuing. 'I don't think, sir, that this is going to turn out to be like the other cases. I think we're going to find that this was done by one of the woman's group at the lodge. It's not likely that she was killed by one of the staff.'

Aramgu looked as if he was about to interrupt, so Odhiambo hurried on.

'If I'm right, it may not be so damaging to the tourist industry. Sexy woman killed by one of her lovers. Something like that has a more glamorous air. Think of the interest in some of the recent books and films. I mean the ones which describe the goings-on of the old white settlers. Delamere and his crowd.'

Aramgu was listening now. Odhiambo could see him formulating his case for the President using the lifeline Odhiambo offered.

'There may be something in that. Which makes it all the more important we get the *mzungu* who did it. Who's in charge there now?'

The question was addressed at a point midway between the policeman and the aide, Gachui. Odhiambo allowed Gachui to supply the answer while he watched Aramgu. It would be easy to underestimate him, Odhiambo thought, as many of his business and political enemies had discovered too late. The aggressive bully-boy manner and an uncouth style of behaviour coupled with his size concealed from the casual observer a sharp and cunning mind.

After a pause, the RA summed up. 'Right. Gachui, get the inspector out there, whatever you said his name is, to give us his notes on the people in this woman's party by tonight. And tell him I expect quick action in identifying a culprit. And you . . .' turning to Odhiambo, 'you will dictate your impressions before leaving for Nairobi. Use the older woman in the office outside. Not the young one, her talents lie in other directions.'

And Aramgu laughed, the laughter welling up like an organ peal from the considerable belly. He felt better now. If he handled things properly, he could even get some credit for dealing with a potentially damaging affair expeditiously without bringing too much attention from outside. Odhiambo needed to be watched though, he thought. Smart, and could be useful, but Aramgu had known other Luos who were too smart for their own good. He belched, a residue of last night's overindulgence. He could do with a drink, but in the light of the summons to the President's office better perhaps to wait.

7

Odhiambo was on his way back to Nairobi before he realized it was Saturday. Government working hours, until recently, had included Saturday mornings, but now a five-day week applied so it was unusual to find an office functioning fully, as was Aramgu's. It hadn't taken the Administrator long to realize the problem and marshal his staff.

On arrival in Nairobi Odhiambo went to his office to prepare a report fuller than the summary he had dictated for Aramgu. His writing finished, he went home, albeit with some reluctance. His wife was away visiting relatives for the weekend, which was why he had planned to spend the extra time in Nyeri. He always felt uncomfortable in the house without her, as if he did not belong. They lived in one of the pleasanter suburbs, courtesy of his wife's employers. He could not have afforded to live there on his salary, but his wife was an executive with the Nairobi subsidiary of an international company. Better still, she had been recruited in the USA and so was treated as international staff with the perks that this distinction entailed. Brought up in the States, because of her father's position as a lecturer at one of the lesser American universities, she had received her education and commenced her working life there, so was in many ways more American than Kenyan although she was Kenyan born to Kenyan parents. Odhiambo's culture did not encompass women who earned more than their husbands and this was yet one more reason for his estrangement from his relatives. But, however much Odhiambo believed he had rejected his cultural inheritance, he, too, was not at ease with the situation. He was honest enough to accept that he enjoyed the better lifestyle his wife's earnings provided too much to renounce it, but it left him feeling somehow inadequate.

Once home, he tried to read, but his mind insistently returned to Hawk's Nest and the doings of the previous night. Finally, he telephoned the Mountain View Hotel in Nyeri and asked for McGuiry. He assumed that night's batch of guests for

Hawk's Nest would have been diverted elsewhere, and this was indeed the case. McGuiry was spending the night at the hotel, which acted as a sort of base camp for Hawk's Nest, and eventually he was located and extracted from the bar. Odhiambo obtained from the warden confirmation of something that was troubling him; he had been cursing himself for not checking it out while at the scene. It was after describing the layout of the lodge in more detail, in answer to the policeman's query, that McGuiry brought Odhiambo upright in his chair.

'Oh, bye-the-bye, Inspector . . .' McGuiry had reverted to addressing Odhiambo formally, now that the policeman was, as McGuiry saw it, on duty. 'There's one other wee bit of news. I had a good nose around today when the fuss died down. I told ye I used to do a bit of tracking in my hunting days. Well, I found the mark of a boot in a pile of dung – the cape buffaloes' doings – between the lodge and where we found the rifle. No good for identification, I mean no clear sole print or anything. But it was made when the dung was fresh and I reckon that puts it at sometime last night.'

'Are you sure we can't get a print?'

'Och, for sure, Inspector. Your colleague was still here, as a matter of fact. Took him to have a look. No good, he said, and lost interest. The laddie probably thought I didn'a ken when the mark was made, but I tell ye from the amount it had dried it was fresh last even', and someone put their foot in it while it was wet. Very skiddy sort of mark, ye ken.'

Odhiambo thought for a few seconds, trying to determine what significance this might have. Then he felt a stir of excitement in his veins.

'Mr McGuiry – Robert, are you sure it wasn't another animal which trod in it?'

'No, no, laddie. You could tell it was a boot or shoe. And I've been thinking. If one of our friends of last night did it on the way to firing that shot, or coming back, of course, why, he'd have a dirty boot.'

Exactly, thought Odhiambo. He pressed McGuiry further.

'Can you be sure it wasn't one of your men, when you sent them out after the stampede?'

'Well nigh sure, Inspector. I asked Daniel. It wasn't him and he checked with the others.'

Now comes the big one, thought Odhiambo. He was frantically trying to picture those first minutes in the bar, running the scene through his mind.

'Hello, are ye still there, Inspector?' The anxious voice of McGuiry summoned Odhiambo from his reverie. 'Dratted phones . . .'

'Yes, I'm here, I'm thinking. Tell me, Robert, and think carefully – do you recollect seeing anyone with muddy or shitty shoes before we found the body?'

'Och, that's it, Inspector, I don't. Of course, we had other things on our minds. But I've inspected the corridor and the escape steps you asked about just now. Found some traces. Canna be sure it's the same bit of dung, but I reckon you're thinking on the right lines. That's how the laddie with the gun got in and out. Or rather out and in again it would be. How about you? Did ye no' happen to spot our dirty boot?'

'No. No, I didn't. I'll think about it again, but I think it would have registered at the time if I had. Anyway, Robert, if I can still call you that, thanks for your help on both counts. Of course, this call is a bit unusual. It's not really my case, you understand.'

'Och well, it may be yet. And Robert it is, mind. If aught else comes up I'll let you know – as well as the police laddies here, of course. Now you look after yourself, do ye hear me, Ins . . . James. And bonnie luck to ye.'

Odhiambo muttered his farewell and returned to his thoughts. But it was two in the morning when he woke and the answer was clear. There was no dirty boot. It was like the old Sherlock Holmes story he'd read many years ago. The dog that did not bark in the night. Now we have, thought Odhiambo, the shoe that was too clean. He smiled to himself, and then slept soundly until his house servant woke him in the morning.

The sound of a car in the drive as he drank his coffee did not surprise him. The driver duly gave the message and Odhiambo was conveyed to the awaiting Chief Superintendent. Odhiambo liked his superior. Masonga was an amiable, honest policeman, not bright but diligent in following a logical course, and he did his best to look after Odhiambo's interests. He was currently trying, as Odhiambo knew, to secure Odhiambo's promotion – but without political backing to put the right word in certain quarters. Odhiambo needed Masonga's goodwill, although he doubted whether it would be sufficient.

Masonga was not one for chatter and got straight to the point.

'So, Odhiambo, your evening off has backfired. I've read your report and, of course, I've heard from the RA. You know he wants you in this and now the President's office has made it official.'

Odhiambo felt it wise to indicate his reluctance which, once genuine, was now fading fast.

'It was a complete coincidence that I was there and now it's a Nyeri *shauri*. I think Aramgu wants me in as a possible scapegoat in case there's political fall-out.'

He got no further before his superior interrupted.

'That's all irrelevant, Inspector, as well you know. The order's from State House and that's that.' He lit a cigarette and gazed at Odhiambo as if searching for the right words. 'There's been progress in Nyeri. They've let the people at the lodge go – the foreigners forbidden to leave the country without permission, of course. That'll be your job – the follow-up interviews here. But they've detained one man for further questioning.' Masonga looked down at his papers. 'Causington. First name Nicholas. A Kenya resident, but British passport holder. They're considering charging him with the murder – possibly by tomorrow. He's demanding access to lawyers and the British High Commissioner and so on.' Masonga paused and then pointed his cigarette at Odhiambo, causing the ash to fall over the desk. Masonga was a messy smoker. He waved his hand cursorily over the ash, merely spreading the particles wider, and continued. 'So, with this fellow as the suspect, go round and see the rest of the group he was with and anyone else you think has something to say and produce some corroborating evidence. They need it in Nyeri to strengthen the case.'

Odhiambo cursed silently. This development was predictable, but confirmed his fears. He must get his superior to see the dangers in the course that the Nyeri police were following. He spoke slowly and with emphasis.

'Superintendent, it's not that simple a case. Causington lied to me and no doubt to the locals. But it's very unlikely he committed the murder. You see, there were two incidents, both strange, and I don't know what their connection is. They might be completely unconnected. One, someone left the lodge with a rifle stolen from the game warden and fired a shot near a herd of elephant causing a stampede. Two, someone, at roughly the same time, hit Mrs Farwell on the head with an axe and pushed her body over the rail where she lay in the path of the elephants. I am almost sure that Causington fired the shot, but someone else used the axe.'

The Chief Superintendent took a few moments in his usual slow way to think through Odhiambo's statement.

'Even if you're right and this *mzungu*, what's his name, fired the shot, why does that alibi him for the murder? He kills the woman then frightens the elephants to conceal the crime. If you can prove that he fired the shot, the rest will follow. *Shauri quisha*,' said Masonga, using a Swahili phrase meaning 'the fuss is over'.

Odhiambo held up a large hand, fingers extended, and ticked off the points.

'He left the main party with the woman, with all appearances of them being on very friendly terms. If she'd been strangled on a bed or something, we could say she changed her mind and refused to have sex with him – but he'd hardly take her out on to the luggage platform for that.'

Odhiambo snapped down his forefinger and continued.

'The only way Causington could get to the ground easily was via a fire escape at the far end of the lodge past the bedrooms. I checked this with the game warden last night.' Odhiambo realized too late his error in revealing a continued interest in the case. He continued quickly. 'If he was going to murder the woman and throw her down, why not do it on his way instead of taking her in a different direction? What's more, from where the elephants were, the body would have been closer to them and more likely to get trampled on.'

Odhiambo lowered his middle finger and leaned closer towards the Superintendent, holding his third finger.

'But most of all, and what I'm saying is confirmed by McGuiry – that's the warden – most of all, Superintendent, there was no way of knowing that the elephants would run on a path that took them under the lodge. Causington has lived in Kenya all his life. He'd be out of his mind to think that. It was either an incredible coincidence that the elephants ran over her, or – ' Odhiambo slowed his speech even further – 'someone took advantage of the approaching elephants and seized his chance to break her skull and hope to get away with it. In either case, Causington, who fired the shot, is not the killer.'

Odhiambo lowered his hand and waited. Masonga stubbed out the cigarette which had burned away between his fingers and lit another. His face, already creased and wrinkled under the grey hair, seemed to furrow further. His questions, when they came, were clearly behind the point where his thoughts had taken him.

'How do you know Causington fired the shot? According to the reports there's no prints on the gun, or rather it's full of prints of all the idiots who picked it up and probably handed it around. And if he did it, why? What point was there in firing at the elephants?'

Odhiambo took the questions in reverse order.

'He wasn't firing at them; he merely wanted a stampede. Why? For excitement – to impress his new girlfriend. Remember, they'd been drinking steadily for hours. I saw him whispering to her as if he was suggesting something. I thought he was suggesting going to his room, but no, he was going to impress her with his daring. And off they went, giggling. It's something like that at any rate, because that's what he did. How do I know? Because he was clearly lying about what happened after he left with the woman. And when I interviewed him he was wearing a safari suit with smart black leather shoes. They seemed incongruous with the fawn suit. Too dressy and the wrong colour. But earlier in the evening I'm sure he was wearing suede safari boots. On his little excursion he trod in a pile of shit and realized that dirty boots would give the game away. So he changed and got rid of the boots somewhere during the commotion. We'll get the Nyeri boys to find them and that will be that. We'll have Bwana Causington for stealing a rifle and illegal firing of same in a national park and so on. But we won't have Mrs Farwell's killer.'

Masonga had risen and was pacing the office. He was a short man, with a careworn and bedraggled air. Odhiambo had seldom seen him look more so than now. Masonga coughed and returned to his chair.

'Odhiambo, you know what you're saying, don't you? You're going to complicate Aramgu's life and delay the case. Unless, of course, you know who did do it and can prove it. The President's office wants this thing over to prevent bad publicity abroad. We have a suspect who is not a tourist, not an African and who kills the woman through jealousy or some such sexual angle. No *shauri*. No foreign reporters. The Big Man and Aramgu congratulating themselves. So you say, no, it's not like that, but I don't know who did it. Tourists are held over in Nairobi for questioning. In come the foreign press. Odhiambo, do you have a death wish?'

Odhiambo was prepared with his defence.

'But, Superintendent, if Causington goes on trial for murder and has a top lawyer like George Albinger, what do you think he will do with the police case? He'll pick holes in it as easily as I'm doing.'

Masonga sighed at the apparent naïvety of his subordinate.

'So? By the time the trial is on no one abroad will be paying much attention. Whether he gets off or not – it will be an old story. And much can be arranged between now and a trial.'

The two men stared at each other, the discomfort rising between them and souring further the already smoky air. At last, Odhiambo spoke.

'What do you want me to do?'

'I can take you off the case. Plead that you're needed for something else, or you're prejudiced by being a witness yourself. I'll put Kamau on it. But that will take me a day or so. Meanwhile, I'm under orders. They want interviews today. So do them, Odhiambo. Just facts. Pin down the locations of everybody and timings and so on. Keep your theories to yourself and hope to God you're wrong.'

Odhiambo rose and turned towards the door, making a visible effort at self-control. Masonga spoke to the retreating back.

'There's no need for you to contact Nyeri. Report through me. Is that clear?'

'What about the boots? They need those even for their own cock-eyed theory.'

'The boots?' Masonga looked vaguely at his notes. 'Oh, yes, the muddy boots. I'll pass on your suggestion for a search for those.' He looked up. 'Be careful, Inspector.'

But Odhiambo had gone.

*

As he arrived at the bottom of the stairs leading to the exit, a policeman in plain clothes accosted him with a summons from another potential source of trouble. Odhiambo sighed and followed his guide to an unmarked office.

W. P. Price-Allen at first acquaintance appeared to be what his forebears actually were – men of minor English aristocratic stock who had acquired their tans and decadent air in the highlands of Kenya. The impression of vacuity was one Price-Allen was careful to foster. He made regular appearances at his Nairobi club bar, engaging heartily in the banal conversations that were a feature of this favoured location for the enjoyment of the sundowner. He was also to be seen at the Nairobi racecourse on a Sunday, but only after attending matins at church near his home. A bachelor in his late forties with a comfortable income, derived from the capital raised by the sale of the family farm at the time of Kenya's independence and augmented through careful and quietly handled participation in business ventures launched by emerging Kikuyu businessmen, Price-Allen was in the position of being able to indulge his fancy. A sequence of chance, initial contact, demonstrated usefulness and reliability over the years, made Price-Allen one of the very few men trusted by successive governments. The unofficial role he played was a dual one: overseer of the intelligence arm of the Kenya police service and arranger of the removal of those deemed to be a threat to senior officials. Such removal ranged from 'voluntary' exile to the more permanent and certain solution that had become known in Swahili as 'vanishment'. Price-Allen regarded it as a failure if occasionally some remains surfaced. He enjoyed planning such removals; ensuring the successful co-ordination of complex and interwoven arrangements fulfilled a need to occupy his devious mind with something more risky than chess. He also liked to be present at the climactic moment of his operations; this fulfilled his other need, to achieve relief from tension akin to sexual orgasm through the infliction of pain.

Odhiambo was aware in a general way of the activities of the man sitting at a steel table in a small and almost bare office. The rumours were numerous, if, as Odhiambo supposed, somewhat embellished. He knew that the truth would be ugly enough and he thanked the Luo gods that his path had not crossed Price-Allen's before. But now it seemed his luck had run out.

Odhiambo guessed the aspect of the Nyeri case that was of concern to this apparently relaxed man who gestured him to a chair.

'This is unofficial, Inspector, so let's not stand on ceremony. I wish to share a little information with you. And get your opinion. I suppose I don't need to say that my interest is on behalf of the government. Intelligence and that sort of thing.'

Price-Allen made a dismissive gesture as if he and Odhiambo, as grown men, knew that such matters were childish, but politicians needed to be humoured.

Odhiambo nodded and waited. He was aware that he was under close scrutiny. He, in turn, studied more overtly the man facing him. Medium height, medium build, tanned as most white Kenyans were, pale eyes, a mouth which in repose had a sardonic twist, dressed in shorts, open-necked shirt and long socks, the traditional colonial attire – everything about Price-Allen seemed conducive to conveying a false impression of out-of-date ordinariness.

Price-Allen allowed the pause to lengthen and then, as if satisfied by what he saw, leaned forward and continued.

'This Nyeri business. Unfortunate, of course. Potentially embarrassing and all that. One hopes the Nyeri people don't screw up, eh? Fortunately, I'm told you are to keep an eye on things. And you have the advantage of personal contact with the main actors, as one might say.' Price-Allen paused again for a moment and then continued. 'And I'm told you're an able and reliable man.' There was just a shade of emphasis on the word 'reliable'. 'That's why I want your views on a matter of some delicacy. I am told a man called Nicholas Causington has been detained in connection with the death of the woman. Tell me, Inspector, how do you assess Causington's role?'

Odhiambo noted how well briefed Price-Allen was about his involvement. He thought for a moment before replying.

'I have just briefed Chief Superintendent Masonga. He informed me that Mr Causington has been detained. I have no information regarding the evidence the Nyeri police have obtained. The Superintendent has asked me to conduct some follow-up interviews here in Nairobi.'

Price-Allen smiled and seemed genuinely amused.

'You are discreet, Inspector, I see. But I'm sure I don't need to produce my credentials or call Masonga to give you permission to talk to me. I can't stand red tape and formality. Let me show my hand, Inspector. Causington is known to me. He is, of course, a man of little intelligence and less consequence, but he has been useful to us on occasion. That sort of man picks up gossip, you know. These social butterflies can be a useful listening device.'

Odhiambo nodded again. His suspicions were confirmed. Causington was a Price-Allen informer. He saw no point in holding back the facts and proceeded to give, for the second time in the last hour, a summary of the events. Price-Allen listened, but his fingers drumming lightly on the table indicated impatience. Finally, he interrupted.

'Inspector, the facts I know. I want your impressions. Causington's involvement is potentially an embarrassment. He may be indiscreet. He has already asked to speak to me, I understand. What do you assess his role as being? I want your frank assessment, and I want it now.'

The last words were spoken with the authority that had previously been concealed. Pleasantries were over: Price-Allen wanted to get on.

'Causington probably was not in the lodge when the murder occurred. He may, however, be guilty of lesser offences – stealing a rifle and discharging it in a national park. In my view the murderer was another member of the victim's group. I don't know who, but Causington may be a material witness even if he is not charged with the murder.'

'There, Inspector, it wasn't so hard, was it? I'm grateful to you. You confirm my impressions. Causington is a fool but not a murderer. So Inspector, it remains only for me to wish you luck with your enquiries. We need the killer quickly. Anyone but a talkative Causington will do.' Price-Allen smiled to indicate that the remark was light-hearted, although, Odhiambo thought, there was nothing light-hearted about Price-Allen.

'You realize, Mr Price-Allen, that my role is merely to assist the Nyeri police. That's all. I am not in charge of the investigation.'

Price-Allen sighed at the stupidity that constantly crossed his path. He rose to his feet and took Odhiambo by the arm as the policeman also rose.

'Inspector. Let the Nyeri police go about their business. You do your interviews and report as appropriate. But, Inspector, keep me informed. I don't drop names to impress people. You know the high level of concern about this matter. Your co-operation will be appreciated.' The smile made a reappearance. 'It's good to have met you. I'm sure you'll be helpful.'

With that Odhiambo found himself back in the corridor. My God, he thought, why did I accept Albinger's invitation? Now I'm caught in the middle between the Nyeri police, the RA, State House, Masonga and now, God help me, the dreaded *mzungu* with the smile of a predator who has cornered his prey.

Half an hour later he left the building, clutching his notes with the addresses that he needed. At least he had a car and driver at his disposal: the only consolation for his high-risk exposure.

8

George Albinger, after arranging for his niece to leave for Mombasa, honoured his commitment to a four-ball golf match, ensured that he signed for the first round of drinks, and then excused himself to return to his spacious bungalow in Karen, a high-income suburban area of Nairobi. Being a bachelor, and Sunday being his cook's day off, Albinger normally lunched at the club, but today he wanted to be alone to think, and to be sober while doing so. The natural curiosity of his golfing companions regarding the events at Hawk's Nest was not only a minor irritant but reminded him of aspects of the affair that he needed to sort out in his mind.

Although his cook was missing, his factotum was on call. The increasing risk of burglary in the Nairobi suburbs made it unwise to leave a house completely unattended. Albinger requested a cold beef sandwich, poured himself a gin and tonic, with a smaller than usual portion of gin, and settled on his verandah. It looked out over his extensive garden, which was filled with overgrown, unpruned shrubs. The laziness of his gardener fitted well with Albinger's preference for a natural wild look to his garden. Only the lawn was manicured so that Albinger, the golfer, could practise his chipping and putting.

There had been no chance to speak to his friend Odhiambo

after the discovery of the woman's body, so he was not privy to any inside information: but it was obvious that the police believed the woman was murdered. Albinger had come to the same conclusion as Odhiambo: if Diana Farwell was murdered it was virtually certain that one of her group was the murderer. Albinger searched his memory to recapture the pictorial images of events up to and including the elephant stampede, but the result merely confirmed that all the potential suspects were absent from the verandah at the crucial time and so outside his scrutiny.

The aspect intriguing Albinger, as he sipped his drink, was the circumstances of the group coming together, which he had happened to witness. It was, ostensibly, a happy meeting of old friends, but Albinger noted at the time an underlying tension below the superficial heartiness. Was the death of the woman linked to her meeting with faces from her past? It seemed a strange coincidence that she should meet her death in such a bizarre way so shortly after the encounter. Did she present a threat to someone, or, as would be the usual case, was it the husband or a jealous lover? Whoever did the deed must have seized a momentary opportunity with all its inherent risks. That spoke either of desperation or a mind used to making decisions quickly and willing to take substantial risks. I wonder what the husband does for a living, thought Albinger.

But the more he mulled matters over, the more certain he became that what was troubling him was something different. There was something relevant in the recesses of his memory, but he couldn't retrieve it. His resolution weakened: another, stronger gin and tonic accompanied his sandwich, and Albinger dozed off. In his doze, faces flitted in and out of a dream. But one face seemed wrong, as if masked. It came into focus, faded and then returned. An hour later the lawyer woke with a start, cricking his neck. After a moment or two to orient his senses, he sat very still for several minutes. His retrieval processes had worked during his sleep. He remembered now. But was it relevant? On the face of it, there was nothing sinister about the connection; quite the reverse, in fact. Still, tomorrow he would initiate some enquiries.

The ringing of the telephone took him into his study. When he heard the voice Albinger was hard put to it to keep surprise out of his reply.

'Shropshire? Yes, of course, I know. We have met, I think. At the club, right? We recognized each other from the Lusaka days.'

His caller, Peter Shropshire, sounded slightly embarrassed. He spoke somewhat hurriedly, as if afraid the lawyer would interrupt him before he had time to put his request.

'I say, Albinger, I'm sorry to bother you on Sunday, but it's this business at Hawk's Nest. Dreadful thing. I only noticed you were there late in the proceedings. Didn't get round to speaking then because the police were all over us. Anyway, I wanted to ask if I could stop by to ask you about something that's troubling me. I know it must seem a strange request, but this Hawk's Nest thing is worrying the life out of me.'

Albinger decided that he would stop being surprised at coincidences. Shropshire was obviously going over the same ground that Albinger himself had been ploughing in his mind.

'Not at all, old boy. It is a terrible business. What is it you would like to see me about?'

'Rather not talk about it on the telephone, if you don't mind. But it's about Mrs Farwell, the dead woman. She and her husband were staying with us, you know. Of course, Morgan, her husband, still is, if you know what I mean?'

Albinger put down the telephone a minute or so later, having agreed to Shropshire's immediate visit. Well, thought Albinger, that suits me. Meanwhile he decided to refer to his old files in his study. He remembered his role in the affair, but the details were hazy. The files would refresh his memory.

In another of the wealthier suburbs, somewhat closer to the city, John Mallow was engaged in an argument with his wife – an occurrence that was becoming increasingly frequent.

'For heaven's sake, Letty. I keep telling you, I don't know why she was killed – if she was killed, that is. Remember, no one has said she was murdered.'

His wife clutched her glass more tightly in an attempt to control the tremble in her hand.

'If she wasn't murdered why do you think the police are making all the fuss? We've been questioned twice at the lodge and now that inspector, what's-his-name, is coming here.'

It was a telephone call from Odhiambo to confirm they were at home and available for more questions that had provoked Letty out of her self-imposed silence into a somewhat tipsy argument with her husband.

'All right. Say she was murdered. Why should it have anything to do with the old Kampala days? Christ, woman, that was twenty years ago. What's done is done. I've served my penance for that little affair. I had no reason to kill her and I didn't kill her.'

Letty Mallow gazed at her husband as if at an imbecile. She spoke slowly, not only because of the danger of slurring her words.

'Because once the inspector finds out that you and Guy Fulton were screwing around with Diana Crandon, he is going to find it very strange that no sooner do you both meet up with her again than she gets pushed under an elephant's foot. Mind you, a girl like that, there must have been scores of bastards like you, both before and after your turn. A tart like her should expect to come to a sticky end. My God! I had to live with this in Kampala and now I'm going through it again. Talk about your sins haunting you. But why should I have to put up with being haunted too?'

Letty was close to tears of self-pity. Her husband felt a different emotion, one of suppressed rage. He fought to control his voice.

'Listen, Letty, carefully. We can tell the police we knew her in Uganda. That's no secret, for Christ's sake. There is no need to go any further. Unless it's you that wants to reveal all so you can wallow in your sanctimonious barbs at me all over again.'

'And what about Mr Guy bloody Fulton? What if he tells all? What are you going to do then to explain why you didn't tell the truth, Mr Smart-Ass?'

Mallow spoke as if to himself.

'Actually, I don't think Guy knows much about Diana other than his own involvement. And that, from something she once told me, could be a real problem for him. No, I don't think we shall hear Mr Fulton telling tales out of school.' Mallow ruminated for a while, then returned his attention to his wife. 'Letty, listen to me. All we need to do is keep our wits about us. The inspector will be here in a minute. Put your drink away, go and freshen up, and act the dutiful wife who hasn't anything to add.' He looked at his wife with a feeling of distaste. 'Not that you could add anything of relevance, as you were drunk as usual.'

Letty rose to her feet with dignified care and turned to go to the kitchen with her empty glass.

'Don't you be so sure,' she riposted as she left. 'I may know more than you think.'

And that was possible, thought Mallow. He had been surprised how incapacitated Letty seemed when she left the group at Hawk's Nest. She was drunk, certainly. But she could hold her drink better than she did that night. Perhaps she hadn't been as drunk as she wanted to appear.

It was Guy Fulton who was the first to receive a visit from Odhiambo that Sunday afternoon. Odhiambo was not sure why he chose Fulton for his first call. Partly, it was a matter of convenience, Fulton's hotel being situated in the middle of Nairobi and close to the Central Police Station. But Odhiambo was also intrigued by the international banker. Apart from Causington, Fulton was the most uneasy during Odhiambo's interviews. Unlike Causington, he had taken pains to be polite and correct, but there had been a defensiveness in his responses, despite their apparent insignificance in terms of substance. The hotel reception desk paged Fulton in response to Odhiambo's request and he was duly located in the residents' lounge drinking a post-lunch coffee. The two men repaired to Fulton's suite on the top floor. The glass doors leading on to a small balcony provided a panoramic view of Nairobi and beyond to the Ngong Hills. The room itself was furnished in a standard up-market hotel manner: sofa, chairs, small table, writing-desk against the wall. Paintings of two types of orchid graced the walls. Fulton gestured for Odhiambo to occupy the sofa and seated himself on the upright chair that served the writing-table, so forcing the policeman to look up at him. Odhiambo was unconcerned by this simple manoeuvre: he was looking for a conversational style of exchange, not a formal question and answer session.

Apologies for the Sunday visit had been offered in the lift, so Odhiambo moved on.

'You understand, Mr Fulton, that, as the enquiries by the

Nyeri police move ahead, it is necessary to fill in more details than it was possible to cover at Hawk's Nest.'

The banker looked more at ease than he had during their last encounter. Understandable, of course: violent death can disturb the most stoic and placid of men, but the change was very apparent.

'Yes, of course, Inspector, er . . . Odhiambo, isn't it? Glad to be of help. Anxious for you to make headway, as a matter of fact. It will be very inconvenient if I am detained in Kenya for very long.' Realizing that detention had a different connotation in Kenya, as in most African countries, Fulton added hastily, 'Detained, I mean, in the sense, er, of not being allowed to leave – to return to Washington.'

'You have already given an account of your movements about the time Mrs Farwell met her death. I want to ask you now about the group that was with her that evening. First, how did you come to join Mrs Farwell's party?'

Fulton looked away towards the window for a moment and then returned his gaze to his interrogator.

'That's easy. I was a guest of John Mallow, manager of the Overseas and Eastern Bank here in Nairobi. He is closely connected with my official business here in Kenya. He suggested a visit to Hawk's Nest, partly as a break, and partly to give us the opportunity to discuss outstanding problems in a more informal atmosphere, before continuing our talks with other interested parties tomorrow.'

Odhiambo was patient.

'I understand why you were with Mr and Mrs Mallow. But I am interested in why your party joined that of Mrs Farwell.'

'Yes. Well, it was really a party hosted by the local man, the scientist fellow, Shropshire, as I recall. Mallow and Shropshire know each other, I believe. Introductions followed. One thing led to another and we joined them for dinner. Mr and Mrs Farwell are, were, staying with the Shropshires, I believe. The other man, they called him Nick. Not sure what his other name is. I'm not sure what his connection is, either. Friend of the Shropshires, I suppose. Seemed pretty fond of Diana Farwell, to tell you the truth. Somewhat embarrassing, as a matter of fact.'

'Ah yes. Mr Causington was on particularly good terms with Mrs Farwell. And she with him. At least it seemed that way to a casual observer. Did that cause any problems? Within the group, I mean.'

Fulton seemed genuinely puzzled.

'Problems? What do you mean, problems? Oh, I see. Farwell himself, do you mean? No, he seemed resigned to Causington sucking up to his wife. No overt jealousy that I noticed.'

'You mentioned that the Mallows and the Shropshires knew each other. What about you, Mr Fulton? Did you know anyone, other than the Mallows, of course? The deceased lady, for instance?'

Fulton looked at the policeman as if reassessing him. He seemed to retreat within himself as if retiring behind fortified defences.

'Yes. As a matter of fact, I did. Bit of a coincidence that. I should explain that both Mallow and I were in the banking business in Kampala in the old days. Pre-Amin, I mean.' Fulton allowed the merest ghost of a smile to appear and vanish in a trace. 'Mrs Farwell, Diana – I mean she wasn't Mrs Farwell then – she was also there. She was a "stenog" – a secretary – in one of the Ministries. They used to bring in British stenogs for senior officials in those days. Probably the rule still exists if they could persuade girls to go there. Still a pretty hairy place when I last visited.'

'Remarkable coincidence, meeting an old friend like that, wouldn't you say?'

'Oh, I don't know. In this business of jumping about the world you keep bumping into people you know. A relatively limited number, all ricocheting around the capitals of the developing countries. Surprising how often it happens, actually.'

Odhiambo decided to change tack and force the issue. Fulton, with years of loan negotiations as experience, seemed prepared to stonewall for ever. He stood up, so reversing Fulton's advantage of being seated above him.

'But it wasn't just another casual acquaintance was it, Mr Fulton? Mrs Farwell seemed to regard both you and Mr Mallow as very dear old friends.'

Fulton seemed to relax. He was no fool, Odhiambo thought. He's like a bridge player. Now that he's forced my hand he feels he can trump my ace. The banker smiled and also rose to cross to the windows.

'You shouldn't read too much into Diana's attitude to us, Inspector. That's Diana all over. She's not changed. I mean, she hadn't changed. Always wanting men in thrall around her. Can't you see, man, that was her way of making both her husband and her new boyfriend jealous.' Fulton paused and looked back towards the policeman. 'Tell me, Inspector. No one has confirmed it yet, you understand. All these questions. Am I to assume that Diana – Mrs Farwell – was, er, murdered?'

'I think you may assume that, sir, yes. We are investigating the matter on the basis that Mrs Farwell met her death unlawfully. Subject to medical confirmation, that is.'

'But who could have done it? Perhaps one of the staff, trying to steal her jewellery or watch or something. Couldn't have been . . . Well, anyway, I'm afraid I can't help you further, Inspector. Surely you must be mistaken? An accident seems so much likelier, slipped and fell or something. She'd had a few drinks, you know.'

'That is what someone wanted us to think, sir. And Mrs Farwell was wearing no jewellery except a cheap watch which she was still wearing when she was found. Well, I won't trouble you any more for now, sir. Thank you for your help. And my condolences.'

'Condolences? Oh, I see what you mean. Yes, poor Diana. Terrible business. Awful.'

It had taken a deal of prompting to elicit any expression of sorrow from the banker. And when it came it lacked even a veneer of sincerity. Diana Farwell's death was either a relief or an irritation to Guy Fulton. The question, Odhiambo thought, as he entered the lift, was which?

Odhiambo's next visit was to the Mallows. He expected little in the way of new information to result from them and his low expectations were fulfilled. He decided that Mrs Mallow was an alcoholic. She sat deliberately still throughout the interview, hands clutched together in her lap, speaking slowly, distinctly, but with the occasional tripping of the tongue that betrays the inebriated. She said nothing specific, but implied by manner and innuendo that she could, if moved to do so, say more about the morals and lifestyles of both the dead woman and Guy Fulton in their earlier days. She was also the most racist of the group associated with the investigation. She was condescendingly polite, with frequent rephrasings of simple statements into even simpler English as if making matters clear to a child, or, as in her mind, to a simple African. Her points were prefaced by such remarks as, 'It may be difficult for you to appreciate, that is, to understand that, well, the expatriate community likes to . . .' 'I know you may think this strange, but, you know, different customs and so on . . .'

Odhiambo was accustomed to the Mallow type of white businessman in Kenya. His prejudices might be the same as his wife's, but he knew how to conceal them more successfully. His manner, the precise opposite of his wife's, was to talk to Odhiambo in a man-to-man, you understand how it is, we're all members of the same club tone: at pains to convey the desired subliminal message. 'I haven't even noticed you are black.' Its constant repetition served to deliver the opposite signal. Mallow stressed the formal nature of his relationship with Guy Fulton. 'Took him away for the night, really, so as to get a chance to fill him in on the local situation. You know how these international experts are – think they know the local situation in terms of their business management textbooks. Not like us who have to experience it every day.' In terms of remembrance of the old chummy Uganda days, Mallow's memory was professedly sadly wanting. He was sure that all concerned were decent people – 'You know, Inspector, how one can tell these things' – including Diana. 'Are you sure she didn't slip? I don't have to tell you what a few drinks can do to a woman's head.' This brought forth a snort from his wife.

Regarding Nick Causington, neither Mallow could contribute much. Mrs Mallow had heard him spoken of in her bridge group as an eligible bachelor. 'Something of an intellectual lightweight, I should think, Inspector, wouldn't you?' was the contribution from the male half of the duo.

Altogether a pair not untypical of many expatriate couples, thought Odhiambo. Bitchy with each other, 'intellectual lightweights', to borrow Mallow's phrase, inclined to drink too much and possibly dangerous if their comfortable lifestyle was threatened. As his car pulled out of the drive he noted the steel fencing, the heavy gates and the standard signs on the gate, 'Mbwa Kali' – literally 'Angry Dog' – and 'Premises Protected by Security Guards Limited'. These days, as burglaries by violent gangs proliferated, the population of the wealthy suburbs, black, white and Asian, retreated behind bars and guards, both canine and human. Spacious gardens surrounding bungalows designed with long colonial verandahs for an open-plan type of living now seemed incongruously shrunk within a protected and opaque perimeter.

Odhiambo's driver made his way towards another suburb, this one, Langata, the home of the Shropshires. Odhiambo had confirmed earlier that Morgan Farwell had returned to Nairobi and remained a guest in the Shropshire house. This, unlike the Mallows', remained open; the low well-pruned hedge which marked the boundary allowed an unrestricted view towards the hills. Odhiambo wondered why the Shropshires remained immune to the pressure for fortified perimeters. As he got out of the car the other popular line of defence made an appearance. Two Rhodesian ridgebacks approached, with spinal hair erect and threatening growls. A female voice from the direction of the verandah ordered them to stand down from duty; this was but reluctantly obeyed, and the lingering growls rumbled on seemingly from deep down in their bellies.

Helen Shropshire was dressed in a grey skirt topped by a simple white blouse. Beyond the verandah, Odhiambo could see the corner of a swimming pool. He suspected that on a normal warm Sunday afternoon, the young and attractive Mrs Shropshire would be in a swimsuit, or at least shorts. He assumed the sober dress was a gesture of respect for the dead, although at his earlier interview at Hawk's Nest Helen Shropshire exhibited no sign of sorrow, real or feigned. She was, in Odhiambo's estimation, a pretty cool customer.

Arriving on the verandah, Odhiambo saw Morgan Farwell seated in a wooden chair at a small table. He and his hostess were partaking of afternoon tea, but the tray was set for two people only. He turned to the lady of the house.

'Mrs Shropshire, I'm sorry to disturb you, but as I mentioned on the telephone, there are a few questions that have to be put. Is your husband here?'

'I'm sorry, Inspector, he had to go out to see someone. He said that on the way back he would call in at the centre to check that all was well. As we've been away. My husband is head of the Livestock Disease Centre, but I expect you know that. I'm afraid he may be some time.'

Odhiambo nodded and turned to the seated man.

'Mr Farwell, I know this is a very difficult time for you. But I wonder if I could go over a few things with you? It would help us make progress with our investigation of the circumstances of your wife's death.'

Morgan Farwell gestured to a chair. He too was composed.

'Please, sit down, Inspector. I'm pleased you've come, as at least you may be willing to give me some information. It seems that the police believe my wife was murdered, but no one will confirm it to me. I think I'm entitled to know how Diana died.' The voice cracked on the last word. 'You must understand that the – the uncertainty on top of everything makes matters so much worse.'

Odhiambo delayed his reply for a moment. He could think of no good reason not to be frank. Helen Shropshire interjected an invitation.

'Will you have a cup of tea, Inspector? And a cake?'

Odhiambo was thirsty and accepted the offer of tea but declined the cake. He then turned back to the man in the chair.

'We are awaiting the results of the post-mortem, Mr Farwell, which is why you have been given no official cause of death. I can tell you, unofficially of course, that the most probable sequence of events was that Mrs Farwell was struck a heavy blow on the back of her head while she was standing on the platform above where her body was found. She then fell or was pushed over the rail. She was almost certainly either unconscious or dead from the time of the blow. In either case we would be dealing with a matter of murder.'

Odhiambo put two large teaspoonfuls of sugar into his tea. He liked his tea sweet. Farwell muttered his thanks for Odhiambo's frankness while appearing to be deep in thought – reviewing, probably, the events of Friday night one more time in his mind.

'And now,' Odhiambo said, 'perhaps I could go over one or two things with you? Is there somewhere we can go?' He looked enquiringly at the woman who was still hovering around them and the tea table. She spoke quickly as if caught out in a social gaffe.

'You can stay here, of course. I . . . I have to go to speak to the cook. It's his day off really, but he offered to do supper in view of the, er, the circumstances. The staff are all very grieved by the terrible tragedy as well.'

With that, Helen Shropshire turned and passed through the doorway leading from the verandah to the interior.

'Mr Farwell, can you tell me how and when you met your wife and what brought you to Kenya?'

'My wife is, was, considerably younger than me, Inspector. I met her only last year at a party hosted by mutual friends. I had been married before, but my first wife died. We married four months ago. She brought new gaiety into my life. I'm afraid I was becoming a bit of a stick-in-the-mud. You know, and boring. Diana made me feel younger and more alive. I was grateful for that.' After a momentary pause, during which he swallowed heavily, the bereaved man continued. 'Diana worked in East Africa for some years in her young days. In Uganda and Zambia. She wanted a holiday in Kenya, which she only briefly visited in the earlier years. By coincidence, I was in touch with Peter Shropshire who is an old friend from university days. So, one thing led to another and here we are, or were. I mean.'

'You hadn't seen Mr Shropshire for some time?'

'No. No, we hadn't been in touch. Our paths differed. In fact, he has spent most of his working life in Africa. This is my first visit.' Again, emotion briefly surfaced. 'And it will be the last. As soon as I can get Diana out of here. I mean, take her body home. When will that be, Inspector?'

'It depends on the enquiries.' Odhiambo was non-committal. 'How did you happen to re-establish contact? With Mr Shropshire, I mean.'

'I am semi-retired, Inspector. Peter wrote to me about a professional matter to do with the Livestock Centre he runs here.'

'Are you a livestock scientist too, then? A vet or whatever.'

'No, no. I know nothing about cattle or any other animal. No, it was a general business question.'

Odhiambo let the matter drop. But it was puzzling. For the first time Farwell seemed to be evasive. Reluctant to give a simple, but full response.

'Now, I believe you told me yesterday you and your wife have been here for about a week. You know the Shropshires, of course, and I believe you know Mr Causington?'

'Yes, we met Mr Causington at a dinner party a night or two after we arrived. He indicated he too was intending to visit Hawk's Nest. So we joined forces, as it were.'

'Your group at Hawk's Nest also included Mr and Mrs Mallow and a Mr Fulton. Were any of these known previously to you or Mrs Farwell?'

'No. Well, that's to say we met them at Hawk's Nest through the Shropshires, who knew them. Or at least, knew the Mallows. But by a strange coincidence it turned out during conversation that Diana knew them when she was in Africa earlier. Uganda, I think, was the link.'

'Mrs Farwell was very animated on Friday evening. Was this normal high spirits? I mean, was her behaviour that evening in any way unusual?'

Morgan Farwell thought for a moment before replying.

'Inspector, I know what you're thinking. You were there, after all. Diana's great quality was her vivaciousness. That what I said just now. She made you feel younger, just being with her. This is the effect she tends to have on males, young and old. I suppose you would say she was flirtatious. But in a harmless way.'

The evasions were becoming more marked as the interview proceeded. Odhiambo decided to push a little harder.

'Are you telling me you didn't object to her flirting, as you call it? If I may say so, Mr Farwell, here in Africa we males would take offence at our wife acting in that way, especially in our presence.'

Morgan Farwell flushed slightly and sat up straighter in his chair.

'I repeat, Inspector, that her love of fun and amusing company was one of her traits that I cherished. As with all such traits you must pay the price for the pleasure obtained. I have no doubts regarding my wife's faithfulness to me so there was no need to act like a young jealous buck.'

Odhiambo switched the point of attack.

'You will be aware that I have to ask certain standard questions. Did Mrs Farwell have assets in her own right, and who will inherit them?'

'Diana has very little. A small cottage in Wales, a few trinkets. Nothing major. We both amended our wills when we married, leaving our estates to each other.'

'What about insurances? Policies on Mrs Farwell's life, that sort of thing?'

There was a momentary hesitation although the answer when it came was smooth enough. Almost, Odhiambo thought, as if it had been rehearsed.

'I believe it to be common prudence to maintain a significant amount of life insurance. I and my wife have similar coverage.'

'How much do you mean by significant?'

'I'm beginning to find this interview somewhat burdensome, Inspector. I am still in shock from my wife's tragic death. The sums involved are substantial. I would have to check with my solicitors to verify the details.'

The reason for evasion this time was obvious. Morgan Farwell stood to benefit from a substantial insurance on his new wife, who, shortly after he had taken out the policy, died in suspicious circumstances. A very common murder plot in both real life and fiction. It made the husband a prime suspect.

Odhiambo prepared to bring the interview to an end.

'I'm sorry, once again, for disturbing you at this time, Mr Farwell. Let me put one last question. Do you know of anyone at Hawk's Nest on Friday evening who had any reason to bear animosity towards your wife? Anyone at all?'

'I can't imagine anyone wishing her harm. She was too fond of life. I'm sorry I can't help you.'

Odhiambo rose to take his leave and as he looked down on the face of the man who started to rise also, he received suddenly but with absolute confidence the impression that he was looking at a frightened man. It was as if, for a moment, the mask slipped only to be quickly replaced. Morgan Farwell would merit careful investigation.

9

As Odhiambo made his way back to the car Helen Shropshire appeared around the corner of the house.

'Oh, Inspector, have you finished? My husband called from the centre a few minutes ago. He will be there for another hour or so. He said if there was anything urgent you wanted to see him about, could you call there?'

Odhiambo nodded.

'Yes, I may do that. He's in his office, is he?'

'Yes, he is. There's a guard at the gate. My husband said he would leave a message to let you in, although I suppose you can get in anyway, can't you? Being a police officer, I mean.'

Helen Shropshire gave a girlish giggle. She was an attractive woman, Odhiambo thought. Young, probably late twenties; red-headed; slim, athletic figure, but with pleasant feminine contours. He wondered how she came to marry a man so much older than herself. But, he supposed, amongst the Europeans this was quite a common practice. Young girls favoured men with power and status more than good-looking younger men. They walked together toward Odhiambo's car.

'Tell me, Mrs Shropshire, did you know the Mallows or the foreign banker before Friday?'

'I don't think so,' answered the woman at his side, puckering her freckled face in thought. 'Peter knew John Mallow, but I don't think I'd met either of them. I'd only met Nick Causington once, come to that. He sort of attached himself to the party. I think he was besotted with Diana.'

She stopped abruptly, as if she realized she was letting her tongue run away with her.

'And the Farwells? They are friends of your husband's, I understand. Not yours.'

They had arrived at the car and Helen smiled graciously at the driver, muttering the universal greeting '*Jambo*,' before turning back to the more senior of the policemen.

'No, that's right, I'd never seen them before. My husband knew Morgan, that's Mr Farwell, long before my time. Before I knew Peter, I mean. Diana, of course, was only recently married. I don't know if my husband knew Morgan's first wife, but I don't think so.'

'Mrs Farwell – she was a very extrovert person, wasn't she?'

'Oh, she was, she was. The centre of attention at a party or whatever. Men flocking around her. She loved the attention. Harmless fun, of course. She was very much in love with Morgan.'

But the last assessment was stated more from form than conviction. Odhiambo was amused that all Diana's intimates insisted on calling her harmless. About as harmless as a mamba, was his own assessment. He wished he knew Helen Shropshire well enough to ask her for her real opinion of Diana Farwell.

'Tell me, Mrs Shropshire, how did Mr Mallow and Mr Fulton react to meeting up with Mrs Farwell?'

Helen Shropshire kicked idly at a stone on the gravel drive. The pause extended while she made up her mind how frank to be. Eventually her innate tendency to respond positively asserted itself.

'To tell you the truth, Inspector, I don't think they were all that pleased. It seems she was an old flame of both of them and neither seemed delighted to be reminded of the fact. Diana can do that to people. Make them wriggle a bit. She gets her fun that way. I don't think she realizes that some people resent it.'

Including Helen Shropshire, Odhiambo thought. He noticed she referred to the dead woman in the present tense when she spoke of her more irritating characteristics. It still rankled, he thought, as he made his farewells and ducked into the car.

The sun was setting into the Rift Valley and the short twilight of the equator would soon mark the end of another day. It had been a hot afternoon and Odhiambo felt his shirt damp on his back. A suit was not ideal wear on a Sunday afternoon in March in Nairobi. He gave the driver the order to go to the Livestock Centre, and, in response to a blank look, gave the necessary directions. God knows where they get some of these drivers from, he thought. No doubt a nephew of some *bwana mkubwa* in the government but too thick to be given a soft office job. As they headed out from the suburbs on the road to Nakuru he watched as the high income residential areas gave way to farmland and humbler houses, many of which were the traditional earth-walled, thatch-roofed huts. Finally, the car approached the gates of the African Livestock Disease Control Centre. The compound contained a set of new modern wood and brick buildings, of which all but one were two storeys in height. The compound was surrounded by a strong steel fence with floodlights for lighting the fence and inner area at night. Security, he supposed, would be good, not only because of the normal risk of burglaries, but because in a place like this there would be dangerous substances, viruses and God knows what else needing to be closely protected.

The gates, pulled by a security guard, opened as the car

approached, the guard saluting as the police vehicle, identified by its number-plate, passed through. Odhiambo lowered his window and asked in Swahili for the office of the Director. The guard pointed to the single three-storey building in the compound and said the Bwana was there on the top floor. The car jerked into motion again, narrowly avoiding a flowerbed placed in the centre of the circular drive.

'How long have you been driving?' Odhiambo asked petulantly in Swahili. The worried look he got in return confirmed his worse suspicions. I wouldn't be surprised if they've given me a driver who had to buy his licence on the black market, he thought. I'll check up on it when I have a minute.

As he got out of the car, a head emerged from a window on the top floor and a voice shouted down.

'Inspector Odhiambo? Good. The door's unlocked. I'll meet you on the stairs.'

Odhiambo raised a hand in acknowledgement and entered the door marked Administration and Management. He was met as promised and ushered into a large office furnished with standard institutional-type steel desks, tables, cupboards, cabinets and fake leather chairs. There were a few personal touches, however. A mahogany table displayed medals and citations that Shropshire had received for his scientific work. There were three original African landscape paintings on the walls and on the window-sill a selection of orchids. Altogether, the office of a man who spent considerable time in it and was proud of his status.

Odhiambo, as he seated himself, surveyed the man now settling back into his executive chair. Heavily-built with a beer-belly, but a strong-looking man who walked with a lightness that indicated fitness. A strong face also, tanned and lined by years in the tropical sun, a firm mouth, a good head of brown hair and an overall impression of amiability.

'I must apologize, Inspector, for being out when you called.' Peter Shropshire opened the conversation in a friendly tone of voice. He gestured at his desk. 'Always a pile-up of papers to read when you take a day or two off. And I needed to see someone who lives on the way here, coming from my place that is. In Karen. Someone you know, as a matter of fact. George Albinger. I saw you together at the tree place. What a business. Terrible. Terrible. Morgan is holding up pretty well and Helen is handling him well. 'Fraid I'm not much good at the hand-holding bit.'

Odhiambo picked up his cue. It made as good a starting point as any. 'Yes, Mr Albinger and I were together at Hawk's Nest. Was it something to do with the events there that you wanted to discuss with him? Or other private business?'

'No. It was to do with Diana Farwell. The story's a bit involved, but let me make it simple. Although Morgan Farwell is an old friend I didn't know his wife, or thought I didn't. But when I was talking to her at Hawk's Nest she spoke of Lusaka and her accident. You may not have realized, but she had had extensive plastic surgery. She mentioned it when she saw George Albinger sitting with you. She said he was a solicitor in Lusaka at the time and handled the insurance claim and subsequent issues. She said she didn't know me but knew of me because her boyfriend who was killed in the accident that caused her injuries – a car crash – worked with me at the time. Bob Harling. I remember him well. Another bad business. Promising researcher still in his twenties. Strange coincidence, the whole business.'

Odhiambo considered this new twist to the biography of Diana Farwell. The woman seemed to have got around all over East Africa in her youth. He wondered why George Albinger hadn't told him that he knew her. Presumably he didn't recognize her. Older, and when he knew her the repairs effected by the plastic surgery might not have been made. He pressed the man opposite him further.

'But why did you need to see Albinger? Is there some connection between her death and the Lusaka incident?'

'No. No. Not as far as I know. How could there be?' Shropshire spoke hurriedly, as if realizing that by linking the dead woman to Albinger he was compromising the lawyer. 'No, I wanted to check that there was nothing germane from her court case and settlement that we needed to bring to Morgan's attention. I mean, there's no point in worrying him with the Lusaka business at this time when he's got enough to handle, unless it was somehow important. I thought Albinger could reassure me on the matter, and he did.'

'Do you have reason to suppose that Mr Farwell is unaware of his wife's past, or at least her accident? It would seem unlikely, given her plastic surgery.'

'I agree it seems unlikely. But I tell you, Inspector, not to speak ill of the dead, but Diana was a funny girl. Funny-strange, I mean. I get the distinct impression that Morgan is not altogether clear about her past. She seemed to like to convey a mysterious air. Here, do you smoke?' Shropshire proffered a silver cigarette box across the desk, but on receiving a shake of the head from the policeman, helped himself and fished around in his safari jacket for a box of matches.

'Well, you've given me something to think about, Mr Shropshire,' said Odhiambo, as Shropshire drew heavily on his cigarette. 'I was intending to ask you about the Kampala connection, not a Lusaka one.'

Shropshire looked puzzled for a moment, then allowed himself a small grin.

'Oh, you mean the embarrassed old boyfriends – our banker friends. I've never seen two men who seemed less enthusiastic about meeting an old friend than those two. Particularly the visiting one. What was his name? Fulton? Yes, that's right, Guy Fulton. Stuffed-shirt sort of fellow.'

'Mrs Farwell seems to have been a very mobile young lady.'

Shropshire laughed. 'She was that. Mobile around the men as well as around Africa, I would think. Well, why not? Poor bitch won't have any more fun now. As a matter of fact, it was not that unusual in those days for a girl like Diana, once they were in this part of the world, to move around. Kampala, Lusaka, places like that were pretty good places then. I mean,' Shropshire attempted to retrieve a gaffe, 'I mean, both before and after independence. Before the economies collapsed, I mean. Before Amin and so forth.'

'Did Mr Farwell seem surprised when his wife discovered old friends at Hawk's Nest? Not at the coincidence, I mean, but that his wife would know former Uganda expatriates.'

'That's what I mean, Inspector. He did seem taken aback. Covered it well, but I think he was playing it by ear for a while. News to him, I think, her Uganda days were.'

'How well do you know Mr and Mrs Mallow?'

'Oh, casually only. Met him at the club and at the occasional do, that sort of thing. I didn't remember her at all.'

'And Mr Causington?'

'Likewise. Knew him casually. Not my type. He latched on to Diana when we ran into him at some party last week. Invited himself along at the weekend as far as I could see.' Shropshire paused and then suddenly his manner changed. The somewhat superficial and boozy expatriate image disappeared and a more serious man was revealed in the body language and tone. 'Tell me, Inspector. Do you suspect that one of the people around Diana killed her? Albinger said that murder was suspected. It's not going to be good for any of us, or for Kenya come to that, if we're in for a lengthy murder investigation.'

Odhiambo gave his usual set piece about murder seeming the most likely explanation, pending confirmation. Shropshire lit another cigarette and gazed intently at the inspector.

'And you're not inclined to believe that it was one of the *wananinchi* or one of the Krauts or Yanks,' said Shropshire, using the Swahili name for the people of Kenya popularized by the first President, the revered Kenyatta. 'No, you're thinking about all the coincidences and homing in on one of us who were with her that night. Can't blame you for that. But it seems unbelievable, looked at from my perspective. These are all respectable people. I guess that gives you a laugh, eh, Inspector? Have you had many murders to investigate?'

'If this is murder, Mr Shropshire, as I believe it is, then it will be an unusual one, as you say. Most of my experience is with murders as a result of robbery and so on. This one has the makings of a story made popular by one of your English thriller writers.'

10

Odhiambo approached his house, head lowered and deep in thought. He had abandoned the car and driver at the point where the side road to his house met the main road from Nairobi. It was twilight now, the air was cooler, and Odhiambo felt the need to stretch his legs. His interview with Peter Shropshire had concluded with a brief summary of Shropshire's own background – a typical progression from colonial veterinary officer, followed by postgraduate studies, a return to Africa, a gradual rise in reputation as a result of research into a major cattle killer, East Coast fever, culminating in his appointment a few years ago as Director of the Nairobi-based centre. Shropshire, in Odhiambo's assessment, was a man who, having fulfilled his life's ambition, was now resting on his laurels, enjoying the status and lifestyle of the head of a research establishment. Odhiambo would check with Albinger the Shropshire version of their talk, but he had no doubt it would be confirmed. The Lusaka connection added a new and unexpected touch which might yet have some relevance, but Odhiambo was most interested in the Uganda link between the dead woman and three of the suspects. He refused to believe that the woman's connections with the group around her were unrelated to her death. Even if her husband was the perpetrator, the murder may have been triggered by the opportunity offered by her African past to spread suspicion over a wider field.

Because of his preoccupation he turned on to the lawn in front of the bungalow before he noticed that the Datsun saloon was parked in the open garage, indicating his wife Cari was back. His mood lightened immediately; he was still sufficiently besotted by his wife that seeing her again even after a short absence caused his heart to race. He welcomed, too, a sympathetic and trusted ear into which to pour his thoughts on the Diana Farwell case. He cleared the two steps to his verandah and the front door with a light step and entered, calling her name. Cari, real names Charity Faith, emerged from the kitchen. She was a striking-looking woman of thirty with the height and lissomeness characteristic of her ancestral Highland tribe, with nothing of the heavy-buttocked look of the women of the major Bantu tribes in Kenya. James Odhiambo was physically captivated by her beauty, but his love was built on more – behind the beauty was an intelligent, modern mind. He could not live with a woman, however beautiful, if she exhibited the docile, subservient, unquestioning behaviour of some of the wives of his acquaintances.

Cari welcomed her husband with a full-blooded kiss, but quickly eased her way out of the embrace before his senses were aroused. As they separated she looked intently into his eyes as if anticipating news, but Odhiambo was still concerned with the question of her return.

'Cari! I wasn't expecting you till tomorrow. What brings you back tonight?'

They spoke in English, Cari's language of choice after her American upbringing. She spoke Swahili, but not the language of her husband's tribe, nor indeed her own.

'I was having lunch with my Nakuru girlfriends. There was a guy at the bar from Nyeri. He told us about a woman being killed at Hawk's Nest, and that it might be a homicide and that you were there. I decided there and then that my guy would need me back pronto. How are you, James? Come and have a beer and tell me all about it.'

Cari Odhiambo's American accent and marked American turn of phrase were, Odhiambo sometimes admitted to himself, a slight irritant. It was a small price to pay for such an otherwise perfect package, but he would consider the price higher if he came to realize that some of the Americanisms were entering his own vocabulary. He allowed himself to be taken by the hand into the kitchen where his wife retrieved a large beer bottle from the refrigerator. Cari was preparing a cold supper, and her own drink of passion-fruit juice was on the work surface. She preferred to do her own cooking when she was free to do so and in any case Sunday was their servant's day off. Odhiambo collected a handled beer mug and they took their drinks to the verandah, cool now in the dusk of evening.

The conversation for a few minutes was sporadic and idle as Odhiambo enjoyed his wife's company. But, when his beer glass was half drained, Cari turned his mind back to the business at hand.

'How is it going, James? Is it tricky, this Hawk's Nest business?'

Odhiambo hesitated momentarily: pouring out his troubles would place the burden on his wife. He had no fear regarding her discretion. They shared business secrets, knowing they would go no further, finding mutual help in talking freely about their current preoccupations. It was this potential assistance which quickly overrode his hesitation.

'Yes, it's a messy one, Cari. You know how sensitive the government is to tourists getting killed and the effect it has on the tourist trade. So there's that to contend with. They want a solution fast. But the man they would like to finger not only didn't do it, but turns out to be a Price-Allen informer. You've heard of the dreaded *mzungu*, Price-Allen. I was summoned to his presence today. Creepy sort of fellow. So you know what complications that could cause. And then, incredibly, it looks as if I've got one of those cases that belong in fiction. A set of suspects with no alibis and all with something to hide.'

As he summarized the basic facts and major players, Cari listened attentively, but her mind was considering the political dimension. That was where the threat was. She waited until her husband raised his glass for a swig of beer.

'One thing I don't get. Why don't they stick to the story of an accident? Tell you to keep your mouth shut. Not that you would be willing. I know that. But do you mean they haven't tried?'

The Odhiambos used 'they' in a sense that both understood. 'They' were the government as represented in this case by the Regional Administrator, Aramgu, and the men around the President in State House.

Odhiambo drained his glass before replying.

'I don't know, really. Aramgu summoned me early yesterday morning. I thought he might take that tack. But he didn't. I suppose he knew that the *mzungu* who runs the place, McGuiry, must know it's murder. And as far as he knew, I'd given the game away already to some of the people I interviewed. I hadn't, but he wasn't to know that. And McGuiry would be difficult to fix.'

To say nothing of yourself, thought his wife, but she kept it to herself. Odhiambo continued.

'Anyway, it's too late now. Everyone's accepted it's murder. I've got three problems now. One, Aramgu and the people here would be happy to arrest Causington, before the world press start treating it as an unsolved murder of a white woman story. Two, Price-Allen is sticking his fingers into the stew and that could be trouble. Three, I don't know who did it and even if I did know it may not be simple to prove. All I know is that Causington didn't. I think I'll have another beer. It's been a long day.'

'You can have another with supper.' Cari rose from her chair. 'It's time to go in anyway. The mozzies are biting me.'

Odhiambo followed her somewhat reluctantly. Mosquitoes didn't bother him and he liked it on the verandah with the sounds from the garden. The incessant clicking of the insects and croaking of the frogs punctuated by sporadic squawking from the trees was to him the music of the African night. And the mosquito-free air-conditioned interior of the bungalow was a luxury out of the range of an inspector's salary. His wife detected the onset of irritability and knew how to deal with it.

'Now, while I put the supper out you get out of that suit and have a shower. You'll feel better then. And after we've talked over your three problems we'll have an early night.' The eyes flashed and Odhiambo went on his way, sensuous images of his wife blotting out his other preoccupations.

Over coffee, after supper, Cari tackled first the issue of Nick Causington.

'Why are you so sure this guy, what did you say his name is, didn't do it, James?'

'Because he was outside the lodge firing a rifle to scare the elephants in order to show off to his girlfriend, who, unfortunately, for him as well as her, was getting killed at the time. The only way he's implicated in the murder is if there was some conspiracy. But if there was, which is doubtful, it's highly unlikely he was in it. No one would trust him in a matter like that. No, someone seized an opportunity presented by Causington's escapade and hit the woman on the back of the head with the blunt end of an axe that just happened to be lying about, or, to be precise, happened to be pinned to the wall.'

'And you say Price-Allen knows him. If he's a Price-Allen man, why is Aramgu setting him up as the fall guy?'

'I doubt whether Aramgu or State House know that Causington is a Price-Allen informer. And Price-Allen is not likely to shout it from the roof-tops either. But he's worried: there's no telling what Causington might say if he really feels threatened.'

Cari knew rather more about Price-Allen's activities than was common gossip in whispered exchanges at the club, but her face betrayed no sign of her deep concern. She was sure that James was underestimating the danger posed by the unofficial security chief with access to unlimited goons. But this was not the time to warn him. Better later when they were in bed and he was relaxed.

'And the others. How do you rate them as priority suspects?'

'The husband, Morgan Farwell, must be number one. The husband is always the prime suspect in a case like this. Jealousy, money, the usual possible causes. I think he's concealing something. I'll try to get a check run on him in the UK. Next, two old boyfriends of the deceased: neither delighted to meet up with an old flame. Both highly respectable bankers. The resurrection of a long-forgotten past could be a threat to one of them. A threat to be squashed. Then Farwell's host, Shropshire. Seems OK on the face of it, but the strange thing is the Farwells were staying with him because he knew Morgan Farwell years ago, but it turns out that he and the dead woman had a link in Zambia also. Shropshire says they never met, but he could be lying. Lastly two wives. Diana Farwell was obviously the sort of woman you don't want around your husband. And one of them already had probable cause to know what Diana could do.'

'I dunno, James. It all sounds a bit thin in terms of motive, doesn't it?'

Odhiambo rose and stretched. He felt his mood becoming depressed again. He knew that the case and its political complications were enough to justify his mood, but, nevertheless, depression irritated him. He looked down at his wife.

'Yeah, you're right. But somewhere in that woolly mess of coincidences and connections lies the true motive and it was strong enough for someone to seize a chance opportunity to kill. Anyway, that's enough of the bloody case. It can wait till morning. How was your trip?'

Cari rose and retrieved the coffee percolator, refilling both their mugs as she talked.

'It was OK. I hate that drive, as you know. Those *matatus* driving at lunatic speeds between here and Nakuru scare the hell out of me. Those and the big trucks going up and down to Uganda belching black fumes. Ugh.' Cari shuddered at the memory. The combination of the unlicensed, badly maintained and grossly overloaded taxis and the large articulated transporters made driving in Kenya a hazardous business and the Nairobi to Nakuru road was the leader in accidents – many of them horrific in terms of casualties. What was once, in the older, more leisurely days, one of the great scenic trips of the world, as the road first hung over and then meandered down into the great Rift Valley, was now to be avoided if at all possible.

'My uncle's fine. His cattle are healthy and fetching a good price. My aunt's not so good. I tried to persuade her to come and see my doctor, but she won't come. And I saw David in Nakuru. He's concerned about the political situation. He was a bit tight-lipped, but I got the impression he thinks the President and the party are overplaying their hand.'

Odhiambo grunted. It didn't need Cari's cousin with his involvement in Rift Valley local politics to tell him that Kenyan politics were getting out of hand. There was a sense of paranoia among the inner circle of the government, driven by their fear of imagined or real plots by other tribes, notably Odhiambo's own. This and greed were the staples of Kenyan politics. The new feature was that, since the death of Kenyatta, the ruling élites were beginning to fall out amongst themselves. Rumours of plots and counter-plots were rife and even the newspapers, careful though they had to be, were reporting the strife, albeit in a somewhat coded manner.

As they discussed the political scene Cari was careful, as always, to hide her fundamental pessimism about Kenya's future. She knew this upset her husband. Tribal politics and local crime, both were getting worse and Cari believed that soon the combination would make Kenya inhospitable for the likes of her honest policeman husband and herself. Her escape route existed. Her firm would place her back in America where she had resident status. James could accompany her and find opportunities in America where his talents would be appreciated. But she knew better than to openly air this possiblity. He was sensitive enough already; things would have to get much much worse before he would contemplate being an accompanying spouse relying initially on his wife and his wife's employers in a foreign land. Well, she thought, it's time to take him off to bed to complete the process of cheering him up. But no sooner had the moment arrived, than the ring of the telephone dispatched it. Odhiambo got up from his chair at the kitchen table, where they were sitting, and went into the lounge where the telephone was situated. Even before he returned, Cari knew the evening was doomed. She heard her husband utter an expletive and start to expostulate, only to stop in mid-word. Presumably silenced by the caller, she thought, which narrowed considerably his likely identity. There was a short silence and then a muttered few words which she caught. '. . . Right. I think . . . OK. Till tomorrow . . .'

Odhiambo replaced the receiver and returned to find his wife staring expectantly and gloomily at him. He made no effort to keep the bitterness out of his voice.

'That was Masonga. Causington hanged himself in his cell this evening. At least Nyeri are claiming he hanged himself.

Nice and neat. Guilty man commits suicide. Christ Almighty! And they expect me to accept it!'

'Oh, James, my dear.' Cari moved towards the angry man. She reached out her arms as she spoke. 'These are muddy waters, James. We're going to have to be careful.' But the intended embrace was avoided.

Cari was right, the evening was irretrievably ruined.

11

Odhiambo was not the only sceptic that Sunday night, nor, as Monday dawned, was he the only one to feel hard done by. Gachui, the long-suffering aide to the Regional Administrator of Nyeri, had had a long night. The news of Causington's death was relayed to him at nine in the evening. It was already too late to bring it to Aramgu's attention. The Administrator had been drinking brandy since four in the afternoon and was now ensconced in his bedroom with two girls from the Black Bull. By this time, in Gachui's estimation, the combination of the brandy and the girls would have put Aramgu into a comatose state from which he would not emerge until the morning. Gachui knew that in the interim he needed to proceed with caution. If, as he suspected, Causington's apparent suicide had been assisted, enquiries would plunge him into sensitive areas, for, as Gachui knew, no order for removing Causington had come through the political channels, either from Nairobi through Aramgu or from Aramgu's own devious mind. If such an order had occurred, Gachui would have caught a sense of something afoot. One did not survive as Aramgu's aide for long without a keen sense of smell for malodorous activities. Besides, Aramgu would not incapacitate himself if he knew of such a pending event. He would sit at the centre of his web ensuring that the fly ceased to flutter without damaging the threads.

To stay aloof from the matter entirely was an option Gachui considered but rejected: although it would be a safer course, the problem was that Aramgu when he emerged on Monday morning would expect Gachui to fill him in with the inside story before he spoke to the police. Intervening in his official capacity and visiting the police station was another rejected option, on the basis of personal prudence. Who knew where the repercussions of this might end. Best to stay officially out of the picture. So Gachui used the good contacts and private den of a business friend in order to get acquainted with the facts from the number-two man in the Nyeri police establishment. The story confirmed his suspicions, but left him worried about the apparent independent decision-taking that seemed to be at work.

The story was simple enough. Causington was being held in the police station, in what was more of a locked internal room than a cell. Because of the potential high-level exposure of the murder and the possibility that the *mzungu* had powerful friends, he was handled with care by the Nyeri police. At five in the afternoon three plain-clothes men arrived in a car with a government number-plate. They announced themselves as Security and authorized to interview the prisoner. About thirty minutes later, according to the solitary police officer stationed next to the room in question, the 'Nairobi men' asked him to fetch them beer, indicating that the prisoner was secure in their charge. When he returned the three men, who awaited him in the guard's area, invited him to join them in a drink. This he claimed unconvincingly to have refused, but in any case the men then left, handing him the key to Causington's room as they departed. Although the guard claimed to have checked immediately, Gachui's informant believed, on the evidence of the time the alarm was raised, that the guard did not check for about one hour. When he did, he found Causington hanging by his own belt attached to a hook in the ceiling that had once supported a large rotating fan.

Gachui sighed as his informant concluded the recital of the facts. Both of them knew without needing verbal confirmation that the Nairobi goons had hanged Causington. The questions were, who authorized it and why? Gachui knew his man could not enlighten him on these, indeed the policeman gently probed Gachui as to his own knowledge.

It was one in the morning before Gachui managed to establish contact with the local liaison man for the State Security Unit. He achieved this by waiting in the man's house for him to return from an evening's entertainment at some location unknown to his wife. The wife, somewhat discomfited by the presence of a *bwana mkubwa* in the absence of her husband, was relieved when he duly appeared. Some nights he did not return at all.

Gachui, in turn, was relieved that his quarry, although inebriated, was able to respond to questions in a reasonably articulate manner. He seemed genuinely surprised at the news of a death in the police station a few hours earlier.

'I assume', Gachui continued, 'that you know nothing of this matter.'

'Oh, definitely.' The Security man Kiwach was starting to sweat despite the coolness of the night air in the highlands of Nyeri. 'No, no, if I had known of anything, I would have been sure to check that your office was in the picture.'

'Yet,' Gachui leaned forward, jabbing a finger at the man in the opposite chair, 'yet, we have men arriving here saying they're State Security and demanding access to a murder suspect and you say you know nothing about it. I thought you're supposed to be the local man here. You don't seem to be in control of your own compound.'

They were talking in the dialect of the Kikuyu and Gachui used the local phrase for a man who has abdicated responsibility to the women in his own place of domicile – a derogatory implication that somewhat stiffened the spine of the unhappy Kiwach.

'No, no, Gachui, this is unfair. How do I know these men are not frauds? Where is the proof they are State Security? I have no knowledge of these men. It would be very unusual.'

'Listen, Kiwach. Listen carefully and think carefully. If you received no message of State Security's interest in this man or this murder, and you received no formal notification of the need to interview this man, Causington, then who could send these men here and do whatever it was they were told to do?' Gachui paused and watched the sweat trickle down Kiwach's neck. 'I don't need to tell you Aramgu is not going to be pleased at this intervention in his area. And I don't need to remind you who Aramgu's friends are. I must know what is going on.'

'But I don't know anything, Gachui. Damn it, even if they were Security people, you know how it is. Some things are better not talked about and certainly not made official. No, Bwana, I know nothing of this matter.'

'Who was Causington, Kiwach? Why are you people interested in him?'

'I don't know him. I heard his name today in connection with the white woman who was killed here. That's all.'

'Your wife told me that you received a call from Nairobi this morning, or rather,' Gachui glanced at his watch, 'yesterday morning, it is now. Who was it, Kiwach? Was that when you heard the name Causington?'

The Security man cursed to himself. He must give his wife another beating to teach her not to talk of his affairs with these people. He swallowed hard before replying.

'I get lots of calls from Nairobi. No, no, I keep telling you, Gachui, I have no connection with what happened to this man. The Administrator can check with the Commandant if you don't believe me.'

Gachui tried one or two more tacks to probe Kiwach's defences, but it was clear that he would get no further. If Kiwach knew anything his fear of his superiors in the Security Unit was clearly greater than his fear of Gachui speaking badly of him to the Regional Administrator.

Kiwach saw his visitor off. He had sobered up now. He remembered well the call to which Gachui referred. The message had been simple.

'Get a message to the *mzungu* being held in connection with the murder of the white woman. Tell him to say nothing about anything until he hears from us. And then forget that you ever heard of this man.'

Gachui was right, Aramgu's wrath was much to be preferred to the consequences of ignoring the latter part of his instructions. Now, Kiwach thought to himself, he must go in and deal with his woman. Teach her the merits of silence. He grinned to himself for he rather enjoyed beating women, particularly his wife.

Regional Administrator Aramgu arrived at his office in his chauffeured Mercedes at 9 a.m. For a Monday morning after a heavy-drinking Sunday he did not feel too bad, but as soon as he saw his aide's face he knew the morning was not going to be a pleasant one. Once given the facts as far as Gachui knew them, Aramgu, rather than exploding into one of his rages as

Gachui feared, sank his huge head on his chest in contemplation. It was a question of whether the happenings of Sunday were, on balance, good or bad news for him. Causington's death was OK as long as the suicide could be made to stick: if it did, it neatly disposed of the murder of the tourist woman as well. If, on the other hand, the suicide didn't stand up, then he was in a lot of trouble with allegations of two murders on his hands – one of them inside a police station. Aramgu could hazard a good guess whose hand lay behind the disposal of Causington. It had taken nerve, decisiveness and efficiency and that narrowed the field considerably. If he was right the executioners would not be talking. The danger lay closer to home in the form of the local police.

Aramgu stared at Gachui who had remained standing while delivering the news and awaiting his chief's reaction.

'Gachui, leave the Nairobi end to me. The important thing is that no fool here starts any rumours to cast doubt on the suicide. Get the superintendent and whoever else matters here in my office now. And make sure they've got that idiot guard under wraps. Best if one of the inspectors tells him he'll cover for his abandoning his post as long as he says nothing about his visitors. And then keep him somewhere safe and away from the bars. We don't want him chattering with a drink-soaked tongue.'

While he awaited his senior police officers, Aramgu debated in his mind his next step. Better perhaps to keep State House out of it; they might not be pleased by him dragging them in. After some thought, Aramgu asked for a number written in his private pad. His secretary informed him a few minutes later that the man he was calling was not in. A message was left for him to call back, although Aramgu had no confidence in messages left with secretaries and clerks, many of whom had been recruited for reasons that had nothing whatever to do with their ability to record or remember messages, or their dedication to ensuring their delivery. His mind still on the Nairobi connection, Aramgu suddenly remembered a source of danger that brought him to his feet with a shout of anger. Gachui, summoned quickly, found his chief at last showing the agitation he had expected earlier.

'Gachui! That policeman at the lodge when the woman was killed. Why didn't you remind me earlier, you simpleton?

You've overlooked our main problem. Odhiambo didn't believe Causington was the killer, so he won't believe he killed himself. That bastard could be dangerous.'

Gachui ignored the attachment of blame to himself for he was used to it.

'We have to assume, sir, that the Nairobi people who are . . . er . . . involved will be aware of Odhiambo's involvement.'

'The trouble with you, Gachui, is you assume too much.' Aramgu continued, spewing obscenities concerning Gachui's inability to find parts of his own body and Odhiambo's reputation for being an honest policeman, a trait that Aramgu seemed to regard as the equivalent of treason. His harangue was finally interrupted by his secretary announcing that the representatives of the Nyeri police force were awaiting their audience.

The next hour served to temper Aramgu's anxiety considerably. The assembled police dutifully digested the story according to the Administrator. Aramgu spelt it out for them in some detail.

'Although the pathologist's report is still awaited, the death of Mrs whatever her name was at Hawk's Nest on Saturday, or Friday, or whatever, is being treated by the Nyeri police as murder. A friend of the dead woman was being detained for questioning over the weekend. This friend, a Mr Causington, hanged himself in his cell on Sunday. During initial questioning, Mr Causington, although not yet admitting to murder, appeared to be depressed. Although investigations continue, the Nyeri police believe it possible that Mr Causington hanged himself out of a sense of remorse for the Hawk's Nest killing. The Nyeri police are being assisted during their enquiries by the criminal investigation unit of the Nairobi Central Police Force.' Aramgu paused and then emphasized the point. 'This is in case the story is put about of a team from Nairobi coming here. Such a visit if it has to be discussed will be confirmed as being part of liaison and assistance from Nairobi with the full knowledge of the head of the Nyeri CID.' At this, Aramgu gazed meaningfully at a somewhat discomfited officer who was part of his audience and then turned towards Gachui, seated on the perimeter of the group, raising his eyebrows in silent query.

Gachui cleared his throat and added a postscript to Aramgu's summary.

'We deeply regret this tragic incident involving visitors to

Kenya, which was a domestic matter in no way involving the staff of the tourist facilities or the people of Kenya. Visitors remain assured of a warm welcome in Nyeri when they come to enjoy the sights and facilities and need not fear for their security when visiting the game-viewing areas.'

'Yes, yes, that's good, Gachui.' Aramgu looked around benevolently. 'Any questions, gentlemen?'

The superintendent who headed the officers present recognized his cue.

'That's all very clear, Administrator. And of course conforms with our preliminary findings. Er . . . there is one small point in connection with Mr Gachui's emphasis on the affair being a *shauri* of outsiders. The man concerned is, I believe, a resident of Kenya. But', the superintendent added quickly as he saw Aramgu stir impatiently, 'that's a minor point.'

After his visitors had filed out, Aramgu called his aide back.

'Even the stupidest of that lot should have got the message, right, Gachui?'

His aide nodded, but the Administrator was moving on with his thoughts.

'Who was the one second from the left? My left, I mean. He smirked when I talked of the suicide. I don't remember seeing him before. Check him out, make sure he knows what's what and if there's any doubt about him I want to know fast.'

At this point Aramgu's Nairobi contact returned the earlier call; the ensuing conversation assisted further in restoring Aramgu's equanimity. His contact was highly placed in the Security Unit and was able to confirm Aramgu's supposition.

'Any interviewing team from here was an initiative taken outside the normal channels of command. You may rest assured, Aramgu, that there is no trail for anyone to follow.'

Aramgu could interpret this code very easily. He had seen the hand of Price-Allen from the time Gachui informed him of the events. Price-Allen officially did not exist. Now he sought reassurance on his remaining concern.

'The inspector who was present when the woman was killed. He had his own theories, which did not include Causington as the killer. Is something being done to keep him from raising any problems?'

'Ah, yes, Inspector Odhiambo,' said the voice into Aramgu's

ear. 'I believe our mutual friend is in touch with him, yes. I think you can leave our Luo friend to us.'

Aramgu was relieved, although he hoped they wouldn't underestimate Odhiambo's potential as a trouble-maker. If he could have listened in to a conversation then going on in Nairoi, his stomach, which was just settling down following the brandy of the previous night and the anxieties of the morning, would have started to rumble again.

Odhiambo had experienced a frustrating morning. Superintendent Masonga was unavailable, he was told, and no one had seen Price-Allen since the previous morning. Finally, at midday, he was summoned to Masonga's office. The superintendent was smoking with a nervous intensity. He quickly took the initiative before Odhiambo's protests could start.

'James, I don't want any foolish talk, you understand. My information is the same as yours. No more and no less. I don't wish to speculate on Causington's actions and I don't wish you to do so either. Your job and mine is to report on the results of your Nairobi interviews. When can I have them?'

'They're waiting for typing. But you won't like them. They show that we have a whole bunch of suspects. Other than Causington. Look, Superintendent, we have to – ' but he was interrupted by his superior.

'I can tell you officially that the Nyeri police believe the Causington suicide will wrap up the Farwell murder enquiry also. No further assistance is required from us. Send me your reports and *shauri quisha*.'

Odhiambo exploded.

'Causington's suicide, my ass! You and I know what we're dealing with here.'

Masonga was on his feet, ash spraying, angry, but also, Odhiambo realized, even in his rage, concerned. Odhiambo stopped; and then continued hurriedly as Masonga reached him and was about to speak from an eyeball to eyeball position.

'Let's go for a walk, or a ride, Superintendent. We have to talk about this. If you don't want to talk in here, let's go somewhere . . .' This was as far as he got for Masonga, containing his anger, spoke with face thrust close to Odhiambo's.

'Inspector, I'm giving you an order. I don't wish to talk with you regarding your views on this or anything. Here or anywhere. You are in no position to comment on the Nyeri incident. You are taken off this case with immediate effect. Is that clear? And as a police officer you will comment about it to no one. No one, you understand?'

Odhiambo struggled for control of his own anger. He could feel the bile of frustration in his throat. When he spoke the bitterness seemed to repel Masonga who withdrew back to his side of the desk.

'No one? Does no one include Price-Allen, Superintendent? You know he called for me yesterday to warn me to tread carefully and tell me Causington was one of his ear-holes? Are you the drum on which he plays his beat? Shall we dispose of Causington's corpse for him in case anyone with one eye could tell he was helped to hang himself?'

Odhiambo knew he had crossed some ill-defined but critical line. Masonga was angry, hurt and – yes, Odhiambo thought, embarrassed. To be accused of being the white man's boy was an insult for which he might not forgive Odhiambo for a considerable time, if ever. Suddenly Odhiambo's own anger evaporated and all that was left was a void, a feeling of being no longer a part of his own world, of being somehow divorced from his fellows. He got up.

'Superintendent, I have quite a bit of leave due me. I'd like to take some. Starting this afternoon.'

Masonga, who had been staring at his desk, a cigarette burning unheeded between his fingers, looked up.

'Permission granted. If you leave Nairobi let us know where you are.'

Masonga watched Odhiambo leave. Damn Odhiambo. Damn his stupid and stiff-necked pride. Where did he think he was? This was Kenya, not England. This was real life, not some training school exercise. And damn Price-Allen. The worst part of Odhiambo's outburst was that Masonga agreed with it. Reluctantly he reached for the telephone.

Price-Allen took the superintendent's call, listened and pondered a moment before replying.

'Thank you for handling the matter, Superintendent. But if he's taken himself off in a huff there's no telling what he may do. We'd better keep an eye on him.'

He listened again.

'Yes, very well. By the way, I understand you have been

recommending our friend for Chief Inspector. Will it help if favourable consideration of this is accelerated? Soothe his ruffled feathers, as it were.'

Price-Allen grinned as Masonga entered his reservations.

'Yes, yes. Obviously not immediately. Don't want him to think he was being bribed. That would never do. But when he's calmed down, it should do the trick. Get him back on the team. Oh, by the way, Masonga, let me see his notes on his interviews, will you? I'd be interested to know a little more about some of the characters around the late lamented lady.'

Price-Allen replaced the telephone, leaned back in his chair, closed his eyes and considered putting into play another counter. As he looked up the number in his private notebook, he wondered if the plan formulating in his mind was too intricate, if there was too much to go wrong. His finger hesitated over the dial only for a second. He loved complex plots and stratagems. Fixing the inevitable hitches was half the fun.

12

The bar to which Odhiambo took himself was a traditional African drinking establishment in a poor area of the city, rather than one of the posher bars in the centre of Nairobi. The room was devoid of ornament except for two murals drawn by one of the bar owner's relatives, who lacked the basic skills of perspective and appreciation of relativities in human and animal anatomies. One was a village scene and the other a lion leaping for the throat of a wildebeest. The colours were garish and jumbled with an abandon that did convey a certain exuberance. Odhiambo found the lion particularly irritating: its face was closer in structure to a human face than to that of a large cat – it gave the whole mural a surrealistic touch which the artist had not intended. The bar and tables were made of plywood and the chairs were cheap metal folding ones. There was sawdust on the floor and Zairian music pounded from two cheap stereo speakers which had seen better days. The clientele at this time of day consisted of the casual labour from the nearby Nairobi wholesale fruit and vegetable market, who had finished their day's work that started before dawn, plus a couple of men who eyed Odhiambo with the careful scrutiny that the underworld gives to suspected policemen.

Both bottled beer and the home-brewed *pombe* were available; cheap local gin and the local distilled spirit – *changaa* – were the other main items on offer. Odhiambo ordered a bottle of beer. The bar girl wondered if he was a potential client for her other services. She was a recent addition to the staff and this was Odhiambo's first visit to the bar for several months, so it was the bar owner who warned her off. Odhiambo favoured this particular bar when his occasional need for a bender arose because the bar owner knew who he was, protected his privacy and sought no favour. This was unusual, particularly as he was a fellow Luo. Odhiambo assumed the day would come when some help might be solicited on tribal solidarity grounds, but at least he spared Odhiambo entreaties on behalf of arrested bar girls, or solicitations for help in reducing the back-handers to City Council employees which were required to protect his licence. Perhaps he knew another better-placed protector.

Odhiambo intended to get drunk. But, as he drank his second beer, he realized he was not even in a mood to drown his sorrows. Instead, there was an unsatiated curiosity about the identity of Diana Farwell's killer. The more he tried to block it out of his mind the more it pressed upon him. But now his curiosity might never be satisfied. He had put in requests for follow-up checks on the suspects, but with the case about to be closed he knew these would not be pursued. And open or closed, he was off the case. In fact, he wondered whether he had any future in the police force. His own personal protector and advocate was probably lost to him this morning. In any case, did he want to stay, given the way things were going? Despite her care he knew Cari's thinking, and perhaps she was right: perhaps it was time for them to move on. Use her connections and go to the United States. Even as the thought came, he grimaced, for he knew he could never do it.

The second beer finished, Odhiambo knew he was at a decision point. A third beer with its successors and bury the Farwell case for ever, or get up now and put some wheels in motion. The bar girl retrieved the empty bottle and looked enquiringly at the large despondent-looking man at the table. She still thought he would benefit from an hour of her ministrations, but obedient to her instructions she stood ready to produce a third bottle. To her surprise her customer suddenly stood up, threw some coins on to the table, smiled at her and strode purposefully towards the door. She collected the money and pocketed the good tip before the proprietor became aware of it and demanded the major share.

Odhiambo walked down the decrepit street, past shops still operated by Asians providing a touch of colour to the drab surroundings, to a nearby post office, found a public telephone in working order and placed a call. He was lucky, the man he wanted was in and available. A short while later a taxi deposited him outside an old colonial-style office building in Kenyatta Avenue, Nairobi's main central street, and without delay, he was ushered into George Albinger's office.

'James! How nice to see you. How are you? And how's the case? Here, come and sit on the sofa.'

Albinger rose from his desk as his visitor entered, came around to shake hands and ushered Odhiambo to the corner of his large office where there were armchairs and a coffee table.

'A lot has happened since we parted company at Hawk's Nest, George. Some of it I'm not at liberty to discuss, but I'm here to ask a favour.'

Albinger looked at the policeman closely. He had picked up the smell of beer on Odhiambo's breath as they shook hands. This, coupled with the rumour he had heard over lunch, gave him cause for concern.

'Ask away, James. You know I'll help if I can.'

'This Hawk's Nest business has taken a strange turn, George. The Nyeri police suspect a man called Causington who was in Mrs Farwell's group that night. Last night Causington hanged himself, apparently. In the police station.'

Odhiambo spoke with careful neutrality. However, his tone did not deceive his listener. Albinger had heard over lunch of the death of a man in custody in Nyeri. The fact that he was in custody naturally led to rumours which, in this case, Albinger was inclined to believe. He prompted Odhiambo to continue.

'So, in the eyes of the Nyeri police, the matter is neatly sewn up. But in your eyes, James . . .?'

'I'm off the case now, George. Well, in a sense there's no longer a case, if it's solved, I mean. But, yes, I still have some questions and you know what will happen to official channels if the case is deemed closed.' His listener nodded, and Odhiambo continued with a rush. 'Actually, George, I'd like to know more about Morgan Farwell. I gather he's a businessman of some kind. Seems a bit young to retire. Plus newly married bride gets killed. You know the sort of questions that come to mind in circumstances like that. But my avenues are closed now. I wondered if through your UK contacts you could find out a bit about him? Say no if I'm asking you to do something improper. It's only a casual thing, really. Not really my business any more.'

Albinger busied himself stuffing his pipe as he listened and there was a pause while he lit it and noisily sucked it into life. He looked up from the pipe-bowl and said gently, 'I'll see what I can do, James, if you ask. But are you sure it's wise to keep pursuing this? From what I hear there are sensitivities involved. If you're off the case, why not walk away from it?'

'Causington didn't kill Diana Farwell, George. I can't go into all the details, but you can take it from me he didn't do it. Which means someone else did. The case may be closed for now but you never know what may happen.'

'But the one who triggers something to happen may not be popular, James. You must realize that.'

Odhiambo bared his teeth in a pleasureless smile.

'Maybe you're right. Why don't I mind my own business and let you get on with yours? I'm sorry, George. I started the afternoon with the intention of getting drunk. I'm on leave, you see. Still with pay as far as I know. Not suspended or anything that you keep warning me about. Perhaps I should return to my original intention.'

Albinger clasped his pipe by the bowl and pointed the stem sternly at his visitor.

'The worst thing of all for you to do, James, is to start feeling sorry for yourself. Damn it, man, even in countries where there are, shall we say, greater constraints on interference with the course of justice than there are here, you get policemen frustrated when they are taken off a case. It's not the end of the world, you know. Look, I'll put a feeler or two out about Farwell. That doesn't commit us to anything. Meanwhile, relax until we see how things pan out. Chances are nothing interesting will emerge that will justify you taking matters any further anyway.'

Odhiambo nodded slowly. Procrastination had its attractions. He rose to go, but then remembered another aspect of the Farwell affair. He raised his hand to ward off protest.

'I'm not making any official enquiry, George. But just out of interest, as I was with you at Hawk's Nest. Shropshire says you may have known the dead woman in Lusaka, some years ago.'

Albinger had also risen. Now he sat down and gestured Odhiambo back to his chair.

'You're incorrigible, James. Yes, it seems I did know her. Didn't recognize her that evening. Of course, she'd had plastic surgery. When I knew her she looked pretty awful. Shropshire came to see me yesterday. Diana apparently recognized me and spoke of her Lusaka accident. He wanted to check if I thought there was anything we should come forward with. You see, Diana had a very bad accident in a car driven by a boyfriend of hers. I represented her in an insurance case that ensued. We won – it was against the boyfriend's insurance company. A tidy sum, nothing huge, but it paid for her medical treatment and left her a few thousand, I daresay. No motive for murder there. I mean, she didn't make a fortune out of it.'

Odhiambo got up once more.

'Yes. That's what Shropshire told me. I mean, about the accident. OK, George, I'll take your advice and forget the Farwell business unless you come up with something. And thank you for your time. I know I'm becoming a nuisance.'

Albinger reassured his visitor and smilingly walked him to the door. He watched as the large man moved through the outer office towards the lift. The stride seemed different, it lacked his usual determined purposefulness; it was more the walk of a man who didn't know how to fill the next hour.

After the policeman had disappeared, Albinger returned to his desk. He had not been quite frank with his friend, but he did not want to raise other ideas in Odhiambo's head at this time. In fact, some enquiries were in hand. Now there were more to start. It would be interesting to see whether his discreet mining produced any nuggets of ore.

When Odhiambo reached the street, he was, indeed, indecisive as to his next movements. He hesitated in the sunshine and warmth amidst the bustling scene involving a mixture of local businessmen, shoppers, shoeshine boys, pavement newspaper vendors and tourists accompanied by a surrounding swirl of touts offering wooden carvings and fake elephant-hair bracelets. Kenyatta Avenue, prior to Kenya's independence, had been named after Lord Delamere, the unofficial king of the white population in the colony. It was one of the older streets in the business part of the city, and broader than any other. Now, it was a strange mixture of the old colonial-style buildings and modern high-storey glass and concrete towers. It was like Kenya itself, thought Odhiambo, undergoing change with currently an uneasy mix of old and new styles.

His wife's office was located in one of the modern multi-storey buildings further up the Avenue and as he stood, gazing vacantly at the hubbub around him, a girl passed whom he recognized as a secretary in Cari's department. The girl saw him, smiled and stopped.

'Hello, Inspector,' she said. 'Has your wife contacted you yet? She was trying to get you earlier this afternoon.'

Odhiambo did not recall the girl's name.

'Good afternoon, Miss . . . er . . . er. How are you? No, I haven't heard from her. Perhaps I'll stop by now.'

With a brilliant smile, the girl went on her way. Ruth, yes, that was it, Odhiambo remembered, Ruth something, part Somali, part coastal Arab. An attractive example of the polyglot nature of the Kenyan scene. A pretty girl in the sunshine served to lift even his spirits as he made his way to his wife's office and they remained buoyant until his wife's secretary announced his arrival.

'Oh, Miss Bito, your husband is here to see you.'

Cari used her maiden name for business purposes, which did not upset Odhiambo, although he knew it was a source of derisive comments amongst some of his associates and fellow-Luos. To such commentators, a wife who didn't even admit her fealty to her husband cast doubt on the manhood of the husband. It was the other part of the announcement which deflated Odhiambo's recently recovered spirits. Yes, he was seeking audience with his wife. He was the husband, partly reliant on his wife's income, who was wanting to distract her from the work that, no doubt, pressed upon her. Cari opened the door of her office and came to meet him.

'James, darling, how nice of you to stop by. Did you get my message? I called the station just a while ago.'

She was looking stunning in her business suit of grey jacket and skirt with a flower-patterned blouse and a matching ribbon holding back her jet black hair.

Odhiambo explained his chance encounter as they entered Cari's well-appointed office together. The window, with a fine view up Kenyatta Avenue towards Uhuru Park, was curtained in good imported fabric. It contrasted starkly with the dirty offices in the Central Police Station, all of which were long overdue for a coat of paint.

Cari gave him a friendly kiss and asked the inevitable questions.

'How did it go, James? What's happening about the Nyeri business?'

'About what you'd expect. Nyeri claim the case is closed. Causington committed the murder and then killed himself. And I'm off the case and on leave.'

Cari showed no surprise at his statement, but uttered some consoling words. Odhiambo turned away and gazed blankly from the window. With his back to his wife, he asked, 'But I'm not here to tell you my troubles. I heard you were looking for me. What did you want?'

'Oh. As you've decided to take leave, I thought maybe they'd got through to you. No? Well, your sister rang me to say your mother is not very well. She'd like to see you. Well, I mean we knew she wasn't well, but perhaps she's gotten worse.'

Odhiambo turned back to face his wife. He was concerned. His mother was not in the habit of sending for him. When his father had died, while Odhiambo was still young, his farm had been incorporated into that of Odhiambo's uncle, but it was now operated by his brother. His brother, sister and he had spent some years under their uncle's roof, but Odhiambo's relations with his kin were now distant, and he had disclaimed any rights as well as responsibilities. He did, however, send periodic gifts of money to his mother and visited her when he had the chance to travel west to Kisumu. Such visits had become less frequent as the years passed.

'No. I took leave on an impulse. I've had it up to here with being buggered about. I don't even know whether I want to go on at all.'

Cari laid a hand on his arm.

'Nonsense, James. You know your mood will pass. You're wise to take a few days off. And, as it turns out, it works out

OK. Go to Kisumu, see your mother and your family and some of your old school friends and then come back looking at things in a new light.'

'You sound as if you want to be rid of me.' Odhiambo was in a mood to take offence and he detected a brittleness in his wife's voice and manner. 'I know I'm not very good company at the moment. But why not? This Causington thing makes me sick.'

'James, it's past time for you to see your mother and she needs you. By the time you get back things may have sorted themselves out.'

'That's what everybody keeps saying. Things are getting sorted out all right. But only to suit Aramgu and Price-Allen.'

But despite his protests, his mind was already working out the logistics of the Kisumu trip. Cari simplified matters considerably by insisting that he take the car; she would arrange to borrow an office car while he was away. She also managed to keep from him her own troubled state of mind, a feat that fully exercised her latent acting abilities.

The journey the next day was uneventful, except for its effect on Odhiambo's state of mind. As always he felt exhilarated at the sight of the mighty Rift Valley, the sloping walls shadowed and covered in trees and scrub, the valley floor, sitting astride the equator, baking under the overhead sun. There was a grandeur about it with the vast panoply of an unspoilt, virgin land, at least when viewed from a distance. From the Rift, he climbed over eight thousand feet above sea level through the tea farms of Kericho, his spirits rising with the elevation, as if the more rarefied air acted as a tonic. The smallholdings of tea pleased Odhiambo. So neat-looking and successful – yes, that was the point, successful. Here was an example of small farmers growing a crop to the very highest standards to the point where Kenya's tea fetched a premium on the world market. This was an example of Kenyans succeeding in the modern world. But as he descended towards Lake Victoria and into his ancestral homeland, Odhiambo's spirits fell. Now the scenery changed. Small plots were cultivated on the sides of steep slopes, becoming ever smaller and more fragmented as land passed from father to sons and needed to be divided and divided again. This was an example, to Odhiambo's eyes, of his tribesmen going backwards, of failing to adapt appropriately to modern times. The urge for large families, the lack of a market in land that would allow viable farms to be put together, the adherence to traditional values in all things: to Odhiambo, these traits were condemning his people to poverty. He had cut himself off from his people but when, as now, he returned, the sense of loss was strong.

It was mid-afternoon when he arrived in his home village, twenty miles past the provincial capital of Kisumu on Lake Victoria. He was greeted warmly enough by his sister and, when they arrived at the compound, his uncle. He was taken to his mother's room. It was cramped and had only one small window, but, Odhiambo noticed, the bedclothes were clean and the room had been swept. His mother was in bed. She had aged considerably since Odhiambo's last visit, which, he remembered with guilt, was over six months ago. She suffered from a weak heart and, although Odhiambo had managed to persuade her to see a heart specialist in Nairobi, she placed more faith in the local healer.

His mother accepted his greetings and gifts gravely. She recognized him, but showed surprise at his presence. His sister said, a little impatiently, 'You know I came yesterday to tell you James was coming. His wife, Charity, called from Nairobi. I told you, Mother.'

They were speaking the Luo tongue. Odhiambo's mother did not speak English and her knowledge of Swahili was scanty.

It soon became clear that there was no particular need that his mother had in mind, indeed she clearly didn't remember issuing a summons for her son. Her mind drifted from time to time, but in her more coherent moments she expressed, not for the first time, a wish that Odhiambo 'now that he was a well-educated man in Nairobi' would take more responsibility for the family and its affairs.

Odhiambo accepted his uncle's hospitality for the night. Since his boyhood days his uncle's compound had been modernized to some extent. The main house was now brick with a tiled roof rather than the mud-and-wattle, thatched structure he remembered. There was now a well inside the compound, so a daily trek to the river was no longer necessary. Also, there was a chemical toilet, an improvement on the earlier hole in the ground cess-pit. The biggest change was the electricity supply, which provided both light and the power for a small refrigerator. That this modest prosperity contrasted with Odhiambo's pessimism about the future did not strike him as a contradiction. He regarded his uncle as being middle-class in the context of his community – more land than the average and the luck or sense to have only one son, a matter regarded as cause for commiseration by most of his uncle's neighbours.

His uncle laid on a fine meal of goat-meat, vegetables, fruits and the staple maizemeal dish, *ugali*. It was the occasion for a large family reunion. Odhiambo realized for the first time that his uncle, too, was getting old. It was very evident how much his relatives longed for him to take charge, to organize the family. This was a commitment that he couldn't and wouldn't make, for with it came the responsibility to play a part in Luo affairs and respect the customs and traditions that had grown up over the ages. His sense of alienation deepened and by the time he retired to his mattress his depression made him feel physically ill.

The next afternoon Odhiambo made his excuses and departed with a sense of relief. A messenger had arrived at his uncle's home, sent by an old school friend, a businessman in Kisumu, asking Odhiambo to come to see him on his way back through the town. This Odhiambo did, arriving at his friend's office in mid-afternoon. Given that Cari was not expecting him back, he was easily persuaded to spend the night at his friend's modern bungalow in the pleasant suburb of the town that provided a splendid view of the shores of Lake Victoria. No reason was vouchsafed for the message until, as the sun started to set over the lake, Odhiambo's host suggested they take their sundowners at the lakeside hotel. In the car, *en route* to the hotel, Odhiambo got the first sniff of the chase. His host confessed that a contact wanted to meet Odhiambo as 'he had some information that would be of interest to him'. Odhiambo grunted and kept his own counsel. He placed little trust in his old school friend: in his experience, businessmen in Kenya who had prospered as well and as quickly as his host were not suitable repositories for confidences.

The contact sidled up after they had been seated for some twenty minutes at a table on the hotel patio. The wait was not irksome, for the sunset over Lake Victoria was a sight that tourists travelled thousands of miles to see: no matter how often he saw it, Odhiambo never failed to be impressed by the dramatic colour show in the sky. The lake, which stretched away seemingly to infinity, was calm tonight with a few fishing boats, sails aloft, framed against the skyline. The sky was aflame, the golden centre spreading yellow and pink tendrils with purple shading where the night clouds had started to form over the lake. The clarity of the air seemed to bring this colourful spectacular to an impossible proximity to the viewer. The same clarity aided the carrying of the voices of chanting fishermen as they prepared to set sail for a night's fishing.

The new arrival was a man in his twenties, clad in a clean white shirt and dark slacks. Odhiambo could not readily identify his tribe, and the man spoke in English. Another round of beers were ordered and Odhiambo waited patiently for the business of the evening to become clear. He had come to the conclusion that this would be a somewhat roundabout way of seeking some favour from him, but the approach, when it came, was unexpected.

'I understand, sir, you are interested in activities of woman in Kampala years ago. Woman just killed.'

Odhiambo made an effort to prevent his jaw dropping. He put his glass carefully back on the table and looked intently at the speaker.

'How do you know of this matter and my possible involvement in it?'

'It was on news, sir. Death of woman and you being there. You are well known here, sir. Then someone say you paying visit to your home.'

'The radio didn't say anything about Kampala, as far as I know. Where did you hear that?'

'I was in Uganda on Monday. Business, you know.'

The young man gestured vaguely with his hands, indicating the unspecified nature of the business. Odhiambo could make a good guess. Smuggling was rife between Uganda and Kenya, with Ugandan coffee and tea coming out and simple consumer items such as soap, tyres and aspirin going in. In Uganda, still experiencing the turmoil of civil war and rampaging soldiers, the economy was in ruins and simple consumer items fetched a chief's ransom. Odhiambo now decided that the man was probably Ugandan. The speaker continued.

'Someone I do business with. He knew of woman's death

from radio. They listen to radio all time in Uganda, not much else to do.' A smile came and went, leaving no humour in the eyes. 'He told me he knows this woman and men she went with when she was in Kampala. He knows something special about one man.'

Odhiambo glared at the man opposite and adopted a more threatening tone.

'Listen, my friend. Even if your Ugandan businessman heard the news of Mrs Farwell's death, there is no way he could connect it with some woman he knew a long time ago in Kampala. She wasn't Mrs Farwell then. So what game are you playing with me?'

Odhiambo's host was beginning to look uncomfortable, but the third man seemed unruffled. He drank from his glass and topped it up from the bottle. His initial deferential attitude was disappearing.

'I not know whole story, Inspector. I just messenger boy. How should I know? But he said the message would make you come.'

'What message? Get on with it. I'm tired of all this nonsense.'

'He tell me to find you and say a banker man was in Uganda wanting something to do with the woman. He not get it, but my friend has it and will show it to you. He said it will be of much help to you.'

For the next few minutes by threat and bluster Odhiambo tried to obtain more details from this mysterious message-carrier. But the man was impervious to Odhiambo's aggression, indeed something close to a sardonic smile seemed now to shape his lips. Odhiambo's school friend became increasingly uneasy, finally laying a hand on the policeman's arm.

'James, be careful. This is a public place. We could attract attention. You don't want that.'

Odhiambo fell silent while his table companions waited. He made up his mind and addressed the younger man. Set-up though it obviously was, he couldn't walk away from it.

'Very well. What does your friend suggest? How do I see him?'

A smile spread across the face, but without humour.

'Ah, good. I take you across in my boat. To Entebbe. You will be safe with me. Boat is better than road. Too many soldiers on road making big trouble. No soldiers on lake.'

'When? I have little time for lake trips.'

'Tonight. Tonight is good. Weather is fine and lake calm.'

Odhiambo gazed out across the water. The lake was now shrouded in darkness with the occasional silver flash as the water captured the lingering streaks of light in the sky and reflected them back. Odhiambo was not fond of sailing and he knew how frequently violent thunderstorms occurred over the lake. Drownings of fishermen were common. Even if the lake proved to be friendly, Entebbe presented all manner of risks. It was dangerous enough to be a casual visitor to troubled Uganda, but Odhiambo knew that this visit could prove to be particularly hazardous. He could be walking, or rather sailing, into a trap. But why would anyone go to such elaborate steps to entrap him? It didn't make sense. Well, there was only one way to find out. He turned back to the messenger.

'What sort of boat? I'm not sitting out there at the mercy of the wind.'

Again the broad-lipped, wide-stretching, non-contagious smile.

'No, no, my friend. Very fast boat. We will be there in few hours. No problem.'

Odhiambo's host had been restraining himself, but now he burst out in opposition to the proposed trip.

'James, for God's sake! You can't just go across to Uganda chasing a rumour like this. I fixed it for this man to meet you, but now I wish I hadn't. Who knows what may happen in Entebbe?'

Odhiambo looked at his friend with a wry smile.

'I'm tired of dealing with intermediaries. You, him,' gesturing at the boatman, 'and whoever. I'm tired of getting buggered about. If there's someone with something to say in Entebbe, I'll go to Entebbe. But . . .' Odhiambo paused, grabbed the shirt of the third man, pulled his head half-way across the table and held it in front of his old friend. 'You know this man, or whoever he works for. I'm not asking for details of their business, but I can make a good guess. Now, if I don't come back by tomorrow night I want you to use all your clout in this town to put them out of business. Will you do that for me?'

Odhiambo released his grip and the young man fell back in his chair. He looked as if he was about to protest and started to get up, but stopped and resumed his place. He contented himself by smoothing down his rumpled shirt. But his eyes for the first time took on life – they burned with the frustration of a man who has to act pleasantly when his desires are very different.

Odhiambo's friend nodded weakly. 'I know this man's boss,' he said. 'Osango. Trucking and freight of a, shall we say, international nature. But why don't you let me check with him first? Before you decide.'

'There's no time,' said Odhiambo shortly, and turned his attention back to the third man. 'Now, you and I are going to stay together. No radio calls to anyone. No messages passed. Anything goes wrong, I blame you for it.'

13

In different circumstances, despite his aversion to large expanses of water, Odhiambo might have enjoyed the crossing. They encountered no storms and the powerful motor boat surged its way over the lake, the bow bouncing into the water and dividing it into two plumes of spray that glistened in the bright moonlight. The bouncing caused a jarring sensation and the noise was greater than Odhiambo had anticipated, but, all in all, it could have been a lot worse. He was clad in his own slacks and shirt, topped by a pullover and wind-cheater borrowed from his Kisumu friend.

Although the cabin was dirty, the boat seemed in good mechanical condition. The availability of such an expensive means of transport across the lake confirmed, if confirmation was needed, that smuggling was the business of the boatman and his boss. In addition to Odhiambo and the boatman there was one additional member of the crew who seemed to be the general handyman and factotum. Little was said; the combined noise of the engines and the boat's contact with the water made conversation difficult. As dawn broke, the boatman turned off the boat's spotlight and throttled back the engines. With the lights off, Odhiambo's eyes became accustomed to the faint light of early morning and he was able to discern a dark mound ahead. He turned towards the man at the wheel, who answered the unspoken question.

'We almost there. We land at place I use near Entebbe. Then I send this man,' gesturing at the crewman, 'to contact my friend. He's Baganda so no problem.'

Odhiambo would have preferred to proceed together into Entebbe, but he could see that three men, at least one of whom was foreign, might arouse attention at such an hour. He deferred discussion and watched as the boat nosed its way into a small sandy bay. As they got closer the light improved and Odhiambo could see that the bay was used for small boats. Two were tied to a makeshift jetty of planks. Neither approached the size of Odhiambo's vessel, which was taken confidently alongside the planks. Odhiambo's companions busied themselves with anchoring tasks as Odhiambo reviewed the situation. The arrival of such a boat should attract some attention. True, the bay was secluded: beyond the few feet of sand, mangroves formed a solid visual barrier and the arc of the bay meant that any boat in it was invisible from other points along the coast. Local fishermen, Odhiambo presumed, had troubles enough of their own without asking many questions about boats from across the lake. Asking questions in Uganda in recent years was a passport to the grave. But whatever officialdom currently ran Entebbe must be aware of big boats coming and going regularly.

Out of the mangroves stepped a man, shabbily dressed in tattered shirt and shorts. He walked along the planks and watched as Odhiambo's companions made fast and climbed down from the boat. Odhiambo joined them as they walked to the beach. He was glad to be back on land even if it was foreign, potentially hostile, land. Words were exchanged in what Odhiambo took to be Luganda, the language of the Baganda. It was of similar origin to that of the Luo, but different enough that Odhiambo could not follow what was said. As the new arrival and the crewman headed back towards the mangroves, Odhiambo's companion offered an explanation.

'He . . .' gesturing to the new arrival, 'has bicycle. He take Latiya to Entebbe to my friend. Then they come for us.'

Odhiambo was not surprised at the concept of hitching a lift on a bicycle. Carrying someone on the back grid was a common practice in areas where better means of transport were inaccessible to ordinary people. He could see no valid objection to the course of action proposed and reconciled himself to waiting for what events fate saw fit to unfold. The sun was now above the lake surface and Odhiambo could already feel its warmth. It was welcome; the spray in the night had left him chilled.

Leaving his companion sitting on the beach smoking, Odhiambo ventured into the fringes of the mangroves. He found a path and followed it a short way. A glance back confirmed the apparent unconcern of his guide. Very quickly the path opened out and the mangroves thinned, giving way to banana trees. Odhiambo could see the thatched roofs of huts and rising along the hill in the background part of a murram road. All very ordinary and everything as it should be. The wait extended a second hour. At last came the noise of an unsilenced engine, and he and his guide set off up the path. Emerging from the mangroves and bananas, Odhiambo saw the crewman coming towards them. It was the two men flanking him that caused Odhiambo's heart to accelerate; they were dressed in the uniform of *askaris*, local policemen. Again, a glance at his guide's face showed no concern and, indeed, as they converged the policemen attempted a salute by raising a hand deferentially to the somewhat battered and misshapen peaks of their caps.

After muttered greetings, Odhiambo was ushered past the huts, outside which children sat and gazed with carefully muted curiosity, to an old jeep parked at the end of the murram road that Odhiambo had glimpsed earlier. He was given the seat of honour in the front while the rest piled into the open back. The first part of the journey was spine-shaking as the old jeep lurched through eroded gullies and potholes, then they emerged on to a tarmac road and the jarring was reduced to more occasional encounters with large holes in the surface. Very rapidly, the dense trees and undergrowth flanking the road on both sides gave way to more open land with the lake showing brilliantly on the left and houses and grassed areas ahead and on the right. Odhiambo gazed around with interest, despite his other preoccupations. This was Entebbe, once the neatly cultivated seat of colonial government stuck out on the promontory into the lake. Odhiambo knew that in colonial times and for some years after, until the day of the notorious Idi Amin, Entebbe resembled one large garden. No town to speak of, no large buildings, merely low colonial-style offices in their own gardens surrounded by bungalows with similar but smaller gardens. All fronting on to the lake.

One could still see the vestiges of what once had been but now it was unkempt and overgrown; the grass was a foot or more in length and the buildings pock-marked and clearly lacking in paint or maintenance. A few other vehicles, all seemingly in need of repairs and servicing, passed as Odhiambo's jeep made its way past an old golf course, and drew up at a dilapidated bungalow once, no doubt, the residence of a colonial civil servant.

Odhiambo, his guide and one of the policemen entered through a makeshift plywood door which contrasted strangely with the original fine-grained hardwood of the surrounding frame. The policeman tapped on another makeshift door and on hearing a command gestured for the other two to enter.

The room was dingy. It contained some relics of the past in the form of old standard supply Public Works Department armchairs, now without their cushions and part of their seat-webbing. These were supplemented with a modern steel table and two upright wooden chairs of local manufacture. Standing awaiting his guests was a man whose insignificance was something of an anticlimax. Odhiambo wasn't sure what he was expecting, probably someone built along the lines of heavy-weight Idi Amin, but whatever his expectations they were confounded by the reality.

'Karonga is the name,' said the little man, advancing towards Odhiambo with hand outstretched and face upraised to meet Odhiambo's own. He was less than five feet in height and slight in build. His suit, European in style, was old and too large for the occupant. Under the suit jacket he wore a roll-top sweater, the neck too big for the small head. The overall impression was that he was about to disappear into his own clothing. Only one feature was not small: a large wide nose which gave his face a curiously bull-like appearance.

As Odhiambo shook the extended hand, the little man continued.

'Inspector Odhiambo, it is great pleasure to welcome you to Uganda. There is so small chance to meet with colleagues these troubled days. Your fame came ahead of you, Inspector, but give me the pleasure of introducing myself: Chief Inspector Karonga, in charge of Entebbe Police Services. You must excuse all this,' as he waved dismissively at his surroundings, 'but I sometimes find it easier to carry out certain business at home. And my home is but humble place, as you can see. We are still living in hard times, Inspector, here in Uganda. Although,' he added quickly glancing for the first time at Odhiambo's companion, 'things are, of course, getting better under the wise direction of our President Redeemer.'

He spoke in English, a stilted English as if he was remembering imperfectly his grammar learnt laboriously at a mission school long ago. He was, Odhiambo thought, around fifty years of age: although he was uncertain how he came to this judgement, for the face could have been that of an old witchdoctor who had seen many things both good and evil.

Odhiambo, fighting off a sense of fantasy, tried to introduce a note of realism.

'Chief Inspector, my arrival here is somewhat unorthodox, as you know, and in response to your message. I find it all somewhat surprising, to say the least. Can you tell me what is going on?'

'Ah, of course. You are, how do you say – mixed by these affairs. No, not mixed, what is the word? Anyway, I bring you to date. Sit down, Inspector, and I will tell the story.' He raised his voice and called and, in response, one of the policemen entered. 'We must have a drink, eh, Inspector? You would like Fanta or Pepsi?'

Odhiambo would have preferred a hot cup of tea or coffee, but these options were not included, so he chose a Pepsi and seated himself on one of the upright chairs; this proved by an instant wobble to be of doubtful stability.

The Ugandan seemed in no hurry to move on to business, chatting aimlessly with queries about police work in Kenya until the bottles of drink arrived. They were warm and, as no glasses appeared, they were to be drunk, it seemed, straight from the bottle. Odhiambo sucked gingerly: he was nervous as to the likely reaction of his empty stomach to warm, gassy liquid. Finally, Karonga put down his half-empty bottle and spoke in a voice indicating business had begun.

'Inspector, long years ago when there were many white people here, my mother worked as housegirl for young English woman – a secretary in government office. This woman had many friends, particularly men. She was good-looking woman, so why not, Inspector? But my mother, she was not too happy. She said things going on in this woman's flat that were not good, not even for white people. One day this white woman leave with no warning. My mother arrive and she is gone. She goes to see man where she worked in government who tells her she has left Uganda. My mother not get her money for that month, but this man he pays her some shillings to go and tidy flat for last time before government give it to new person. My mother find few things left behind so she keeps them. Why not, eh? After all, she is owed wages. But these things not worth anything, or . . .' with a sudden touch of candour, 'at least these things I find. My mother not able to read, but there was a diary and few photographs. I think she kept them because woman might come back, but she never did. I found them when my mother died, locked in drawer with her own charms and medicines.'

Odhiambo's interest was quickening. He asked the question to which he was certain he knew the answer.

'What was this woman's name? The woman your mother worked for?'

The man across the desk smiled. It was a smile that combined cunning with triumph.

'Ah-ha. That's it, Inspector. You ask right question straight away. You go, how do you say, to point. She was called Crandon, Inspector, Diana Crandon.'

The pronunciation of Diana made it sound like Dee-Ian-A, so that for a moment Odhiambo was confused. But Crandon, he remembered, was Diana Farwell's maiden name. One or other of the bankers had mentioned it.

'The real right question, Chief Inspector, is how do you know I am interested in this woman? And the next real question after that is why contact me in this peculiar manner?' Odhiambo gestured towards the boatman who was still present, lounging against the back of one of the old PWD chairs, his sardonic grin ever present as he watched the two men at the desk.

Karonga held up his hands, palms towards Odhiambo, in protest. 'Give me time, Inspector Odhiambo. What do you say? Patience is a goodness.' His voice took on an almost theatrical quality. 'I look at diary and photos, of course. They are, what do you say, dirty ones. Pornographic, that's it. The pictures and bits of the writing show what this lady did with her friends. I tell you, Inspector, some of it was new to me.' Karonga smiled salaciously and Odhiambo half expected him to lick his lips. 'But so what, those were old days and what the white people did was no concern to me in Amin days. Little time to think of dirty games then, Inspector. My brother, he was taken by Amin's men, it was not nice what they did.' Karonga paused for a moment, then he gave a little shake of his head and continued. 'Inspector, I forgot all about them until one day at Entebbe airport see a visitor arriving and it made me remember. There was likeness, yes? I took his immigration card. It said he is bank man. One of international banks that wants to lend us money now we have new President. So we are told to treat these people well. His name is Mr Fulton. G. Fulton.'

Karonga paused, looking at his visitor expectantly, but Odhiambo held his tongue: he wanted to hear how much Karonga would reveal unprompted.

'Yes, Inspector. Yes. Mr Fulton was in photos that had come to me. Not with Miss Crandon, you understand. Perhaps she took photos. But with boy, Inspector, Uganda boy. There, what do you say?'

Odhiambo still waited and Karonga pressed forward. It was as if he could not abide a silence. He seemed almost pathetically eager to get a dramatic response to his story.

'It will not surprise you, Inspector, Mr Fulton was anxious to get photos. And diary. A respectable man – it is not nice for such things to be about. But I remember property belong to Miss Crandon. I am not free agent to dispose of it.' Karonga paused for thought and seemed to come to a decision. 'Also, Mr Fulton want negatives, but negatives I do not have.'

So now it was becoming clear, thought Odhiambo. Karonga tried to blackmail Fulton and extort money for the diary and photos. Fulton, reasonably enough, wanted the negatives of the photos before paying.

'So,' Odhiambo interjected, 'you decided to trace Miss Crandon to test the market value there or check the whereabouts of the negatives.'

'It seemed right thing to do, is it not so? Problem is, how to find her. Then gods smile on me, Inspector. Miss Crandon was in Zambia after she left Uganda and there was court case, insurance claim. Office of insurance company here made official enquiries about her Uganda days. Many, many records were destroyed during the bad days, Inspector, but gods were kind for this record I find. I check with insurance people here. I told some story or other. They found for me address in England where they paid her money. I have friend in London High Commission so the rest is simple.'

Karonga's smile contradicted his words. He obviously thought he had been very clever indeed.

'And so you found that Miss Crandon was now a Mrs Farwell. And your High Commission friend, perhaps, was able to tell you she was coming to East Africa on holiday. Perhaps she thought of including Uganda in her visit and applied for a visa.' It was clear from the expression on the Ugandan's face that his dart had hit the bull. 'And then you hear she is dead and your chance of cashing your assets is shrinking. But still you haven't answered my question. Why contact me this way?'

Karonga got up from his chair and paced about behind his desk. While he answered he fiddled with papers piled on a small filing cabinet against the wall.

'Inspector, you must realize Miss Crandon's death makes difficulty for me. Property is now rightfully mine, perhaps, but how to dispose of such sensitive things? Mr Fulton told me he will return to Uganda near this time, but now, perhaps, he will not come. You can help me, Inspector. If he did not kill her you can give him message. If he did, you can tell me so. We talk what to do. I think he has much money, Mr Fulton, and we are poor men.'

Odhiambo was certain that Karonga was lying now. His eyes and ears gave the signals to his sixth sense that this was so. Nevertheless, he needed to be careful. He glanced at the boatman. It seemed odd that Karonga was willing to discuss his blackmailing activities in front of an associate. It must mean that the boatman was already fully in the picture. He chose his next words with care.

'I am willing to respect the confidentiality of this visit if that is your wish, Chief Inspector. The information you have given me may be of significant help in our enquiries into the death of Mrs Farwell, the former Miss Crandon. Any business you have with Mr Fulton is, I'm afraid, your affair. I cannot facilitate your contacts with him. Nor can I condone any implication of extortion. If you are willing to collaborate officially, I shall make sure your collaboration receives official recognition by my superiors. I must ask whether I can see the diary and the photos? And whether I can take temporary possession of them, as they are clearly of importance in the ongoing investigations?'

Karonga did not seem upset at the rebuff; this confirmed Odhiambo in his view that the true reason for the contact lay elsewhere. The Ugandan resumed his seat and addressed Odhiambo's questions.

'Diary and photos not here. You understand, I must arrange safe keeping. But I knew you need proof I have them. I have friend in forensic laboratory in Kampala. Or what is left of it. All equipment is very short these days, Inspector. He took photo of page of diary and one photo.' Karonga fished in his trouser pocket, produced a small key, opened a drawer in his desk and produced an envelope which he slid across the desk. 'Here you are, Inspector.'

Odhiambo opened the envelope and glanced briefly at the contents. The copy of the photo was poor in quality, but seemed to portray a homosexual activity between a white man and a black boy. The photostat copy of a page from the diary was a description of a party which involved, it seemed, a sex orgy. Odhiambo wondered briefly about the dead woman's motives in keeping such a diary – this reminded him of one of his earlier, and as yet unasked, questions.

'Tell me, Chief Inspector, why do you suppose, Mrs Far . . . Miss Crandon, as she was, why did she leave these things for your mother to find? I would have thought she would be careful to take them or else destroy them, however much of a hurry she was in.'

Karonga did his best to portray a man whose sensitivities have been hurt. The performance was not a very convincing one.

'I hope, Inspector, you not suggest my mother get them in a way not proper. Miss Crandon go very fast, possibly to avoid much trouble. She forgot these things. That is what it must be.'

Odhiambo was unconvinced. The likelihood of a woman leaving behind such embarrassing materials to fall into the hands of someone, she knew not who, was remote. But Karonga was unlikely to implicate himself in having possession of stolen property. He moved on to another topic, although he expected a response as unforthcoming as the last.

'How do you know so much about the Farwell death? Such details were not given out on the radio.'

Karonga opened his arms and leaned back in his chair. 'Inspector! One needs friends, you know that. With my interest in this lady I ask friends in Nairobi to keep me in, what do you say, in picture.'

Odhiambo considered for a moment. They had arrived at the crucial point. If Karonga's story and motive were as he had indicated, the arrest of Fulton would not be in his interest, so the return of Odhiambo to Nairobi with the intention of questioning Fulton, rather than blackmailing him, would not be in his interest either. He felt without turning his head the eyes of the boatman focused on him and could picture the widening of the unpleasant grin.

'Chief Inspector Karonga, you will be aware that the evidence you have shown me provides a possible motive for Mr Fulton to kill Mrs Farwell. She may have tried blackmailing him.' Odhiambo stopped himself saying, 'As you are.' 'She may have other things she did not leave behind. Should this prove to be the case then the diary and photos will be needed as evidence. This may not be altogether the way in which you wish to proceed.'

Odhiambo could feel the satisfaction oozing from the man opposite. His bovine face showed the expectant but confident look of a bull who has got the red rag firmly impaled on its horn and has the matador at its mercy. The hands extended palm upwards in supplication.

'Inspector, you must not judge me badly. In other circumstances, well, we see what can be done. But now there is murder. I understand your duties, my other interest must go. You go home, Inspector, and when you are ready you let me know. I will have the helping hand, no?'

Odhiambo was relieved that his return was to be unimpeded, but his ignorance of Karonga's motives concerned him. He replaced the scraps of evidence in their envelope, looked enquiringly at Karonga and, receiving a nod, put the envelope into his back trouser pocket. There seemed to be no point in prolonging the interview. Karonga had given him what was intended and, seemingly, achieved his immediate objective. He tried one possible new line.

'There was another man in the group associated with the

dead woman when she died who knew her in Kampala. A married man. I presume there are photographs of men other than Fulton? Or references in the diary?'

Karonga shrugged.

'The photographs, they are not many. I think Fulton is in nearly all. In some it is difficult to say. The diary has many names but I cannot remember them now.'

'Any women in the photographs? Other than Mrs Farwell, I mean. Or does she not appear herself?'

The shrug was repeated.

'I never have the pleasure of meeting the lady, Inspector. So I would not know her. There are women in the photos, yes. Sometimes two together. These white people, Inspector, they have strange behaviour. Yet they ruled us, Inspector. There is lesson to be made from this, you think?'

Odhiambo smiled. He supposed it was the release of tension, but he felt happier than he was entitled to be.

'It was like the Romans, perhaps. The decadence signalled the end of the empire. The trouble with us today, Mr Karonga, is that too many of us are greedy at the beginning of our empires.'

Karonga declined to find any personal allusion in this.

'You are right, Inspector. Our rulers . . . ahh . . . they want to be emperors.' Again, a defence mechanism cut in. 'That is why we are so lucky with our President now. A humble man, dedicated to serve the people.'

Odhiambo rose and the meeting ended with fulsome best wishes from the Ugandan. As Odhiambo turned to go, Karonga laid a hand on the boatman's arm and held him back.

'He will be with you in a short moment, Inspector. I must give him directions for looking after you.'

Odhiambo left and the door closed. He would have liked to hear what was being said, but the constables awaiting him precluded any keyhole listening.

Karonga's voice to his partner was low and incisive, contrasting with the shriller, bear-with-me tone adopted with his visitor.

'You know what to do. Contact Nsolwa and tell him to tell the *bwana mkubwa* all went as he wished. It took much organization and care and risk was heavy. His gift to us is very well earned.'

The boatman nodded acknowledgement, but added a warning.

'This man Odhiambo worries me, Karonga. He is dangerous man. He will not make good friend. Now he knows or can guess much about our business. This is not good for us.'

Karonga again laid his hand on the other man's arm, this time in reassurance.

'Do not fear anything, my friend. With our new friend in Nairobi we do not need this Odhiambo. Nor need we fear him. If necessary he will be dealt with. Now go before he becomes suspicious.'

During the return journey across the lake, Odhiambo had plenty of time to think. Karonga was clearly trying to use him for some purpose by providing information that moved Fulton to the head of the suspect list. Was it to frighten Fulton because he was proving recalcitrant in meeting Karonga's blackmailing demands? Alternatively, Karonga wanted Fulton arrested. Odhiambo refused to believe in his devotion to the course of justice, so either this was a false trail to protect the real murderer or someone was using Karonga as a means of bringing Fulton to justice. Someone with a motive for not allowing Causington to be branded as the murderer while the real killer went free. If Karonga was laying a false trail, who was he protecting? Mallow was the only other suspect with Ugandan connections, as far as Odhiambo knew. If Karonga was a puppet, who was pulling the strings? And where, Odhiambo thought, time and time again, where does all of this leave me? I'm officially off the case already. Well, the only thing to do was to get back to Nairobi and see what was happening.

14

Back in Nairobi several things were happening as the repercussions of the Hawk's Nest murder worked themselves out.

Regional Administrator Aramgu was in town on Thursday to give a press conference in collaboration with the head of the Kenyan CID and the long-suffering superintendent of the Nyeri police force. The story and Gachui's soothing words for potential tourists had been polished and cleared with State House. Aramgu was prepared to refuse questions should the foreign journalists prove excessively inquisitive, but the only awkward questions related to security in the Nyeri police station and how a murder suspect could hang himself unnoticed. Aramgu was content to let the Nyeri superintendent squirm his way through excuses for this lapse. Aramgu made much of the efficiency of both the Nyeri and Central police officers who, firstly, detected a murder which, dealt with by less skilled and dedicated officers, might have been thought to be an accident and, secondly, had solved the puzzling crime within two days..

One journalist representing an American news magazine asked about Odhiambo.

'I understand a policeman, a detective inspector, was at the lodge when the murder occurred. What was his role in this affair?'

Aramgu took the question himself.

'Inspector Odhiambo from the Nairobi CID happened to be a guest at the Hawk's Nest on that night, yes. He had no connection with, er, with Mrs Farwell and her party. Due to his fortuitous presence he was able to ensure that the scene of the crime was undisturbed until the arrival of the investigating team from Nyeri. The whole investigation is a good example of co-operation between the various police units. I, as Regional Administrator, extend my congratulations to them.'

The journalist persisted.

'Where is Inspector Odhiambo now? I would like to hear about events at the time in the lodge.'

The CID Commissioner fielded that enquiry, referring to Odhiambo's many other duties and regretting there was no time for idle chatter about this unfortunate tragedy.

In response to another question, Aramgu announced that the Regional Administration would review the reports of the pathologist, the police investigators and the manager of Hawk's Nest, and statements made by key witnesses, and would produce a summary report of this sad affair incorporating relevant key evidence. Nobody present showed any great excitement at this prospect – everyone knew what such official summaries were worth. With that the conference was brought to a close and Aramgu left well pleased. One of Aramgu's options towards fulfilling his ambitions involved promotion to a Cabinet position as the next step. For that he needed a safe seat at the forthcoming elections and a promise of office to follow. Only one party would be allowed to contest the elections, but, often, two or three candidates were allowed by the party to contest a seat. It was important to secure a seat where the national party would discourage any other serious aspirants. The President, when Aramgu was given an audience, remarked that he needed men like Aramgu in government who were loyal and able to dispose of problems rather than cause difficulties. This gave Aramgu hope that his upward mobility was to continue. Of course, there were other options to consider that offered hope of even faster and more dramatic advancement.

Three of the foreign journalists took their liquid lunch at the bar of their Nairobi club. A press agency representative voiced his suspicions regarding the death of Nick Causington.

'Knew him slightly. Typical Kenyan-born, thick-in-the-head sort of chap who thinks himself superior to both the Africans and temporary residents like us. Wonder if he really hanged himself or did Aramgu hasten the wheels of justice a bit?'

The American who had raised the question about Odhiambo snorted.

'Surely you've been here long enough to know you never believe any official version of what goes on in police stations? But this one, I don't know. The Kenyans are mighty concerned about their image and its effect on the camera-toting travelling goddamn public. I guess they're not so stupid as to start hanging white guys in their cells. Africans, who Americans have never heard of, complaining about the lack of democracy is one thing. White guys is something else. What a story it would be if there's anything in it.'

The chatter drifted on as they drank their excellent local lagers and nibbled at a plate of samosas. The third member of the party suddenly returned to the subject of the press conference. He had been in Kenya longer than the others, freelancing articles, particularly for business, airline and tourist magazines.

'Of course, we're assuming Causington knocked off the woman. If he didn't, where would that leave the suicide theory?'

The American looked at him sharply.

'Do you have any reason to suppose the guy didn't do it?

Jesus Christ, if that were the case . . .' His voice tailed off in speculation.

'No, not really. Only that policeman you asked about: Aramgu said it was Odhiambo. He's one of the good guys. Competent and honest. I got the feeling Aramgu was sweeping his involvement under the carpet. Strange he was at the lodge when it happened. Don't get many Kenyans like him at a place like that, particularly in the height of the tourist season.'

At the Shropshires' home in Langata, Helen Shropshire was once again looking after the bereaved husband alone: her husband was away on business and wouldn't be back until Saturday. A police visit earlier in the day gave Morgan Farwell news of the pathologist's report confirming that his wife was murdered. There would be a brief formal hearing to make the matter official and then he would be free to fly the body back to England. On the question of the identity of the murderer the police spokesman was non-committal. Enquiries were proceeding, but one suspect had hanged himself in his cell and it was likely that the case might be closed.

Helen was interested in her guest's reaction to this news. He seemed relieved, restricting his questions to the administrative ones of what he was required to do to obtain the right papers for removing the body and how to get the official death certificate. Helen could understand Morgan's reaction; he was glad to have things settled so that he could leave, taking Diana's body with him. She sympathized with his impatience, but, even so, he seemed singularly incurious about the actual sequence of events at Hawk's Nest. She broached the subject when, once again, they were taking tea on the verandah. Morgan had returned from the city where the necessary paper work was initiated and facilitated by an Indian administrative officer from Peter Shropshire's centre who knew government offices. He sat looking both hot and drained, gratefully sipping a cup of tea. Helen waited until he sat back in his chair looking slightly more relaxed.

'Morgan? I know it's good that the police have got on with things and you'll be able to get away from all this, but are you totally happy – oh dear, what an ass I am – are you sure in your mind that that young man Causington did it? I don't see why he would. And he doesn't, or didn't, seem to me to be the type.'

Morgan Farwell looked intently at his hostess. When he spoke his delivery was slow and measured.

'It is very difficult for me to believe Diana was murdered, Helen. I don't really believe it. Perhaps I will some day. But if she was, then it must have been Nick. Who else? One of us or one of those bankers? And after all, my dear, it seems he committed suicide. No, I don't want to think about it, but when I do, perhaps in months to come, I'm sure that things will appear the same. Diana rebuffed some advance he made and in momentary frustration he hit her and then tried to cover his tracks.'

It seemed to Helen that 'tracks' was not the most fortunate choice of word considering his dead wife had had elephant tracks all over her body. She spoke after a pause.

'Yes, I suppose you're right. But I don't know. Something seems wrong with it all. I don't think that policeman who was there when it happened thinks it was like they're saying either.'

Farwell sat forward, closer to the young woman.

'Listen to me, Helen. Don't distress yourself worrying about it. It was a terrible thing, but it's happened and I have to live with it. It won't make it any easier for you to be raising questions at this stage.'

'Oh. Oh no, Morgan. I wouldn't do anything to complicate things. And I don't have any questions to ask. Not really. Just a feeling.'

'That's just because it seems so unbelievable. But any other explanation would be even more unbelievable. I am told that the policeman you're talking about, Odhiambo, is no longer on the case. Diana's gone, that's the fact that dominates my mind. She's gone and all I can do for her now is to take her home.'

To Helen's embarrassment, her guest turned his head and pulled a handkerchief out of his pocket and used it to muffle his sobs. Helen was unsure what to do. Then, remembering her mother's dictum that a woman should always have a shoulder to cry on but a man needed to cry alone, she rose quietly and slipped away.

*

George Albinger had been sitting quite still in his study for some time. His enquiries both on his own behalf and for Odhiambo had resulted in replies received at his office that morning. After lunch he left the office, went home and retired to his study, telling his house servant that he was not to be disturbed. He needed to think things through and conduct another check. He placed one call to the office where he knew Mrs Odhiambo worked to be told she expected her husband back on Friday or Saturday. She agreed to ask him to call the solicitor when he returned. After this brief conversation, Albinger allowed his thoughts full rein. At first, they were chaotic. The simple explanation was probably correct, but could the other information be explained by a coincidence? It seemed very odd. Slowly he again thought through the events of the previous Friday night in the context of what he now knew. Now, finally, as he looked out of his window at the setting sun, he believed he knew the answer. He shivered a little and decided to catch the last of the sun, although the cool of his study was not, he knew, the reason why he suddenly felt cold.

He left the house through the french window of his study and descended the steps to the garden. On his left he could see the verandah and noticed his tray of drinks already in place on the table. Time for my sundowner, he thought, but first a turn around the garden. The gardener had gone, but Albinger made a mental note to pass a compliment when he next saw him: the lawns were velvety and smooth, and the climbing roses, now in full bloom, were cascading everywhere.

He paused to sniff the roses and admire the lilies of the Nile. It was as he turned back towards the verandah that he noticed two men who, already within his property, were approaching him from his right. Two Africans, dressed in old trousers and long jackets and wearing woolly hats that covered their heads from their ears upwards. Albinger wondered where the night-watchman was. He should be on duty by now and should have stopped these visitors, for they were strangers. The first momentary puzzlement gave way to alarm. These men looked like burglars. Alarm gave way to terror, for suddenly as they reached him the men pulled pangas from under their jackets. The first blow to the head he parried with his arm, but the second from the side sliced into his skull: for a brief second the incredible pain from arm and head registered in Albinger's brain. Mercifully, the next blow severed his nerve system at the neck and he knew no more as the sharp blades brutalized his falling and then prostrate body.

The only sound he uttered was a shout cut off before it reached full volume. It was not heard by his house servant, who was at the back of the house. Neither was it heard by the missing nightwatchman who had been waylaid as he walked the two miles from his hut. A stranger approached him with a story of great magic by a man with a powerful *juju* in a nearby compound. He could, according to the story, make five-shilling notes change into twenty-shilling notes. Intrigued, the nightwatchman allowed himself to be diverted. By the time he discovered that the magician had disappeared and did not seem to be intending to reappear quickly, he was late for taking up his duties. Despite hurrying he arrived fifteen minutes late – five minutes after Albinger's neck was severed. As he looked up the drive, flanked by large hibiscus bushes, two men burst through them and raced past him. A half-hearted move to intercept them prudently changed to one of retreat as he caught sight of the pangas. The two men ran through the gate and up the road towards an old Peugeot saloon, standing some twenty yards from the property the nightwatchman was so ineffectually guarding.

Albinger's house servant had been on his way from the kitchen to the verandah to see if his master was settled there when he heard a noise in the study. Opening the door he saw two men ransacking his master's files. As soon as they saw him they fled. The house servant shouted, more in fright than in anticipation of raising support. Then, after a momentary pause, he followed the burglars through the french windows. As he reached the lawn he saw his master's body and changed direction towards it. The horror of what he saw as he drew closer brought him to a trembling standstill. One arm was completely separated from the body. The head lay forward on the chest at an unnatural angle and the left side gaped open through the remains of the shirt that, together with the body, was drenched in blood still trickling from the terrible wounds. The house servant crouched, covered his eyes with his crossed arms and commenced a low wailing of grief mixed with terror.

*

Cari Odhiambo went to bed early that Thursday evening. Since the phone call from Price-Allen and James's departure for Kisumu, she had felt as if she had betrayed her husband's faith in her. Price-Allen had been reassuring and she had allowed herself to be persuaded at the time, but doubts soon returned. To subdue the feelings of guilt and foreboding which oppressed her she had flung herself into her work and forced herself to concentrate on winning a keenly contested tennis match in the club championship. After a solitary supper, she settled herself in a chair and attempted to read a biography of Martin Luther King. Even the stirring tale of the Alabama and Mississippi marches, however, could not prevent her mind returning to her husband's problems and her contribution to them. Of course, what she was doing was in his interest. Wasn't it? Are you sure? she asked herself again and again. Or is it selfishness to protect the pedestal James has put you on?. At ten she abandoned the struggle, put away the book and went to bed. But sleep took some time to come. There was George Albinger's call that afternoon to worry about: she thought she detected excitement in Albinger's voice, excitement and, yes, nervousness. Oh dear, she thought, I hope I can prevent James getting dragged back into the Hawk's Nest mess. Then there was the second call, from an American journalist wanting to see James. She had put him off, saying she didn't know when he would be back, but it looked as if the matter was far from closed. It had to be over, or at least James's part in it. Price-Allen had promised, but what was that worth? Oh, James, let's get the hell out of this benighted place.

Round and round her mind raced, until, mercifully, physical fatigue took hold and she fell asleep.

She woke, it seemed almost instantly, hearing the sound of tyres on the gravel and a knocking on the door. The knocking turned out to be the nightwatchman with the message that the Bwana was back, and, sure enough, James emerged from the garage. Cari checked her watch, and saw that it was one in the morning. As her husband entered the house she put on the lights and saw the fatigue and strain in his face.

'Oh James, you don't look rested at all. Why did you drive back in the dark? I wasn't expecting you until tomorrow.'

Odhiambo looked at his wife and thought how beautiful and enticing she looked even with her hair dishevelled, eyes full of sleep and his dressing gown over her pyjamas. He mustered a tired grin.

'I couldn't wait to get back to you, Cari. But I'm sorry to have woken you up.'

'You need a drink by the look of you. Have you had any supper?' At the slight shake of the head from her husband, she continued, 'I'll fix you a sandwich. And a beer? Or something hot?'

As he ate his snack, Cari was able to coax a little more information.

'I took your advice. I did go on the lake, but not fishing. I went over to Entebbe.' Odhiambo watched the surprise on his wife's face give way to concern. 'It's all right. I'm safely back. It was an odd thing. I was set up, really. A messenger waiting for me at Kisumu, with a boat. A big boat. The Entebbe police chief wanted a meeting. It was almost as if they knew I was coming.'

Cari's pulse started to race and she felt physically nauseous. What have you done? – the question beat inside her mind.

'But what for, James?' Her voice sounded shrill and bordering on hysteria. She fought to control herself. 'What did he want?'

'Well, that's the strange thing. Would you believe he wanted me to help him blackmail one of the people involved in this Nyeri business? And the reason for the blackmail? Because the dead woman, Diana Farwell, had dirty photos of this now very respectable man. Photos, some of which, at least, my Entebbe friend has got hold of. Plus a diary. How about that?'

'Oh, my God! What is going on? James, you've got to drop this business. I'm frightened for you.'

'Steady, Cari, steady. There's no need to get so uptight. I'll report to Masonga in the morning and he can decide who should follow it up. I thought it over on the journey back. I'll insist on recording the evidence as I know it, but if they decide someone else is responsible for following-up, I'll let it be.' He paused for a moment and then, as he so often did, used his wife as a sounding-board for his summary. 'It looks to me as if those in the group who knew Diana Farwell in Kampala in the old days had a motive for getting rid of her. It seems she was not averse to a spot of blackmail. For all I know that could include the woman, Mrs Mallow. According to the Entebbe fellow, some of the photos involved two women. Of course, that doesn't eliminate the rest of the group. What we have is one of those bizarre situations where a woman is surrounded by people who may have a motive to do her in and, indeed, she gets done in. All I can do is make Masonga take account of the evidence. After that it's out of my hands.'

Cari was listening intently but her preoccupation was not with who had killed Diana Farwell. She couldn't care less who killed the silly bitch.

'Listen, James,' she said, grabbing his arm. 'What I'm worried about is what you said just now. You're being set up. This trip to Entebbe nonsense. They want to keep your head in the noose: have you available as a scapegoat. It's time you thought about yourself . . . and . . . and me.' Oh God, she thought, what would he think if he knew she had set him up? How could she ever explain? He would regard it as a terrible betrayal. Should she tell him now? She couldn't. He would never understand.

Odhiambo watched the obvious strain and distress on his wife's face. He was puzzled. This business was getting to her more than it should. He knew, as she did, that he was in a delicate situation, but Cari seemed to be actually frightened for his physical well-being. He took the hand that was laid on his arm and pulled her to him.

'Come on, let's forget all these *mzungus* and their dirty little games. I'm ready for bed.'

It was as well for his peace of mind that, for all his instincts, he could not read his wife's mind. She lay awake long after he was asleep: she could not rid herself of the incessant, drumming self-reproach – I have betrayed him and now because of my betrayal he is in danger. For Cari, dawn was a long time coming.

15

The ringing of the telephone woke him. As he opened his eyes the brightness of the sunlight told him he had overslept. His journeys combined with his mental struggles as to his future course of action had left him physically and emotionally drained. He had slept heavily and, it now transpired, late. The sleep had obviously done him good for he felt alert. Cari's side of the bed was empty, but as he sat up she appeared at the bedroom door.

'It's for you, James. Inspector Ntende from the station.'

At the back of his mind he noted the concern in her voice and from his memory he recalled her state of mind the previous night. She was getting paranoid about his situation. He picked up the telephone, while gazing with some concern at Cari, hovering in the doorway.

'Odhiambo. Yes, Ntende. Good morning. I'm afraid I've overslept. I drove back from Kisumu late last night.'

A glance at his watch confirmed the evidence of the sunlight: it was past nine o'clock. He listened to his colleague with growing incredulity.

'Odhiambo, I wouldn't have disturbed you with this business: I know you're on leave. But I know you knew him and that he was with you last week when that woman was killed. So I thought I'd better let you know. Albinger, the lawyer, he was killed yesterday evening. The usual, it looks like. Burglar gang armed with pangas. He was cut up pretty badly.'

Odhiambo felt a disorientation akin to dizziness: he was in the middle of a centrifuge which was spinning out of control. He struggled to digest the import of the news.

'Odhiambo. Are you there? Are you hearing me?'

'Yes, yes, Ntende, I'm here. I'm trying to get my wits together. This is terrible news. I liked him a lot. Are you sure it was an ordinary burglary? Did you get any of them?'

'No, not yet. There were two, according to the servants. They had a car outside, probably with a driver. Why do you ask if it was an ordinary burglary? Why wouldn't it be?'

Odhiambo realized he must tread with care.

'No reason, Ntende, no reason. It was just that he was getting some information for me. I wonder if he'd got it and whether any papers were stolen? I'll come on in to see you. Perhaps I can visit his house? I take it he was at home when it happened.'

'Yes, he was killed in his garden. Of course you can check his things if you want. But first get in touch with Masonga. He told me to tell you to contact him before you do anything and to remind you you're still on leave.'

Odhiambo cursed to himself. Masonga was becoming an old woman. Scared shitless.

'OK. I'll be in as soon as I can. Half an hour. Call Masonga's office for me, will you? Tell him I'm on my way. See you then, and . . . er . . . Ntende, thanks, eh. I mean, thanks for calling me first.'

He put down the telephone and looked again at his wife. She looked like a scared little girl. But as he looked she seemed to shake herself and when she spoke it was in a deliberately casual voice.

'I was just going to say I'm off to work, James. I didn't want to go until you were awake. Then the phone rang. What was all that about a burglary?'

'George Albinger. He was killed last night. Gang with pangas. Terrible business. He was a nice man. What the hell is happening to this place? We're not doing enough to stamp on these gangs.' He headed for the bathroom. 'If you can wait ten more minutes, Cari, you can give me a lift in.'

Cari's hand was at her mouth.

'George Albinger! Oh, no! I liked him too. Oh, how awful. He lived alone, didn't he?' Then, as she remembered her last contact with the dead solicitor, she paused, hesitated for a moment, but realized she had to deliver the message, even though it was too late. She called through the bathroom door. 'James. He called earlier yesterday. Albinger, I mean. He said he had some information for you. For you to call him today or tomorrow. When you got back from your trip.'

From inside the bathroom she heard a string of obscene curses. She returned to the lounge and mindlessly tidied the cushions on the chairs. But when her husband appeared, showered and dressed, she was composed. She drove carefully and kept the conversation on light domestic matters: as he vacated the car at the Central Police Station she kissed him.

'Goodbye, James. Take it easy, big guy.'

She drove on to her office. She knew what she was going to do. She was going to reverse the process and issue a few threats of her own. She had to get Price-Allen off her husband's back.

Odhiambo found himself back in Masonga's dingy office for the third time in less than a week. Masonga greeted him with the hope that he had enjoyed a few days of rest and continued in a very matter-of-fact voice as he lit another of his chain of cigarettes.

'If you're ready for work again, Odhiambo, I've got plenty for you. A company fraud case. Two big, or formerly big, people. We've got the green light to put them under the microscope. Needs someone with your insight.'

Odhiambo sat forward and kept his voice low and even.

'Superintendent, I'll do whatever you want. But first let me say two things about the last business. Please don't . . . just give me two minutes. I was in Kisumu on Wednesday. Information was passed to me that provides a possible murder motive for one of Diana Farwell's crowd at Hawk's Nest. Blackmail arising from sexual activities in the past. Guy Fulton, the international banker, is the man. I will file a report and then brief Kamau, if you wish. Obviously, he has to be interviewed. Particularly in view of the way the information came to me. I can tell you about it if you have time.

'Second, Superintendent, George Albinger who was killed last night rang my wife yesterday to say he had some information for me. Possibly about Diana Farwell's husband. He gets himself killed before I have the chance to get back to him. I need to go with Ntende and see if he left the information for me in writing. If only to protect ourselves, Superintendent.'

Masonga sighed heavily and sucked so hard on his cigarette that the end glowed red. More ash fluttered on to his tie and shirt.

'I see you still have your obsession, Inspector. The Nyeri people have given me the result of the tests on the axe you identified as the murder weapon. You were right; the dead woman's hair and blood were on it. Also Mr Causington's fingerprints. So forget the banker and the husband.'

Odhiambo gaped at his superior and for a few seconds he considered the possibility that he was indeed making a complete ass of himself. Then assurance returned. Masonga was watching him with a stony, discouraging look, but Odhiambo's good intentions to fall into line disappeared with this latest outrage.

'Aramgu and his tame policemen are making a bad mistake, Superintendent. I explained to you why Causington couldn't have done it.' As Masonga opened his mouth, Odhiambo raised his hand. 'No. Wait. You know me, Mr Masonga. I looked closely at that axe: it looked to me as if the handle was wiped. It was clean. I said as much to the policeman who collected it that night, and as I was leaving Nyeri the next afternoon I ran into him. He said they'd sent the hairs and bloodstain for analysis, but he couldn't get any prints. You know what they've done now, don't you? They're hostages to fortune. If it turns out that Farwell or Fulton killed her, how do they explain faking the prints? It's one thing to say Causington confessed or something. No one can disprove that. But if someone else wielded the axe, how could they find Causington's prints on it?'

Masonga turned his chair through 180 degrees and sat staring through his office window. He seemed to shrink as his shoulders bowed. The smoke from his cigarette rose unheeded through his fingers. He turned back and when he spoke there was a weariness in his voice.

'Inspector Odhiambo, you will report on Monday to Chief Inspector Kilembe who will instruct you as to your working with him on a possible fraud. Until Monday you will take no – '

He was interrupted by his secretary knocking on, and then immediately opening, the door.

'Mr Masonga, there's an urgent call. Confidential. State House.'

Masonga reached for the telephone.

'Wait outside, Inspector.'

Odhiambo followed the secretary out of the office. He was a youngish man with a pronounced limp incurred when he was hit by the car of a gang of Ugandans he had attempted to intercept at a road-block. It was Odhiambo who had pulled strings to get him into a secretarial course when it was clear he would never be able to return to police duties. As Odhiambo waited the secretary returned to his desk, considered a moment, looked up at Odhiambo and mouthed quietly, 'Bwana Price-Allen.'

Odhiambo gave a slight nod of acknowledgement. It figured. The whole machinery of government was working to keep the case closed with Causington branded as the killer. Why then the elaborate ruses to feed him with information that led to Guy Fulton? He was sure that the answer to this question involved Price-Allen. Rarely had one of his feelings received quicker confirmation.

'Odhiambo, come back in, will you?'

As Odhiambo entered he thought Masonga seemed to be ageing. He always looked old and sagging, but now there was an air of defeat about him which accentuated these characteristics. He stood facing Odhiambo.

'Mr Price-Allen asked if you had any news. He did not seem too surprised at hearing about the banker . . . what's his name? It seems he is currently in Mombasa on business. Price-Allen thinks it would be helpful if you followed up with him.'

There had to be more, so Odhiambo waited. Masonga picked up a thick government report that was lying in his in-tray. He looked at it idly for a moment or two and then slowly tore it in half. He placed one half on top of the other and carefully placed it in his out-tray. Odhiambo was not sure whether it was himself or Price-Allen that Masonga had just executed.

'In Mzee Kenyatta's day, we knew where we were. Right or wrong, we knew what State House wanted. Now there are too many people who think they're the *bwana mkubwa*.' He looked up at Odhiambo. 'Are you one of them?'

'You know that's not right.' Odhiambo defended himself, but he felt only compassion for the older man. 'This confirms my suspicions, sir. Aramgu wants the matter closed and Price-Allen wants it open. God knows why, unless he shares my dislike of seeing a murderer go free. Some chance!'

Masonga straightened up. He detected the sympathetic note in his junior's voice. Christ Almighty, he thought, he's so stupid he doesn't recognize that he's the one needing sympathy.

'I'll get the booking made for you on the evening flight. And I'll inform the Mombasa end. Enjoy the sun and sand.' He paused and then went on, 'Don't feel pleased with yourself. You're swimming in very dangerous waters now. Take care, because there's little I can do, you know that. Now go on.'

Odhiambo turned to go. As he reached the door, Masonga gave him one parting gift. 'If you need to see Ntende, deal with it before you go to the airport.'

The sun was directly overhead as Odhiambo stood with Ntende in George Albinger's garden. It was hot and Odhiambo felt the sweat dampen his shirt collar. He'd better take more casual clothes to Mombasa, he thought. If it was hot here at nearly six thousand feet what would it be like there at sea level? His companion spoke.

'Here is where it happened. Evening, just before dark. The nightwatchman was late. May have been deliberately delayed, or he knew something and stayed away. We're still after him, but it looks like he didn't know anything. Houseboy has been with him for twenty years and seems to be in the clear. No, it seems like a routine case of burglary with violence.'

'And yet you're not completely satisfied?'

'Well, it's just the coincidence. He's lived here for years. Why does he get chopped the week he's with you when the other *mzungu* gets killed? Then this morning you said he had something for you.'

As they talked they mounted the steps to Albinger's study. Ntende gestured at the scene.

'It seems they came in here, after the killing. Opened the drawers, grabbed a few things before they were interrupted by the houseboy.'

Odhiambo looked around. There were papers strewn around the floor, scattered from files that, presumably, had stood on the solicitor's desk. There was a filing cabinet in the corner with the bottom drawers open and a key attached to others in the lock. He walked over to the cabinet and peered at the keys: it was easy to see the dried bloodstains. He turned towards Ntende, eyebrows raised. He received confirmation.

'The burglars took his keys and opened it. The houseboy says the Bwana always kept it locked. They hoped he kept money in there, perhaps. Although he didn't, according to the servant. He kept some money and valuables and a gun apparently in that safe over there. It's a combination lock. Undisturbed and we haven't been able to open it yet.'

Odhiambo grunted and continued his perusal of the filing cabinet. On the side was glued a list of files. Many, presumably current ones, were listed individually and included personal financial files and files concerning Albinger's social interests. There were only a few dealing with his legal practice: Odhiambo assumed that all the official documents were filed in the offices of his Nairobi firm. One heading was merely 'Old Cases'.

Odhiambo moved over to Albinger's desk. It was difficult to tell whether anything was missing: papers were scattered about and the desk was devoid of ornaments such as paper-weights or pen sets. A desk diary still sat on the left side of the desk, sitting atop a small pile of magazines that revealed themselves to Odhiambo's casual inspection to be technical journals – legal and scientific. The diary interested him more. It was of the type providing two pages for each day, with an hourly log on the left and a blank page for notes on the right. It was open for Thursday, the previous day. There were no entries in the hourly log, but on the right there were some jottings consisting of letters and numbers. Half-way down the page was written 'M 1 m' and underneath this appeared 'H 1 p'. A large question mark bracketed the two lines. Odhiambo flipped back the pages. The log for the previous Tuesday had an entry for 6 p.m. which read 'TB O1-762 1841 re MF'. Odhiambo considered this. 'MF' could very well mean Morgan Farwell and the entry was probably the number of someone that he intended to call to follow up Odhiambo's request. The number was probably a London number, in which case 6 p.m. made sense as Nairobi time was three hours ahead of Britain. Odhiambo checked his watch. It would be mid-morning in London now. He reached for the telephone on the other side of the desk and muttered to the burly policeman now leaning against the wall near the window.

'I don't suppose whoever inherits Albinger's estate will mind one extra phone call on the last bill.'

His companion looked doubtful, but Odhiambo was already dialling. He got the international operator, asked for the number and told her it was urgent police business in the hope of getting priority. While he waited he sat at the desk drumming his fingers lightly on the polished surface and looking again at the entry for the previous day. It was the sort of doodle a man would make while he was considering options or choices, but the symbols were meaningless without a key. The other policeman shifted restlessly and looked impatient. Odhiambo spoke in a placatory tone.

'I'm sorry, Ntende. Let's just give this a couple of minutes. Just playing a hunch. It could be the source of the information he had for me just before he was – '

He was interrupted by the ringing of the telephone. The operator said his number was on the line. A click, followed by a pleasant female voice.

'Hello. This is Mr Barton's office. Who is this calling?'

'Good morning. This is Detective Inspector Odhiambo calling from Nairobi. Is that London 762 1841?'

'It is, yes. Somerville, Barton and Barton, Solicitors. Mr Tristan Barton's office.'

'Is Mr Barton in?'

'Just a moment. I'll put you through.' There was a short pause. 'You're through now.'

'Hello, Mr Barton? This is Detective Inspector Odhiambo. I'm calling in connection with an ongoing enquiry. Do you know a Mr Albinger, George Albinger, a solicitor here in Nairobi?'

'Hello. Yes. Good morning. Upon my word, this is a coincidence. Yes, yes, I know Mr Albinger. Spoke to him this week, as a matter of fact. Twice. How can I help you? Did you say Adambo?'

'Odh-i-am-bo. Inspector, Kenya CID. I regret to tell you Mr Albinger died yesterday. We are pursuing our enquiries and I wanted to ask you about your conversation with Mr Albinger.'

'Died! But, bless my soul, I was talking to him early yesterday. When you say you are pursuing enquiries, what do you mean? How did he die?'

'I'm afraid he was murdered at his home; it seems by burglars. But we need to look into matters that he was dealing with when he died.'

'This is terrible news . . . er . . . Inspector. Adiambo, did you say? Actually, I do believe George mentioned your name. In connection with his request to me, you understand.'

Odhiambo sat up straighter. At last, he was getting his listener to the point.

'Not Ad . . ., Od . . ., Odhiambo. I asked Mr Albinger to institute a check on a certain gentleman in connection with another ongoing enquiry. Was this the request he put to you?'

'Correct. He asked me to see what I could find out about a certain individual. Bit unorthodox, of course. But George and I go back a long way. Owe him a favour, as a matter of fact. But what has this got to do with his being killed? Oh, goodness me. It's difficult to take it all in. Murdered, you say?'

'Yes, I'm afraid so. His enquiry to you probably has nothing to do with his death, but as you understand, I'm sure, we have to eliminate all possible connections. Did you pass on your findings to him yet? He tried to contact me yesterday with some information, but unfortunately he died before I could get in touch with him.'

'Yes, I did. Yesterday morning. Bit of luck, really. Found out what he wanted quicker than I expected. Ran into the right chap, that sort of thing.'

Odhiambo tried to keep the impatience out of his voice.

'What did you find out?'

'Well, Inspector Odombo. I'm not sure that I can reveal such confidential exchanges on the phone. I mean, I don't know who you are.'

'But you remember Mr Albinger saying he was asking on my behalf. There's no need to mention names for I know who I was asking about. Tell me anything pertinent you found out about a certain anonymous man.'

There was a lengthy pause while Mr Tristan Barton thought through this suggestion. Odhiambo started to worry about the cost of the call and Ntende was looking ever graver.

'Yes. I suppose there's no harm in that. After all, it was a personal matter, not in my capacity as a solicitor. And if you're not the right man you won't know who I'm talking about, will you? Yes, I think a brief summary of the salient facts would be in order. No names, no pack drill, what. Or don't you have that expression out there? Bit colonial perhaps for Kenya today.'

Odhiambo closed his eyes and waited for the chuckle to cease. Mr Barton seemed to have forgotten his grief at his friend's death.

'Yes, yes. A summary would be fine, Mr Barton. Perhaps we should get on in case the line becomes disconnected.'

'Yes, I suppose that happens a bit out your way. Happens here, come to that. Modern technology, gone too far in my view. Although I have to say this line is clear. It's as if you're in London. Yes, well . . . where were we? Yes. George asked me to check on Mr A., shall we call him? Poor George. Terrible business. Can't believe it. Well, I was lucky, as I said. Could have been a difficult business. But, anyway, I got what he wanted. Mr . . . er . . . A. was a financial adviser of sorts. Consultant sort of fellow. Went bust a year or so ago. Got sued by a client. Forced him out of business.'

Odhiambo intervened.

'Did you find out anything about his recent marriage and what Mr A. might stand to gain from his wife's death?'

'Well, that's it. That was the nub of George's request. That was the hard part, in fact. That's where the luck came in. It seems that Mr A. met and married a lady some years his junior last year. Quick affair. Met one week, married the next; that sort of thing. Always a mistake in my experience. He'd been married before but his first wife died so he was a free man, although I gather there was another girlfriend who got tossed aside when he met this particular lady. Well, yes, as a matter of fact I got what George was after. There was a life policy on his wife. The better part of half a million pounds. Policy was in dollars, I think.'

There was a motive big enough, thought Odhiambo. Husband in financial trouble, marries in haste, insures his wife's life and she falls off a tree.

He disentangled himself from the chatty Mr Barton with fulsome thanks. Barton was a strange sort of solicitor, he thought. Solicitors were supposed to be silent uncommunicative people. Still, he was lucky that the garrulous Barton was not a stereotype; he had given Odhiambo what he needed.

He smiled at his colleague Ntende and sought to reassure him.

'Ntende, my friend, that's very useful. I've got what I needed – the information that Albinger was going to give me. Thanks a lot for your help. It doesn't look as if my business has anything to do with his death.'

Ntende nodded.

'OK, Odhiambo. Glad you're satisfied, and that eases my life. Burglary it is, although why they allowed themselves to be frightened off by the houseboy when they were willing to kill Albinger to get in we won't know till we catch them.'

Once back at the station, Odhiambo rang the Shropshires' number. Helen Shropshire answered the call, sounding responsive but with the underlying nervousness Odhiambo had detected during their previous meeting. She confirmed that Morgan Farwell was still staying with her. He was planning to leave with his wife's body on Sunday. Odhiambo explained that he might have a few more questions, but would let Farwell know if another interview was required.

There was no time to interview Farwell before the flight to Mombasa. Odhiambo assumed he would be returning to Nairobi the next day, Saturday, so that still left time for him to see the now prime suspect.

It was later, during the short flight to Mombasa, that an explanation for one of the cryptic entries in George Albinger's diary occurred to Odhiambo. Barton had said that the value of the life policy was nearly half a million pounds, but taken out in dollars. At just over two dollars to a pound the policy was probably for one million dollars. 'M' for Morgan and 'm' for million. Morgan Farwell and one million dollars – that was the meaning of 'M 1 m'. Now if only I could fit 'H 1 p' into the picture I could close down another loose end, Odhiambo thought to himself as the plane commenced its descent into the evening light over Mombasa.

16

Odhiambo had not been in Mombasa for some years. The airport was unrecognizable – what had been a small sleepy affair was now a bustling international terminal catering for the European and American tourists. Many tourists now came primarily for the sun and sand, with brief excursions inland to see wild animals, rather than the older-style safari holiday.

To Odhiambo's slight surprise, however, the town, as his driver threaded through the evening traffic, seemed dirtier and more decrepit than he remembered. He knew that the modern hotels and the well-maintained gardens and beach frontages lay north and south of the city: yet he had expected more of the money generated by the enormous tourist industry to have been spent on the city itself. He had heard that the Mombasa City Council was even more ill managed and corrupt than its Nairobi equivalent, but, still, the incredible pot-holes, the broken lampposts, the blocked drains that caused parts of the road and pavement to be flooded in dirty, evil-smelling water bespoke of neglect on a truly heroic scale. Yet seedy or not, as one passed through the great carvings of elephant tusks that arched over the entrance to the main avenue, it was impossible not to be affected by the cosmopolitan air that Mombasa still purveyed. It had the true atmosphere of a world seaport. Seamen of every nationality mingled with tourists, and the polyglot variety of local traders, hustlers and plain local residents. These last included Moslem women gliding through the streets in their purdah-prescribed robes and veils, Asian shopkeepers clad simply and carefully to conceal any signs of wealth, and white-suited, prosperous, African businessmen flaunting their wealth, power and prestige with Mercedes-Benz cars, gold chains and mini-skirted girls of various races around them.

The Arab influence over the architecture of Mombasa was still very much in evidence, but the police station was of modern rectangular design, although already it had acquired the run-down, ill-kempt look of most government buildings. Odhiambo was directed through to a small office occupied by a plain-clothes man who in introducing himself as Hassam did not volunteer his rank or unit. Odhiambo made his own diagnosis: the smiling, slightly built man belonged to Special Security. A Price-Allen man, to be handled with suspicion and care.

'Your man is staying at the Grand – it's on the beach on the North Coast. Just a couple of miles out of town.' Hassam spread his hands, palms up, his mouth drawn down and eyebrows raised in an expression derived from the Arab part of his ancestry. 'Don't know what it's about, but was told to help you so we've kept an eye on him. He's spent a lot of time with the Mulathi brothers who own the Grand. And the mayor and one or two of his henchmen. Perhaps it's to do with the Mulathis' latest scheme for developing a part of our poor city: a new marina and skyscraper right here in town. There's some opposition because the site would involve clearing a lot of low-grade housing. But there'd be a lot of shillings in it for many.'

Odhiambo doubted Hassam's ignorance regarding Fulton's connection with events. If he was a Price-Allen man he was probably well briefed. However, he went along with Hassam's preferred role, giving him a brief summary of the Farwell murder and the position of Fulton as a suspect. Hassam listened, his smooth brown face impassive. When Odhiambo had finished, he reached a hand towards his telephone as he spoke.

'You'd like to get on with it, I take it, and interview him tonight?' Receiving a nod, he lifted the receiver and spoke in Swahili. After a delay, he said, 'Good' in Swahili and put down the telephone. 'He's there, at the hotel. Shall we go? I will accompany you if you have no objection. Glad to help out in any way.'

The intention was a statement, not a question, and Odhiambo saw no excuse to object. Twenty minutes later they stepped together to the reception desk of the Grand and Odhiambo asked for Guy Fulton. Fulton was not in his room and needed to be paged. This gave Odhiambo an opportunity to assess his surroundings. Most of the beach-side tourist hotels on the Kenyan coast were modern or modernized to international standards, with spacious rooms, air-conditioning, large swimming pools and luxurious restaurants and bars as well as beach frontage and sea. The Grand was at the top end of the scale, more opulent and exhibiting better taste than many. Here the décor was restrained; the fittings in local wood and brass were functional, not garish. Many hotels catered exclusively for large charter groups, homogenous in composition, of German, Swedish or Italian origin. The Grand catered for smaller parties from more varied origins, but, in particular, it was popular with the top end of the American market.

From his vantage point in the reception area Odhiambo could see through into the bar. It was busy at this cocktail hour and, indeed, the barmen were mixing cocktails in shakers – a certain sign of an American clientele. As far as Odhiambo could see, there was not a single black face at the bar.

Guy Fulton now appeared from the patio outside the bar that overlooked the beach. He was dressed casually but smartly in slacks, shirt and cravat, so Odhiambo assumed correctly that he was taking a pre-dinner drink in the evening air. When Fulton caught sight of the waiting policemen his stride checked momentarily before he resumed his advance towards the desk. He greeted Odhiambo without warmth and Odhiambo detected worry behind the blue eyes.

'Inspector, er . . . Odhiambo, isn't it? I hadn't expected to see you again: especially here. Am I to take it that it is you paging me? I was expecting . . .' Fulton ground to a halt as if he was about to say too much.

'Good evening, Mr Fulton. I'm afraid there are one or two matters needing to be cleared up. This is Mr Hassam of the local police. We're sorry to disturb you, but we need some minutes of your time.'

Fulton nodded briefly at Hassam before returning his gaze to Odhiambo.

'I am expecting someone later. But I suppose if I must put up with more questions on the Hawk's Nest business, I must. I'm sure I can't think what else I can tell you. You've probably had a wasted journey. Anyway, if you insist, let us go to my table outside, if you don't mind the mosquitoes. The tourists are hurrying in for dinner so that they finish in time for the native dancing later.' Fulton snorted sardonically. 'So the verandah is becoming empty now.'

The policemen followed Fulton across the reception area, through the inside bar area to automatic glass doors that opened on to the patio. As they stepped outside, the contrast with the air-conditioned interior was sharp. Although night had fallen and the air was cooling, it was still very warm; however, Odhiambo was grateful for the major improvement since he got out of the plane an hour or so earlier. Odhiambo was in a short-sleeved thin cotton shirt with no jacket. Hassam was wearing a light-coloured tropical suit with shirt and tie, but seemed immune to the humid conditions. Fulton gestured to seats at a table on which stood a tall glass of lager. As they seated themselves, Fulton gestured to his drink and raised his eyebrows questioningly. The policemen shook their heads and Odhiambo went straight to a direct frontal assault, thinking this most likely to breach the experienced banker's defences.

'Mr Fulton, I have received further information relating to your relationship with Mrs Diana Farwell. Namely, that she and other persons were – are – in possession of photographic and written materials of an embarrassing and possibly criminal nature. Further, that these materials are being used to blackmail you.'

The lights on the verandah were dim, but good enough to show the increase in the pallor of Fulton's face. A tic started to stretch the corner of his mouth. He attempted to bluster away Odhiambo's statements.

'What on earth are you talking about? I have told you repeatedly, until we met last week I hadn't seen Mrs Farwell since the days we were both in Uganda. Nor were we in communication in any way. Talk of blackmail is nonsense. It was a chance meeting at the lodge. I didn't even recognize her at first.'

'Mr Fulton, are you aware that Mrs Farwell, or Miss Crandon as she then was, took, or arranged to have taken, photographs of you engaged in various sexual activities?'

There was a lengthy pause before Fulton replied. Odhiambo noticed that Hassam, seated with folded arms, was watching the banker with something akin to amusement. Like all Price-Allen's people, he thought, he likes to see people wriggle like a butterfly impaled on a pin.

'Any relationship between Mrs Farwell and myself was a private matter and remains so and has no bearing on her death. I can say no more without consulting my solicitor.'

'You would be well advised to be more co-operative, Mr Fulton.' Odhiambo turned the screw a little tighter. 'You are subject to the laws of Kenya. You may find the rules about arrest and subsequent interrogation of suspects somewhat different from those in your own country. I have direct evidence that you are trying to secure certain photos and diary entries from an individual in Uganda. You then run into the primary holder of these photos and papers who is killed within hours in circumstances where you have no alibi. Why should I not request my colleagues here to arrest you now?'

Fulton glanced from one face to another, swallowed and surreptitiously wiped a palm on the side of his slacks.

'Look, Inspector, you don't understand. That crooked little bastard in Uganda is one thing: Diana was something else. She wasn't interested in blackmail. She was worse than a blackmailer in a way. She just liked to have power over people: to know something about them that would make them uncomfortable knowing she knew it. She hadn't tried to take advantage of our former relationship all these years. Why would she suddenly do so now? And it wasn't only me. She knew things about Mallow, and his wife I daresay. Probably about everyone at the table. If she hadn't got something over the other men already she was no doubt trying. Certainly I despised her, but I had no reason to kill her.'

'Women can change, Mr Fulton. She may have decided now was the time to cash her deposits. Especially as you had risen to be a senior international banker. Her long-term investment was paying off, so to speak.'

Fulton seemed to be recovering a little of his poise.

'Pure speculation, Inspector. Pure speculation. I have said I had no hand in Diana's death and I have nothing more to add.' He paused and then continued in a rush. 'Except one thing, which I offer as indicative of my wish to co-operate. When I was on my way to fetch my camera, just before the elephants stampeded, I saw Diana go on to that luggage area, or whatever, from which she fell. The door to it was open and she was passing through as I came from the bar. She, or someone, shut the door: I assumed it was her at the time because I thought she was alone. I can tell you this, Inspector, the door was in my sight from then until the elephants reached the lodge. No one went through it in either direction.'

Odhiambo's interest was heightened: Fulton's statement was important, whether he was guilty or innocent. If guilty, he now admitted knowing that the woman who presented a threat to him was alone on the luggage platform and that he was in a position to have followed her. If innocent, he introduced a new possibility that the killer was on the platform ahead of the victim. Had she met her killer there inadvertently or in response to a summons? Odhiambo followed up quickly as Fulton lapsed into a defiant silence.

'If the door to the platform was constantly in your view then you did not go to your bedroom to fetch your camera. Why not? Why did you hang around in the lobby area? Or did you join Mrs Farwell on the platform?'

Fulton seemed to realize he had said too much. He pounded his flat hand on to the table, making the glass and ashtray rock. He grabbed the glass with his other hand and snarled his reply.

'Damn you, damn you and damn this benighted country. As well as that woman. Yes, I thought of following her to ask how that bastard of a policeman in Uganda had come by some of her things. But I thought better of it. If I had followed her I might have saved her life. That would have been ironic, wouldn't it? Now that's it. I've nothing more to say. You've got it all. The truth. Now I have other business to attend to.'

He got up and the others rose after him. Odhiambo wondered what his next step should be. He was tempted to have Fulton detained, but first he needed to check with Masonga and consult Hassam. He might be foolhardy, but to detain someone for a murder that State House deemed solved without seeking any clearance would be suicidal. Also, as he reflected on Fulton's statement he found himself half inclined to believe it. He spoke as Fulton turned to go.

'We will be in touch with you again. What are your intended future movements in Kenya and when do you plan to leave?'

Fulton grunted in what might have been exasperation.

'I will be returning to Nairobi on Monday for final discussions with the local bank and one or two individuals regarding the project on which I am working. I intend to return to the United States on Thursday. Perhaps Wednesday if all goes well.'

The two policemen made their way back to Hassam's car and driver. As they settled in the back, Hassam spoke for the first time since the interview with Fulton began.

'A very stupid man, Odhiambo, don't you agree? You frightened him badly and his tongue gets faster. Tell me, from interest only, what are these photos and so on?'

'The only one I've seen involves him and a boy. Seems his first choice in sexual partners was not girls like the young Farwell woman.'

'Ah. Yes, I see. We get a lot of that sort of thing down here, you know. The tourists. I tell you, Odhiambo, we get some strange visitors to our shores. It's a good job you and I are honest men – we could have some fun with these people, I tell you.'

Hassam laughed like a man who is in very good humour indeed. Odhiambo wondered why.

Back at the police station, Odhiambo attempted to call Masonga, but could not get through to his home number. Hassam offered his driver to take Odhiambo to a hotel and promised to continue efforts to contact Nairobi.

The hotel, one which charged within the very limited allowance for government servants, was predictably uncomfortable. A desultory ceiling fan did little to cool the small room, and the bed was hard and not too clean. The mosquitoes were active and the mosquito net over the bed was full of holes. This made it worse than useless. The mosquitoes found their way in, but were then trapped inside with their victim. Odhiambo took a long time to get to sleep and then slept but erratically. In one of his restless dozing states he had a nightmare in which the dead woman appeared to him, muddied, bloodied and face terribly distorted.

'Arrest my murderer,' the ghost cried. 'You must revenge me. You owe me that.'

'But I never knew you,' cried Odhiambo in his sleep. At his denial the ghost vanished and he awoke. He cursed for he had given the wrong response. He should have asked, 'Who was it? Tell me who it was who did it?' He lay awake as dawn broke over the Indian Ocean. His mind kept returning to Albinger's desk and diary. He had no idea what the second of the entries meant. He needed a clue, a pointer, before it could be of help to him. But the image of the desk itself kept floating into his mind. The rumpled papers, the diary, the books, there was nothing untoward there given the circumstances. What was it that was wrong with the pictures in his mind? At last he groaned, rose, splashed a little water on to his face from the jug provided, and from the balcony watched the sun rise with the promise of another scorching day. As he watched, the towers of the mosques sent out their wailing calls summoning the faithful to prayer.

It was seven thirty when Hassam arrived.

'You may have the weekend off yet, Odhiambo,' was his greeting. 'I got through to Nairobi later. They are satisfied. They say you can come home. *Kasi quisha*.'

I wish my work was over, thought Odhiambo. He asked whether Hassam spoke to Masonga himself, but Hassam smilingly shook his head.

'No, but word was got to him. The message was passed. I have a seat for you on the early flight.'

I wonder who he called, thought Odhiambo. Price-Allen, almost certainly. Now Hassam seemed anxious to be rid of him. Well, why not? The coolness of his garden seemed infinitely preferable to the heat and humidity of Mombasa. He was already dressed and his overnight bag packed, so within minutes he was on his way to the airport. The streets were already busy with traders in fruit, vegetables, maize and small haberdashery items. Young men pushed carts piled high with goods, sweat already covering their bare chests and soaking their tattered shorts. Odhiambo broke the silence that had prevailed for some minutes.

'And what about Fulton? Did Nairobi give you any word on him?'

Hassam glanced at his passenger, the ever-present sardonic grin in evidence.

'Our distinguished banker is to be allowed to complete his business here without further disturbance. I told them you rattled him badly; that pleased them. I think you've done your job, Odhiambo. As I said, *kasi quisha*.'

It was already hot and Odhiambo felt a rivulet of sweat roll from his neck down his chest. Hassam looked cool and comfortable. This further raised Odhiambo's feeling of frustration and irritation. He spoke as the car stopped in front of the terminal, his voice harsh.

'You keep saying "them", Hassam. Who is "them"? Price-Allen? What does he want from this business?'

Hassam did not reply immediately. There was a queue at the ticket counter but Hassam guided Odhiambo towards an office. At the door he paused, turned and faced Odhiambo.

'You are still preoccupied with the murder of the woman.' Hassam clicked his fingers dismissively. 'I think this is a thing of the past to the men in Nairobi. I think there is interest in your banker for the money he can provide, not because he might have killed your woman.' Hassam chuckled and opened the door. 'We are all hoes in the hands of the gardener, Odhiambo. We must learn to be happy turning over the weeds as the gardener directs. Do not worry so much.'

As Hassam dealt with the Kenya Airways clerk to obtain a boarding pass, Odhiambo felt his mood darken further. Christ, he was fed up being used as a tool, hoe or otherwise. The picture was becoming clear. Price-Allen did not care one way or the other whether Guy Fulton killed Diana Farwell. His interest in Fulton was the potential loan to the Mulathi brothers and their connections. Getting the banker to approve the loan was the objective. Threatening him with exposure, or worse, arrest for murder, was a means to that end, coupled with the assurance that all could be smoothed over in the interest of national development, namely the flow of hard currency to the Mulathi brothers. And Odhiambo himself was being moved around like a pawn, first to Entebbe, now to Mombasa, just to apply the pressure. Now that he had done so his services were no longer required. All this didn't mean that Fulton was not the murderer; just that nobody but Odhiambo cared whether he was or not.

Odhiambo scarcely spoke as Hassam gave him his pass, made his farewells and left. He wandered through to the departure area and watched the incoming flight from Nairobi disembark its passengers prior to boarding Odhiambo and his fellow passengers for the return flight. Suddenly he stiffened. The passengers, mainly tourists, emerged down the steps blinking in the sudden bright glare after the shade of the plane's interior. They walked across the tarmac, some already wiping their necks with handkerchiefs as the humidity took its toll. In the middle of the crocodile of people was a lone woman, colourful in a print cotton dress. Tanned and wearing dark glasses, she could easily have been one of the tourists, but Odhiambo knew better. What on earth was Helen Shropshire doing in Mombasa?

Acting on impulse, Odhiambo hurried back to the office, found the clerk, told him to book him on the next flight, thrust the boarding pass into his hand and headed back to the main concourse just in time to see Helen Shropshire getting into a taxi: she was obviously travelling light with no luggage. Odhiambo took the half-dozen steps at a run, grabbed one of the taxi drivers and for the first time in his police career uttered the tired old cliche, 'Follow that taxi!'

As they proceeded back towards Mombasa, Odhiambo considered the woman he was following. He had sensed in both his encounters with Helen Shropshire that something was worrying her. It was not what she said – she was open enough in replying to questions – but there was about her person a feeling of tension. Odhiambo was not surprised when her taxi entered the hibiscus-bordered drive of the Grand Hotel.

Following his quarry at a discreet distance, Odhiambo soon found himself looking out on to the same patio he had visited the previous evening. Fulton was clearly a man of habit for now he was breakfasting at the same table. He did not seem surprised to see his visitor, rising and ushering her into a chair at the table. As Odhiambo watched, the woman shook her head, probably refusing the offer of breakfast. There followed a brief period where the banker seemed to be the main conversationalist, but, at last, the woman seemed to gain courage, leaned forward and spoke at some length. Following this, the conversation became more animated.

After a few minutes Odhiambo withdrew, found a coffee shop where he could keep an eye on the lobby, ordered himself coffee, and, realizing suddenly how hungry he was, a plate of eggs and sausages. An hour passed, then Odhiambo's vigil was rewarded as Fulton and the woman walked through the lobby to the entrance. The banker ushered her into a taxi and watched as she disappeared down the drive. He gave a huge sigh, as if, thought the watching Odhiambo, he was finding things getting on top of him, and then returned through the lobby.

Odhiambo made his way back to the airport to find he had a lengthy wait for his flight. He located Helen Shropshire sitting in the bar nursing a large cold drink. She saw him as he neared the table, her face exhibiting a range of emotions in quick succession: first surprise, then puzzlement and finally alarm. The ice in her drink tinkled against the glass as the hand holding it trembled.

'Good morning, Mrs Shropshire. We are, perhaps, fellow passengers on the plane to Nairobi? May I join you?'

The woman nodded and stammered a greeting. Odhiambo seated himself and smiled at her. Was she the type who constantly needed reassurance, a private worrier? Or did she have something very real to worry about? He let the silence develop, knowing that the woman would feel compelled to break it by offering an explanation.

'Inspector, how odd meeting you here. I'm just making a quick trip. Needed to see somebody on a private business matter.'

She blushed as she spoke and brushed a strand of her red hair away from her eyes in a gesture like a nervous twitch. She was a poor, transparent liar and knew it.

Odhiambo smiled and his rejoinder betrayed no scepticism.

'I, too, am completing a quick trip. Arrived yesterday afternoon. Follow-up enquiries concerning Mrs Farwell. Mr Fulton, the banker who was in your party at Hawk's Nest, is here on business, I believe.'

At the mention of Fulton's name, Helen Shropshire looked shocked and her glass trembled so violently that some of the liquid spilled on to the table. She gazed at Odhiambo, who realized as he met her eyes that he was looking at a very frightened woman.

'How could you, I mean, I was . . .' The hand went once more to her hair. 'Oh dear, I don't know what I mean.' Then suddenly she demonstrated that Odhiambo was not the only one at the table with sound instincts. 'You know, don't you? Have you been following me? You see, I had to clear something up, something that's been bothering me. I thought he might be able to help.'

'And was he? Able to help, I mean?'

'Well, yes, he was. He was able to confirm something, which if he hadn't, I mean, if the thing that was troubling me was so, then I ought to have told you about it. It's silly really, because I understand you've closed the matter. With the death of Mr Causington, I mean.'

'You saw something, didn't you, when you left to look for your husband? Something you didn't tell me. Didn't think was relevant, perhaps. Well, why not tell me now?'

Helen Shropshire bit her lip and stared at the table-top. Then, her mind made up, she raised her glass and drained it. Now she was ready, thoughts marshalled.

'You see, Inspector, I went to look for Peter. This took me through that central area and I saw Mr Fulton. I wanted to ask him if anyone came back through the door from where Diana was . . . was, well, was killed. He says no one did while he was watching. Well, you see, I saw Nick Causington and Morgan coming from the bedroom area. This was just as Peter came out from the loo. As Mr Causington was there, I don't see how he could have killed Diana. I mean, he was in the wrong place.'

'You're very observant, Mrs Shropshire. There is some problem regarding Mr Causington's movements, although there is a possible explanation. You see, an agile man, or woman, could climb down the structure below the luggage platform, nip under the lodge and back in via the fire escape. Which is at the bedroom end. But let me ask you a question. Did Mr Fulton leave the lobby area?'

'I . . . I don't know. He was there when I went through and he was there when I came back. So I assumed . . . Oh, I see what you mean, he could have . . . could . . . Is that why you're here?'

'Why so surprised, Mrs Shropshire? When you came to see Mr Fulton, you hadn't considered questioning his movements?'

'No, no, I hadn't. I took his presence in the lobby as a sort of reference point, if you see what I mean.'

Her awareness that Fulton was a suspect, after the initial surprise, seemed to be a source of relief. Odhiambo spoke gently.

'If you're willing to trust Mr Fulton as the alibi source for all those you met in the corridor, including Mr Causington, who are you worried about, Mrs Shropshire?'

The lower lip was subjected to further gnawing. Lipstick marks were visible on the woman's teeth. But as he studied her face, Odhiambo was conscious of the sex appeal of this woman.

'Well, no one really. Well, it's just that . . . I shouldn't put silly ideas around. But you must know this too. I couldn't help noticing that the one man who wasn't in the bedroom area was John Mallow.'

Her mind suddenly veered to other matters. She looked around and shivered slightly.

'It's funny me being here. Morgan and Diana were supposed to be at the coast this week. They were going to Malindi.'

Over the tannoy system, Odhiambo heard the announcement of the Nairobi flight. He leaned forward and spoke quietly, but with great conviction.

'Mrs Shropshire, please let me give you some advice. Don't do any more private investigation. You run the risk of complications from the authorities, and the people involved. If after thinking things through you want to talk about it any more, come to see me. Will you promise me that? I'll give you my home number too.'

The woman looked at him in a way that Odhiambo found gratifying to his male ego.

'Thank you,' she said with a small smile, the first Odhiambo had seen from her. 'I'll remember that. You're very nice.'

Odhiambo, as they rose from the table, wished he could believe her.

17

As his plane descended towards Kenyatta airport, Odhiambo resolutely put the jumble of facts, ideas and theories regarding the Farwell murder out of his mind. He would relax with Cari, using what was left of the weekend. On Monday he would make a decision. Beard Price-Allen in his den and force a resolution of the issue or turn his back on the whole affair. He would talk to Cari about her ideas of moving to the States. Maybe this was the time for him at least to consider the idea.

As the plane circled one last time, Odhiambo could see the city, dominated by the office tower of the Conference Centre. In one of those offices the further disruption of his weekend was being considered.

Price-Allen was angry. One of his men close to the President had just briefed him regarding the substance of a meeting between the President and Aramgu. The Nyeri Administrator had somehow learned that Odhiambo was tracking down Guy Fulton in Mombasa at the instigation of Price-Allen and had quickly used the opportunity to put in the President's mind the thought that Price-Allen was jeopardizing Aramgu's success at extricating Kenya from the embarrassment of an unsolved Farwell murder. A call from Hassam in Mombasa confirmed to Price-Allen that his plan was working. Hassam reported that Fulton was now completely co-operative regarding the Mulathi contract, including the padding in the estimates, needed in order to make the necessary contributions to certain persons. Unfortunately, in terms of spiking Aramgu's guns, Price-Allen could not use this as justification for keeping the Farwell affair alive, for he was reasonably confident that the Mombasa mayor and one of the President's henchmen from Coast Province had not cut the President in on the Mulathi deal. It was another straw in the wind, in Price-Allen's view, that the President's position was weakening. He himself would soon have to decide on his best course of action: loyalty to the President and work for the downfall of his enemies, or switch sides. One option was closed. He could not join Aramgu: there had been bad blood between them for years. In view of this, Price-Allen was concerned that Aramgu was gaining in strength and momentum. Something needed to be done to thwart his ambitions. A whispering campaign that he was plotting against the President would be the standard ploy, but first an example was needed that would shake the President's confidence in Aramgu as a handler of events. The Farwell business provided an opportunity.

Price-Allen had used one of his hit squads to deal with Causington. It provided, after all, a dual benefit: removal of a potential embarrassment to him and a favour done, albeit unsolicited, that helped to solve a political problem. But, now, if he could show that Aramgu was making silly mistakes . . . Odhiambo was back in Nairobi – this was included in Hassam's report. Perhaps it was time to set Odhiambo loose. But on whom? Price-Allen knew of Odhiambo's visit to the Albinger bungalow, and the call he had made. He had listened to the recording that was routinely made of all international calls from a large number of private telephones. This had needed some pressure, given the number of recordings and the inefficient system for locating a specific piece of tape, but Price-Allen had persevered. He knew, therefore, that Morgan Farwell was a logical suspect. Then there was the Diana Farwell diary and its revelations about the other banker, Mallow. He reached for the telephone: it was time to bring in Odhiambo.

Cari saw the taxi pull into the drive and went to meet her husband. The telephone call, half an hour earlier, had worried her. Also, she had made a decision that would lift her sense of guilt, but she was nervous as to her husband's reaction.

Cari took Odhiambo's hand as they went into the house.

'James, darling, I'm so pleased to see you. Someone said you were on the morning flight. I was getting worried.'

'Someone said? Who do you mean, Cari? Someone rang from the station?' Odhiambo was puzzled by Cari's statement, but also by the brittle brightness she exuded. As he collapsed into a chair he added, 'What's wrong? Has something happened while I've been gone?'

Cari sat on the arm of his chair and started to massage his neck. She spoke softly, but he could detect the effort made in keeping the tone light, and his puzzlement gave way to the first intimation of alarm.

'Gotta promise, James, that you'll sit quietly and hear me out. I've got something to tell you, that I should have told you before, only I didn't want to worry you. I hope you'll understand.'

Odhiambo looked up at her.

'What are you talking about? Cari, what's up?'

He started to get up but her fingers, surprisingly strong, pushed him back.

'Listen quietly, my love. First I've got a message for you. Price-Allen wants you to contact him as soon as possible. He was surprised you hadn't arrived. He was the one who told me you were on the morning flight. He was more than surprised, I think, but concealed it pretty good.'

Good old Hassam, thought Odhiambo, reporting faithfully to his master.

'I've got a few things I want to say to him, too. I'm tired . . .'

'Sshh, James. Wait a mo'. Hear me out. I want to tell you

about Price-Allen and me. You see, he's used me a couple of times, most recently last Monday.'

This time, Odhiambo was out of the chair. He grabbed his wife by the shoulders so fiercely tears came to her eyes.

'What the hell are you talking about, Cari? What's that creep got to do with you? This is the limit – '

'James, James, please. It's hard enough as it is. And you're hurting me.' Her husband's grip relaxed, but he did not let go. 'You see, when I was a student in the States, I got in a little bit of bother once. Those were the days when everyone experimented with this and that. I was at a party which got busted by the police. There was marijuana and . . . and a little cocaine. I wasn't really involved. Just a hanger-on, you know. But I knew one of the boys who was supplying the stuff. It could have got awkward. Could have cost me my scholarship. One of the men in the embassy helped me out with the police. I didn't get charged or anything. But Price-Allen knows.'

Odhiambo's senses were in a whirl. Seeking to grasp something, his policeman's mind focused on the obvious.

'Oh my God, Cari! Why didn't you tell me? But so what if that bastard knows? Nothing can happen to you now because of some student escapade, what, ten, twelve years ago.'

'It was you, James, you. He threatened to tell you that your wife had been a drug user. Well, he didn't exactly threaten, just said it would be better if you didn't know. I didn't want you to know, James. I'm sorry.' Cari buried her head on his shoulder and Odhiambo could feel the tears through his cotton shirt. He grabbed her head and tilted it back and gazed into the wet eyes.

'But you don't take anything now, do you? I mean, you haven't touched anything like that since?'

'No, no, of course not.' Cari sniffed and wiped her fingers across her nose. 'It was just a student thing.'

'Then sod Price-Allen. Tell him to get stuffed.' Odhiambo paused. 'What does he expect you to do for him?' Awful thoughts started to pour into his resisting mind.

'Nothing much, honest, James. Once, when he first brought the matter up, he wanted some details on a man we were doing business with. I don't know why. Just harmless details – no confidential stuff. Well, I suppose it was confidential in a way, but not sensitive stuff. Nothing that could hurt him. At least I hoped not. I was naïve, James. I know that.'

'I'll kill that bastard myself.' Odhiambo let go of his wife and turned and crashed his fist into the wood panelling on the wall. One piece splintered and his knuckles were grazed, but he noticed neither.

'James, shut up.' Suddenly his wife's voice took on more strength and timbre. She was approaching the climax of her confession and somehow confidence was flowing back into her. 'The second and only other time was Monday last. He wanted you to go to Kisumu. Said it was for your own good. Get you out of the political flak. When you told me about the Entebbe business, I realized he had other motives. But it was me who arranged for your mother to call for you.' She looked at her husband's face, but for the moment it was mask-like. 'He deceived me and that did it. I rang him, told him what a shit he is and that I was going to tell you and you'd be mad as hell with him, not me. He laughed, James. And then I realized to threaten him with you was also foolish. God, he could do anything. I've been so stupid. Can you forgive me?'

Forgiveness, however, would have to wait. Her story confirmed to Odhiambo that he was being manipulated like a puppet. He felt a burning, imperative desire to confront the puppet-master.

'Did he leave a number? Price-Allen, I mean.' As Cari nodded, Odhiambo moved towards the telephone, holding his wife by the arm. 'Get him.'

But Cari hesitated.

'James, you mustn't do anything foolish. He's too dangerous. Please, promise me, James. That would be my worst crime of all, to make you Price-Allen's target.'

'Cari, I already knew what he was doing. Only I didn't know you were one of his bloody agents. Just get him or give me his number.'

Reluctantly, Cari took the telephone and dialled. At the third attempt the call went through and she heard Price-Allen announce his name. Wordlessly she passed the receiver to her husband.

'Hello. Price-Allen. Who is that?'

'Odhiambo. Your messenger boy. Reporting back from Mombasa and with another message. If you ever contact my wife again, I'll personally break your miserable white neck. You hear me, Bwana?'

The voice came back unruffled.

'So your dear wife has carried out her promise. That's good. It shows she trusts you. She's matured. There was never any problem, Inspector, only her own concern. You can be a little volatile, I'm told . . .'

'I'm not interested in listening to you, Price-Allen. It's over. I want no more to do – '

'Wait, Inspector. You're not naïve. You know I can pass orders through others. But I want to tell you direct. Go after the killer of the Farwell woman. Forget Fulton. He didn't do it. But you've got a free hand with the others. And I've got something for you on one of them. Why don't you let me pass it on to you?'

'Why have I been chasing leads on Fulton all over East Africa if you know he didn't do it? No, don't bother to answer because I know. You want him to approve a certain loan.' Odhiambo heard Cari gasp and knew that he was being indiscreet, but he was past caring. 'Well, I haven't ruled Fulton out. And if he did it, I'll nail him for it.'

There was a small pause before Price-Allen replied, still in the same even tone.

'I know you are pursuing other leads as well as Fulton. Fine. There's nothing more to know about Fulton anyway. Then there's this new lead. You'll receive a small parcel within a few minutes. And, Inspector, good hunting, but get on with it. Your available time may be short. And my congratulations to your wife.'

The line went dead. Odhiambo replaced the telephone and turned to his wife. She was gazing wide-eyed at him, the fear apparent on her face and sweat on her palms as she raised them towards him.

'Oh, James, I'm sorry. But I'm frightened. Being rude to that man is not wise. You know what he can do.'

'Never mind Price-Allen. In fact, I don't want you to mind Price-Allen ever again. Do you hear me? And, Cari, don't ever deceive me again. Why didn't you trust me?'

The words were harsh and on Cari they made an impact as visible as physical blows. She opened her mouth, but no words came. Abruptly Odhiambo turned away. He could hear, in his mind, his forebears reproaching him as less than a man, unable to control his woman and unable to punish her properly when she erred. But what he found unbearable was this proud, beautiful woman crushed into tears of self-abasement.

18

Peter Shropshire arrived back at his Langata home on Saturday afternoon after spending two days at a livestock ranching scheme in the highlands of Kenya. On the way home his mind dwelt on the death of George Albinger: he wondered what Odhiambo made of it. His curiosity was soon satisfied for when he answered the telephone in the early evening it was the inspector on the line.

'Inspector Odhiambo? How are you? How's your detective work going, or shouldn't I ask?' He listened to Odhiambo's question and replied, 'Yes, he's still here, but he's leaving tonight. The British Airways flight just after midnight. My wife and I have to go to an official dinner. Can't get out of it, but we'll be taking him to the airport later. He's resting now. The body is going out on the same flight. Your people are taking it there, I suppose . . . You want to see him later. Shall I check with him now . . . No? . . . OK, you call him in an hour or so . . . No trouble . . . Fine. Good speaking to you. Oh, by the by, Inspector, what a terrible business about George Albinger. You were a friend of his too, weren't you? You were with him at that damned place last week . . . I suppose it was the usual – burglary, I mean. These gangs going around armed . . . Not your case?. . . No, I suppose you've enough on your plate. Although Helen tells me the Hawk's Nest thing is closed. She said there was a press conference. Was that you?. . . Oh, I see . . . Who?. . . Oh, the Nyeri man, the Administrator. Yes, I met him once . . . Fine, and take it easy. Goodbye.'

A minute later Helen emerged from the shower and looked startled when he told her Odhiambo had called.

'Inspector Odhiambo. Oh dear. What did he say? I haven't had a ch . . . What did he want?'

'Nothing much. He wants to see Morgan later. I'll tell him before we go. He's going to call to confirm a time. Wonder why he's still nosing about. I thought the case was closed.'

Helen sat at her dressing-table and debated with herself whether to tell Peter about her Mombasa trip and the reason for it. She had used her own bank account, maintained for household expenses, so it was unlikely that Peter would notice the expenditure. She didn't mind telling him from that aspect; her concern was his likely incredulity and impatience at her nagging worries over Diana's murder. She was convinced now that Causington did not kill Diana and that Odhiambo knew this too. His story of shinning down the poles and running under the lodge was just to put her off. Anyone doing that would have run into the elephants and would have finished like Diana. Unless, of course, someone killed Diana first, but in that case Fulton was lying when he said she was alive after the shot that disturbed the elephants. But if he was lying then he was the most likely murderer. If Fulton was innocent then Causington was innocent too, and that meant someone else did it. Her woman's instincts led her to distrust John Mallow. Letty was a drunk and Helen believed her husband had made her so. There was something about him that made her skin crawl. With a start she realized her husband was speaking.

'He's a queer fish – Odhiambo, I mean. Why doesn't he let sleeping dogs lie? Has he said anything to you about why he's still sniffing around? Does he suspect Morgan?'

Helen looked at her husband. She knew he was particularly busy with the approach of the annual meeting of the Board of Directors, representing the financiers of the centre. He had shown due sympathy for his house guest, but it was Helen who had looked after him this week. He was so distracted that she hadn't broached the other matter that was bothering her. Should she do so now? Better not. He would be cross with her. 'Why didn't you tell me before what was bothering you?' That's what he would say. But she didn't like to disturb him with her fancies, for he was such a busy and important man.

'I don't know, Peter,' she said. 'I'm sure he thinks it was someone other than Nick. I think, perhaps, he's investigating Fulton the banker. You know, the one they called Guy.'

Peter Shropshire sat on the bed and watched his wife. She was fretting over something – the question was what. Perhaps it was time to probe a little. He knew her well enough to know she would withdraw within herself if faced with a direct attack.

'What's troubling you, dear? You're in the clear, you know

that. I saw you in the corridor ahead of me when I came out of the bog. I didn't catch you up until we were back in the bar, but I know you weren't bopping Diana on the head.'

'Oh, Peter, it's not that. It's not me I'm worried about. Well, I'm not really worried at all. Anyway,' her voice took on a defiant ring, 'if you want my opinion, John Mallow did it. So there!'

Her husband found it difficult to restrain his laughter. That would never do.

'I hope you're not giving your slanderous theories to Odhiambo,' he said. 'We don't want him more agitated than he is now.'

Helen's theory was brought quickly back to mind on arrival at their host's, for two of their fellow guests were John and Letty Mallow. Peter turned a half-amused, half-concerned glance at his wife as they greeted the Mallows and reference was made to the tragedy at their last meeting, but Helen was discreet and demure. It was later, after dinner, that Helen contrived to settle next to John Mallow as the guests retired to the verandah for coffee.

'Have you thought any more about that dreadful night at Hawk's Nest? I mean, do you accept the official line that Nick Causington did it?'

John Mallow surveyed her more closely. He was surprised and disturbed.

'What do you mean? Why on earth shouldn't I accept it? You have reason to believe he didn't do it?'

'Well, if the facts the police have on how and when she died are correct, then I can provide an alibi for Causington. And for Diana's husband, come to that. I already have, of course, in giving my story. That's why Inspector Odhiambo is still on the case, or nosing around as Peter puts it.'

John Mallow cursed to himself. The last thing anyone needs is this bloody woman to start the police chasing around again, he thought. Just as it looked as if he was through and in the clear. He had thought Letty was the danger, but she had the sense to keep her mouth shut despite the gin, and now here was this stupid woman putting her oar in.

'I don't know what the police know and I don't care. The important thing is, Helen, that the case is closed. In Kenya, my dear, it's best to let sleeping dogs and the Kenyan police lie. Raising wild theories at this stage isn't going to help any of us.'

'You see,' said Helen as if thinking aloud, 'you see, if he didn't do it, Causington I mean, then one or other of our group probably did. And how many of us have cast-iron alibis? You, for example – can you prove you weren't on that platform thing with poor Diana?'

'Stop this, Helen, it's not funny. This is dangerous talk. Stirring things up can hurt you as well as others. I don't want to talk about it. Now, if you'll excuse me.'

With that, Mallow rose, ostensibly to fill his coffee cup, in reality to resettle away from Helen's questions.

Later, as they were driving home to collect their guest and deliver him to the airport, Peter Shropshire accosted his wife in an amused tone.

'Whatever did you say to upset John Mallow? Don't tell me you accused him of murdering Diana?'

'Not exactly. I asked him if he could prove he wasn't with Diana. I think his reaction is interesting. Why should he take on so if he's innocent?'

Her husband's tone sharpened.

'Look here, Helen. You can't go on like this. Accusing, or virtually accusing, people of murder. We'll end up with a libel charge to answer.'

Helen replied briefly, if inelegantly.

'Balls,' she said.

Even stronger language was being used in another car. John Mallow was cursing fluently and lengthily. Letty listened with her eyes closed. Even alcohol was losing its ability to ease the stress. Finally, she opened her eyes and turned towards her husband.

'If you're such a spotless paragon why are you so worried? Just 'cos that little Shropshire bitch gets under your skin. You should have given her a dose of her own medicine. I would have, if I'd heard her. Want my opinion? She was terrified that Diana, God rot her, would get her precious husband into bed. Same as she's done with all you weak bastards. Ask her where she was?'

'Don't be ridiculous. Start a witch-hunt and where would it stop? Can you prove you were in the bedroom all the time?'

Letty felt tears coming to the surface.

'If you think I care enough to risk my neck knocking her off, you're stupider even than you seem. There was a time perhaps. But now I couldn't care less what you or she or any other of your fancy women get up to.'

Mallow shook his head slightly. How stupid could a woman get? She persisted in her belief that the problem with him was his eye for other women. She had never suspected the truth. Or was she burying her true suspicions in her subconscious?

Odhiambo was ready for bed after a busy evening. He had confronted Morgan Farwell with his knowledge of the large insurance policy on Diana's life. But Farwell was unfazed. 'There is nothing to connect me with her death, Inspector. And I didn't kill her,' he said, and to Odhiambo's ear it had the ring of truth. And yet there was something he detected behind the man's eyes. Earlier, Odhiambo had considered it was fright, but now he changed his mind: it was not fright and not guilt, but something. The only fear Farwell exhibited was of Odhiambo's power to delay his departure with his wife's body. Odhiambo considered doing so, but he didn't have sufficient grounds, and he was in no mood to inflict even more gratuitous pain this evening. On his return home, he discovered Cari had gone to bed. He did not disturb her, but helped himself to a whisky and sat in the lounge to read the contents of Price-Allen's package. He had deferred opening it in order to see Farwell, but now he read with interest further extracts from the infamous diaries of the dead woman. Odhiambo wondered idly whether Price-Allen now had the originals from Karonga. The extracts revealed that Diana used cocaine and that her supplier and co-user was John Mallow. What a woman, thought Odhiambo. It was surprising she had lasted as long as she had. Was John Mallow still a drug dealer? If so, the threat posed to him by Diana was not only historical, but a very present one: one that provided a strong motive for murder.

He went to bed, taking care not to disturb his sleeping wife. It was well for his peace of mind that he was not aware that she had cried herself to sleep. As he lay awaiting sleep, various permutations floated through his head. If Fulton was speaking the truth, Diana joined her murderer on the luggage platform just before the elephant stampede. Odhiambo was convinced that the murderer seized a chance opportunity when the stampede occurred. If the murderer called to Diana it was probably to have a private word, to plead with her, perhaps: then a more permanent solution presented itself. Carrying on the presumption of Fulton's truthfulness, it followed, by definition, that he was not the murderer and nor, in all probability, were any of those seen by each other in the bedroom corridor. In which case the only logical suspect was Mallow. Alternatively, if Fulton was lying it meant in all probability that he was the murderer. In either case Morgan Farwell seemed to be in the clear.

But there were several points about his reasoning that worried Odhiambo and kept him awake. The timing seemed too constrained. Did either Fulton or Mallow have sufficient time after leaving the verandah and the tunnel respectively to set up the meeting with Diana on the platform? If Fulton was lying, but was not the murderer, most of the alibis were weak. But why would he lie if he was innocent? Come to that, why would he lie even if he was guilty? An intelligent man, he must have realized that he was providing an alibi for most of his co-suspects.

The next morning, Sunday, his luck was in. An early telephone call produced McGuiry who was breakfasting at Mountain View, having returned with the Saturday night guests from Hawk's Nest.

'Good morning to you, Jimmy. I tell ye, laddie, I've felt passing strange at the Nest these last days. You dinna need me te tell ye, these tourists are a morbid lot. All they want to be shown nowadays is where the poor lassie was killed. 'Tis a sad commentary on the human condition, James, that it is.'

'Robert, I've got a strange request to make. I need the name of a tourist who was there with us last week who took a video of the elephants from beginning to end of the episode. At least from the time they started milling about. I need the timing, Robert. Then I need to go to Hawk's Nest with you and check the timings of the various leading players. As far as we can remember them.'

'Och, laddie. Are you still on this business? I thought it was all over and done.'

'I'll explain when I see you. But first I need a video of the elephants.'

"Tis a difficult task you set me there, James. But leave it with me and I'll get back. Where can I get you?'

After giving McGuiry his number, Odhiambo called the station. Again he was lucky to find the inspector who specialized in tracking the drug trade in Nairobi on duty, writing up a report. In answer to Odhiambo's request the inspector summarized the situation.

'As far as the *mzungu* trade goes, Odhiambo, I'd say it was fairly small stuff here in Nairobi. Bit different down at the coast. No single big *bwana mkubwa* here amongst the *mzungus*. It's mainly what is called social use. Helps them to muster the energy for their sex parties 'cos most of them aren't up to much without a little artificial aid.' The inspector laughed uproariously. The joke that white men did not have the sexual vigour of African males was one that was highly relished. 'There's a lot of *totos* in the business, though. Smallboys just supplying enough for themselves and their friends. They get it through one of the bigger Indian boys usually.'

Odhiambo couldn't resist a comment, although it risked affronting his colleague.

'I don't hear of many of these social users getting themselves arrested.'

Another high-volume laugh came down the line.

'I don't suppose you do. That's not how the game is played, you should know that, Odhiambo. Some of these *mzungus* have good friends in high places. Anyway, we have no time to worry about these *totos*. Stopping the high-volume stuff is all we can cope with.'

Odhiambo got to the point.

'Have you heard the name Mallow in terms of small fry in drugs? M-A-L-L-O-W. John Mallow. *Mzungu*, early fifties. Banker.'

There was a short silence. Then the negative rejoinder.

'I don't think so. Don't remember hearing that name. But I'll ask around. Why? You interested in him for something else? Drugs is not your *shauri*, Bwana.'

'Yes. He's a witness in another case of mine. I need to know if he's hiding something.'

'Most of these *mzungus* have something to keep from you, Odhiambo, my friend. Even if it's not drugs. I'll see what I can do.'

Odhiambo now joined Cari for breakfast. Conversation between them was stilted, as if they were new acquaintances being careful to be more than usually polite to each other. Odhiambo was in the middle of the meal when McGuiry rang back from Nyeri.

'Is that you, James? Listen, I had a wee word with Daniel. You remember Daniel, do ye no? Well, Daniel reckons the most avid cameraman that night was one of our Japanese friends. He got talking to Daniel, asking about the girls of Nyeri. They're sex-mad, ye ken, these Japs. Or some of them. So Daniel remembers he mentioned he was at the Ngong Hotel. He was going on to visit the Mara, but the Ngong was his base. He might still be there, if your luck's in.'

'What's his name? Or is that asking too much?'

'All in the service, laddie, all in the service. I checked the register. Only two of our Oriental friends gave the Ngong as their last place of stay. Now let me see, I've got the names here somewhere. Ah, here they are. Hakimu and Ozashi. Do ye want me to spell them? No? Yes, Ha-ki-mu with a U, and Oz, as in Wizard of, followed by ash and an i, Ozashi.'

'Robert, I'm in your debt again. Look, if I can get hold of the video, expect me up there. Will you be available?'

'Tonight and tomorrow I'm off, James. So I'll be free in the morning to accompany ye. Give me a tinkle when you know. 'Bye for now.'

Cari watched as her husband looked up a number in the directory and dialled. She didn't know whether to feel more or less frightened. If James was getting close to cracking the case there was no telling what the repercussions would be. But at least his spirits were rising and his mind was moving on from thoughts of her betrayal. She listened to his conversation with what seemed to be a hotel telephonist. After a pause, he grunted, told the operator to do nothing and replaced the receiver. He looked at his wife and she could feel his excitement.

'Somehow, I think I'm getting to the nub of the thing. Now I've got a fifty-fifty chance that I've nabbed the right Japanese. Mr Ozashi has left, but Mr Hakimu is still here. Let's hope that he's the film fan.' He picked up the telephone again and called Masonga's home number. A servant answered and went to call his master.

'Odhiambo? What's the problem?'

'Superintendent, I've got a lead, but I need to check the timing of events at Hawk's Nest. I've traced a Japanese tourist who may have a video. He's at the Ngong.'

'Why bother me, Inspector? I thought you were dealing direct with others these days?'

'Hey, Superintendent! That's not fair. It was you who passed on Price-Allen's instructions. But Price-Allen doesn't want Fulton for this murder. He wants me to get someone else. To embarrass another mutual friend of ours. At least he's not blocking the investigation. But I don't have much time.'

'So what do you want?' Masonga's tone was still disgruntled, but Odhiambo detected a slight thaw in the chill.

'I need a couple of men to meet me at the Ngong. I want to put on a bit of a show. Impress the Jap. In case he's reluctant to part with his film.'

There was a silence before Masonga replied.

'Odhiambo, I'll provide the men if you insist. But I tell you as a friend that no good will come of this. You're being used.'

'I've been buggered about enough, Mr Masonga. Entebbe, Mombasa, like a clockwork doll. I've had it. I'm going to see this through now and I hope the result embarrasses both Price-Allen and Aramgu. A pox on both of them. It may be my last case, but by God I'll do it right.'

19

As soon as the door opened in response to his knock, Odhiambo sensed he had the right man. Hakimu's reluctance to open the door more than a crack and to let Odhiambo in was sufficient to prepare the policeman for the local prostitute in the bed. Mr Hakimu was still pursuing an active sexual holiday and Odhiambo hoped his passion for his camera matched his sexual appetite. Odhiambo's bluster, backed by his silent supporting cast, overcame Hakimu's resistance and Odhiambo found himself surveying a frightened tourist and his one-night-stand companion who sat up in the bed making only a desultory attempt to conceal her nakedness. She was young and good-looking and the clothes tossed on a chair were not cheap. Mr

Hakimu had hired the best and was probably paying a good deal for his pleasure – and in hard currency.

The setting made things very easy for Odhiambo. The Japanese, when he realized that all that was needed from him was a little co-operation in the form of handing over a film on loan, was only too willing to oblige. His English was good and his film-filing system efficient.

'There you are, officer.' Hakimu had rummaged through a metal case containing exposed films. 'This is the one I used to film at tree hotel. It was good night until unfortunate events overtook.' He looked at Odhiambo more closely. 'Have we not met before, officer? Yes, I know, you too were in tree hotel. I remember now. I have good memory for faces I meet.'

'Thank you, sir.' Odhiambo took the film. 'I'll give you a receipt.'

The girl in the bed laughed and spoke for the first time.

'If you want to buy dirty movies, Mr Policeman, I've got some hot ones.'

Hakimu looked alarmed and anxiously ushered the police contingent towards the door. Odhiambo checked the film. It was in the form of a cassette. As he left he spoke to the Japanese while looking directly at the girl.

'Thank you, Mr Hakimu. I don't think we need question you on other matters. I'm sure the lady there has explained to you the rules about using hard currency.'

The girl snorted and the sheet slipped from her fingers, exposing completely her splendid body.

'Piss off, Mr Policeman,' she said pleasantly enough. 'You don't frighten me. I've got friends too.'

Odhiambo took the film to an Indian friend who he knew was a keen amateur cameraman. Sure enough, his friend settled him in a comfortable armchair, pressed a cold beer into his unresisting hand, and up on a portable screen came a view of the hotel in Nyeri. With the use of a fast forward device the scene rapidly shifted to Hawk's Nest. Prior to the crucial elephant scene, Odhiambo was interested in one frame. Hakimu had scanned the dining-room during dinner and the camera dwelled a second on the Farewell table. Facing the camera was Diana, with a three-quarter profile shot of Letty Mallow. The look she was giving Diana Farwell was one of clear, undiluted hatred.

The elephants' arrival was duly captured and, after a gap, the herd's restlessness rekindled the cameraman's enthusiasm: the film captured the subsequent minutes, including the stampede. Odhiambo timed both the period from the restarting of the film to the point where the elephants were startled by the shot, and the period from then to when the elephants passed from the camera's view under the lodge. Watching, Odhiambo could almost hear and smell once again that thundering mass of flesh. The film confirmed what he supposed – the entire episode was briefer than it seemed to be at the time. Odhiambo now had confirmation of two facts: one, whoever fired the shot could not subsequently have tossed Diana Farwell to the elephants, and, two, if the murderer decided on the act after realizing the elephants were stampeding he, or she, had very little time to grab the axe, hit the unfortunate woman on the head and tip her over the guard rail – Diana and her killer must have been on the platform in advance of the shot.

A sense of urgency now gripped Odhiambo. His friend volunteered to make a copy of the film and was even willing to return the original to its owner, so Odhiambo took himself back to his house to break the news to Cari that he was off once again. He felt constrained to offer an apology even though the spontaneity of their relationship was still suffering from Cari's confession of the previous evening.

Cari shook her head.

'It's not you rushing off, James. You know that. Gee, I'm used to this sort of thing. I surely should be by now. It's the whole business of you going up against these people – Price-Allen and Aramgu and God knows whose toes you're stepping on. These people do nasty things James. I want you out of this whole affair.'

Odhiambo sighed audibly and spoke slowly with an exaggerated show of patience.

'You know I'm in too deep now to just walk away. You know me better than that, or I thought you did.' He paused and resumed in a softer, reasonable tone. 'When this is over we'll talk about the future, I promise.'

'Damn you, James Odhiambo. You and your stiff-necked pride.' Cari's voice was lighter than the words, reflecting the slight easing of the tension between them.

'You realize I don't have official backing for this trip. I need the car, Cari. Is that all right?'

To his surprise, she laughed with genuine humour.

'Oh, James, you fathead. As if I'm worried about the car. The office will send one in the morning if I need it. Now get on.'

As he was reversing the car in the drive, Cari suddenly signalled and ran towards the car.

'Oh, James. I forgot. There were two calls for you. One from Sentongo. You called him earlier. He said to tell you that there was no firm evidence, but the *mzungu's* name had cropped up once or twice as a small dealer.'

'Thanks, Cari. That's the sort of vague response you get from Sentongo's people. Either they don't know much or they like to play their cards close. What about the second call?'

'It was that reporter again, the one I told you about. He'd found out you were back. I put him off again by saying you were going out of town.'

'Well done. With all my present problems that's one I can do without. So here goes. See you later.'

Odhiambo reached Nyeri at what British tradition insisted was teatime. In answer to his query at the reception desk of Mountain View he was directed through to the verandah, where, indeed, Robert McGuiry was taking tea. As he approached, Odhiambo remembered his previous visit to this verandah when his conversation with George Albinger proved to be the start of the whole sequence of events. It seemed a long time ago – was it only ten days or so? Now Albinger was dead. As this thought entered his conscious mind Odhiambo was aware that something else in his subconscious was close to being retrieved at the same time. Something connected with Albinger's death. Something to do with Albinger's study. Impatiently he shook his head and came up behind the warden he had come to see.

McGuiry greeted him warmly and pressed tea, sandwiches and cake upon him. Odhiambo found that he was hungry and enjoyed the, for him, unusual meal in the middle of the afternoon. During tea McGuiry kept the conversation at a gossipy level, as if realizing that Odhiambo needed to unwind, but, finally, Odhiambo broached the matter in hand and McGuiry nodded.

'I suggest we take one of my wagons and pay a wee visit to

the Nest, James. There's nearly a full house there this even', but we can creep about without announcing our presence.'

'That's great, Robert. I know it sounds corny, but revisiting the scene of the crime may help me sort out my thoughts.'

McGuiry cleared his throat, which sounded as if it was lined with gravel. 'Ahem, James. Stop me if I'm trespassing, mind. If you're still tracking whoever killed that poor lassie, what's Aramgu going to think if ye find him? They've dotted the i's and crossed the t's, James. They won't take kindly to anyone dirtying up the neat wee scenario they've put together.'

Odhiambo laughed and patted the older man on the shoulder as they rose.

'Robert, Aramgu is the least of my worries. You should see some of the sharks in Nairobi. I'm out on a limb, Robert, but if they're going to cut it off at least I'm determined to take the murderer down with me. If I can find out who it is.'

McGuiry's concern was unallayed. He followed his tall companion through the hall of the hotel and then took the lead as he guided Odhiambo towards an ancient Landrover in a corner of the hotel car-park.

'Don't underestimate yon Aramgu mind, James. I could tell a tale or two of our Administrator if I had a mind and you weren't a policeman.'

They left the hotel and passed the guard in the hut at the gates at the end of the drive without stopping, for McGuiry's vehicle was well known to him. As they disappeared up the hill towards the forest the guard gestured to one of the several curio sellers clustered outside the gate. He spoke softly in Swahili; his listener nodded, repeated the message and then turned and trotted down the hill towards the town and the government buildings.

When they arrived at Hawk's Nest, Odhiambo looked around the interior with more detailed interest than he had given it during the hectic hours following the murder. Unobtrusively, he and McGuiry paced through the movements as claimed by the various suspects. Odhiambo satisfied himself on one point: if Mallow left Albinger's niece, Jennifer, at the end of the tunnel at the time she claimed – just after the initial uneasiness in the herd manifested itself – he had time to reach the luggage platform before the shot was fired and possibly before Fulton reached the lobby. But, Odhiambo asked himself, why would he have gone there unless an assignation with Diana was already arranged?

The two men walked down the narrow and dimly lit corridor that connected the bedrooms to the central lobby. On the right side nearest to the lobby was the toilet and shower area. On the left the bedrooms ran the whole length of the corridor with bedrooms also on the right side for the second half of its length. At the end of the corridor there was a door marked FIRE EXIT. Pushing it open, Odhiambo inspected the narrow iron staircase that spiralled its way to a point about a foot above the ground. McGuiry had with him a copy of the bedroom occupancy plan for the night in question. The Mallows' bedroom was about half-way down on the left, with the Farwells' two doors further along. Causington had been allocated a room near the fire escape end of the corridor on the right-hand side. Fulton and the Shropshires both had rooms on the left side nearer the beginning of the corridor, opposite the toilet and shower area.

Odhiambo ran his mind over the witnesses' statements. Morgan Farwell and Nick Causington agreed they met in the corridor as both headed back towards the lobby. There were others ahead of them, but they did not recollect anyone in particular. Odhiambo was convinced that Causington had come from the fire escape door and was just passing Farwell's bedroom door when he emerged. Helen Shropshire, in her statement, claimed to have visited her bedroom in search of her husband; on leaving it she had seen Farwell and Causington behind her in the corridor and her husband emerging from the toilet almost opposite. Shropshire himself confirmed seeing his wife, but not the other two men. This was not surprising given the dim lighting, indeed it was Helen Shropshire's ability to recognize them at a distance that was questionable.

McGuiry ushered Odhiambo back to his office and produced a whisky bottle from a cupboard.

'How about a dram afore we set back?' he asked.

'I'd prefer a beer if that's possible.' Odhiambo replied.

'Surely, James, surely. Just let me give the barman a shout a moment.' McGuiry disappeared briefly and then returned. As he poured himself a generous measure of whisky he mused aloud.

'Mallow forgetting he was escorting Albinger's niece, you tell me. Sounds a wee bit thin, that.'

'I don't know, Robert. You've got to remember they'd all had quite a few drinks. And then the noise of the elephants. He could be telling the truth.'

'Talking about Albinger and his niece – that was a terrible business in Nairobi. Poor George. Cut down in his own *shamba*. Nothing to do with this business, I suppose?'

'Doesn't look like it, Robert. He was doing a bit of digging for me, but the killing seems to have been coincidental.'

Once again, as he spoke, Odhiambo felt the tug of his subconscious. Something about the Albinger study. What the hell was it?

McGuiry's mind was on a different tack.

'What about the niece? What happened to her? Was she staying with George at the time? Nasty for her if she was.'

'No. The inspector in charge told me that she was at the coast. George's office was arranging to contact her. She'll probably be at the funeral on Monday. Tomorrow, that is.'

Odhiambo's beer was brought in on a tray by a steward. He sipped the cold lager as his thoughts continued to mill about in his head. Yes, he should attend the Albinger funeral. Out of courtesy to the dead man, but also he'd like another word with Jennifer. His thoughts were interrupted again by McGuiry.

'James, we know that fellow Causington was outside blazing away with one of my guns. What puzzles me is what made him do that?'

'Again, remember they were all far gone in drink. I think he was besotted by the woman and his nose was put out of joint by the attention she was giving to Fulton and Mallow. He wanted to do something to thrill her. Oh, by the way, did they find the boots?'

'Ay, the Nyeri boys and my lads gave the place a good search. Shouldna' been too difficult, really. He'd wrapped them up in a bit of paper and stuffed them in one of the waste bins. We were right, James. There was shit on his left boot. The Nyeri police didna tell ye, then?'

McGuiry smiled the smile of a man who knew that the answer to the question was well known to both, but better unspoken. Odhiambo, however, had passed the point of reticence.

'All they're interested in is shutting the case and keeping it shut. I expect the boots have disappeared again by now. There's one thing about Causington's escapade that puzzles me. If he'd seen the gun left lying about here and collected it when he was off to thrill his girlfriend, he'd have had to walk all the way through the lobby and down the bedroom corridor carrying it. Somebody was almost bound to see him and wonder why a guest was carrying a rifle.'

McGuiry replenished his whisky and turned back to the policeman.

'I thought about that, James. The gun and the cartridge belt were left by a window just down the corridor from here. He could have helped himself to a cartridge, dropped the gun through a window and come back under the building to collect it after going out at t'other end. Didna' ye tell me one of the women saw someone moving under the building? That would have been yon Causington on his way back after retrieving the gun.'

'God, I must be getting stupider. Yes, that's probably how it was.'

Half an hour later the two men left, stepping down the stairs from the platform where Diana Farwell had met her end. One of the lodge staff with a rifle walked with them to McGuiry's vehicle, parked a hundred yards away. The gap between the parking space and the lodge was deliberate. The short walk through the bush accompanied by an armed ranger was one of the introductory thrills for each night's customers. Odhiambo was deeply conscious of the noises of the forest night. The caustic laughter of monkeys above his head, the clicking and chirruping of the insects reaching a decibel level that implied many thousand contributors and, close enough to make him start, the sudden heavy sigh of a larger animal, probably a nearby buffalo. I am an African, he thought, yet in this very African environment I am the stranger, it is McGuiry who is at home. Somehow this triggered his lurking depression, which it took supper at the hotel and two of McGuiry's malt whiskies in his cabin to partially dispel.

McGuiry insisted that Odhiambo stay with him in his cabin in the grounds of Mountain View. Late in the evening McGuiry looked over his glass at his guest and returned to the subject of George Albinger. The whisky he had consumed throughout the evening was making him a little maudlin.

'Poor old George. You say the funeral is tomorrow. Would have liked to go down but it's impossible. Don't suppose

George will mind. I'll drink a toast to his memory here. Knew him since way back, James. Good man, ol' George. Never married, but I never heard ought about him and other males. Just liked a lonely life. Bit like me there. I was married once. Poor Sheila died here in Kenya in the full flush of her beauty, as the poet says. Never wanted to marry again.' He sipped from his glass, his eyes looking watery. 'I said to him more than once, you need more interests, George. Always stuck in your law books. Stayed with him once. Nothing but law books. Not a novel or magazine in the place. I like a good yarn. Like that South African chap, Wilbur Smith. And the British jockey fellow. As well as my old copies of Burns. But George, nothing. I've got my golf, he said to me. Golf, I said. Well, if you like golf so much, how come you don't even have a golf book? 'Cos they keep the magazines at the club, he said. Couldna best ol' George in argument. But he never read them, though.' He inspected the dry bottom of his glass. 'Shall we be having a nightcap, James? One for the road to bed.'

'No more for me, thanks, Robert.'

Odhiambo put a hand over his glass. McGuiry's ramblings recalled his picture of Albinger's study. He scanned it again in his mind. But only as he lay in bed did it click. Yes, that was it. That's what was odd for a lawyer – and McGuiry said he had nothing but law books. Could it have any connection with Diana Farwell? If so, he needed to view the whole affair from a different angle.

He left just before dawn, dressing quietly and creeping out to avoid disturbing the snoring McGuiry. He left a note:

Robert,
Thanks for a great evening. Something you said may have given me a clue. I have to check it out. Will be in touch later.
                 James

Making his way from McGuiry's cabin to his car, Odhiambo almost tripped over a dozing nightwatchman. He moved on as the embarrassed man scrambled to his feet searching for his spear. I don't suppose it matters, he thought. Not many panga-wielding burglars here. As he unlocked his car a light from a torch suddenly focused on him. He turned to face the source as the voice, speaking Swahili, came from behind the light.

'Inspector Odhiambo? You are wanted by the RA, Bwana Aramgu.'

20

Odhiambo drove through the early light, his hands clutching the steering wheel with a combination of tension and anger. There were low-lying clouds around these highland hills and ahead of him as he approached Thika it was raining with a tropical intensity. This wouldn't make the remainder of his return journey any easier. The early morning traffic on the Nairobi-Thika road was enough to frighten the careful at the best of times.

The man who had accosted him in the Mountain View carpark turned out to be an *askari* from Aramgu's office placed on guard in case Odhiambo left during the night. He was unable to produce any identification, which provided Odhiambo with the excuse he needed to browbeat the man, alleging he was to lead Odhiambo into a trap set by robbers. As Odhiambo, pushing the *askari* aside, got in his car and drove away, he saw in his headlights the unfortunate man crouching on the grass verge, no doubt wondering how he was to explain his failure to his master. Odhiambo was under no illusions about the likely consequences of his action: his excuse would not deceive Aramgu who would know he had been defied. Odhiambo guessed that Aramgu intended to have him picked up by official policemen in the morning to find out why he had returned to Nyeri. The suspicion that Odhiambo was about to expose his cover story and reopen the Farwell murder enquiry would be sufficient for him to hold Odhiambo under one pretext or another until Odhiambo's limited time was exhausted. Now it was likely that Aramgu would attempt to have him arrested and detained for contempt of the government.

Surviving the rainstorm and the skidding *matatus* overloaded with early morning passengers making their way to work, he reached Nairobi before eight. He drove around the fringe of the city and arrived at Albinger's bungalow. The gates were closed, but the nightwatchman was still present and opened the gates when Odhiambo produced his identification. He parked in front of the main door which was opened by the servant he had seen during his previous visit.

'Are you alone here?' Odhiambo asked the man in English.

'No, Bwana. Memsahib is here. Bwana Albinger's relative.'

Odhiambo was momentarily nonplussed. Then he remembered – Jennifer, back in town for the funeral of her uncle.

'Is Memsahib Jennifer out of bed? I want to see her.'

'Yes, Bwana, she is taking breakfast. Today is day of funeral of Bwana Albinger.' At this the man keened quietly to himself, rocking slowly on his heels in grief, then, returning to his well-trained role, he stood aside and gestured Odhiambo to enter. As he did, Odhiambo saw Jennifer emerge from a door on his left. She was dressed in a simple floral-patterned dress, below which legs that gave evidence of recent tanning ended in local-style sandals. She wouldn't have had any reason to pack black mourning clothes when she set off for her Kenyan holiday, thought Odhiambo. She was composed, although startled at seeing Odhiambo.

'Inspector! I didn't expect . . . I mean, oh, please come in. What can I do for you?'

'First allow me to express my grief at your uncle's death, miss,' said Odhiambo. 'I hope you have had some assistance since he died.' He shook her hand and bowed slightly. 'I mean, I assume his friends or office people are making all the necessary arrangements.'

'Yes, his partners and secretary have been very helpful.' Jennifer ushered him into the lounge, asking the servant over her shoulder for coffee to be brought there. 'I came here as I had nowhere else to go. I thought uncle wouldn't mind.' Her voice gave just a slight quiver on the word uncle, but she seemed fully in command of herself and her surroundings. She sat, hands demurely in lap, at ease despite Odhiambo's unexpected presence. 'They didn't know where I was at first, so I didn't find out until Saturday morning. I came straight back . . . I was at the coast, you know, near Malindi. They're picking me up at eleven. For lunch at his partner's house and then on to the funeral. I'm his only relative here, you know. My mother, his sister, is not very well so she isn't able to come. He doesn't have other close relatives.'

'I hope to be able to attend,' said Odhiambo. Aramgu permitting, he thought. 'But I've come here this morning because I wanted to check something in his study. With your permission.'

'Oh, of course, Inspector. Are you in charge of investigating poor uncle's murder?' The girl's frame shivered. 'I can't believe it really happened. Why did they have to kill him if all they wanted was to steal something?'

Why indeed, thought Odhiambo. He answered her first question as Jennifer rose and led the way to the study.

'No, I'm not in charge of the inquiry into your uncle's death. I'm still looking into the Hawk's Nest business. George . . . your uncle was trying to get some information for me just before he was . . . he died.'

As they reached the study door, Jennifer called for the house servant who quickly appeared.

'Oh, John. Has anyone been in the study the last few days?'

The servant looked quickly at Odhiambo before replying.

'No, Memsahib. Not since this man and other policeman come see it on Friday. Other policeman say keep study locked.'

Jennifer dispatched him to fetch the key. As they waited for the door to be opened, Odhiambo turned to the girl.

'It might be wise if you and the, er . . . John, here, stayed while I have a look. Just to verify that I disturb nothing.'

They went in. The study now had a musty smell. Somehow it seemed suitable to a lawyer's study. Odhiambo crossed to the desk and scanned the top. It was as he remembered it, except that the loose papers had been collected together into an uneven pile. The diary sat on top of the journals. Odhiambo looked again at the double entry, 'M 1 m' and 'H 1 p'. He lifted the diary off the journals and quickly flicked through them. All but one were legal, the exception being an old copy of the journal of a British scientific society. Odhiambo opened the cover and saw a stamp on the inside indicating it belonged to the University of Nairobi library. On the right-hand side was printed the list of contents giving the titles and authors of the papers included in the volume. The titles were virtually unintelligible to a layman like Odhiambo, but as he scanned them he felt a shiver of excitement in his muscles and a tension in the pit of his stomach. He didn't understand yet the precise significance of what he had found, but he felt the anticipation of the hunter as he sights his prey. He didn't have time now to pursue the matter in detail. He reassembled the pile of journals and reinstated the diary on top. He turned and crossed to the filing cabinet; as he remembered, there was the list of files stuck with sellotape to the side of the cabinet. He checked the list and found the heading 'Old Cases'. He pulled open the top drawer and checked the headings on the closely packed files with the list of contents. Yes, they were filed in order. He flicked quickly through and moved on to the lower drawers. The bottom drawer was less than half full. He went back to the top and checked again. Finally, he was sure; there were no files headed 'Old Cases'.

After a minute or two of reflection, Odhiambo checked that the french windows were locked and then led the way out of the study. He watched the house servant lock the study door and then addressed both him and Jennifer.

'It's very important that no one goes into the study until you hear from me. OK? Me, or the other inspector, Inspector Ntende.'

Both his listeners nodded. Odhiambo and Jennifer walked together to the door and down the steps on to the drive. Odhiambo's thoughts were racing. Finally, as they stood by the car he came to a decision.

'Jennifer. May I call you Jennifer?' She smiled and nodded. 'I think your uncle's death may have some connection with the murder of Diana Farwell. It may not have been a simple case of burglary. He may have known something that was dangerous to someone. Someone who probably killed Diana Farwell.'

He was interrupted by the girl, who was staring at him wide-eyed with one hand at her throat.

'What do you mean, Inspector? You mean whoever killed Diana, killed Uncle George? How can that be? I mean, he was cut to . . . I mean, the way he was killed . . . and, and, John, he saw them. They were Africans. Two or three of them.'

Odhiambo placed a hand on her bare arm.

'I'm afraid that here in Nairobi it's not too difficult to hire violent men. Now listen, I'm not sure about this. And I won't be able to prove anything unless I get some help. I wondered if you would be willing . . .' He allowed his voice to tail off and watched the girl closely. He remembered thinking at Hawk's Nest that there was more to this girl than appeared on the surface. He could see her trying to make sense of his statements.

'Inspector, I liked Uncle George a lot. He was always kind to me, since I was a little girl. But I would want to help you in any case. How can I help?'

'The Shropshires will probably be at the funeral and maybe the Mallows as well. I was with George when Mallow came to chat with him at Hawk's Nest. Fulton probably not. And the husband is back in England. I was thinking of asking you to . . . But I'm not sure. It could be dangerous.'

'Oh, come on, Inspector!' Although Jennifer did not actually stamp her foot her tone indicated that only her manners prevented her from doing so. 'Don't be coy. What can I do? Tell me and I'll decide if it's too dangerous.'

Odhiambo's respect for his companion rose further. Beneath the shy demeanour lay a great deal of spirit and, he suspected, intelligence. He swallowed his reservations and spoke in a quiet voice.

'We have to flush the murderer out. If you were to mention to the Shropshires, the Mallows and, if you can get hold of him, Guy Fulton that your uncle sent you a letter just before he was killed and you're puzzled by the contents, their reaction would be interesting. Tell them, separately of course, that you're intending to sleep on it, but think you'd better consult me. If one of them is the murderer he will try to dissuade you. The trouble is he may not stop at argument. If I'm right, he may have arranged your uncle's death. I keep saying "he", but I want you to understand that it could be one of the women. If you do what I suggest you have to be on your guard. You wait here with me around, of course, to protect you if the murderer should pay a call. But this is frightening you. That's why I say it's a stupid idea.'

The girl's face revealed the fear that Odhiambo's suggestion conjured up. Waiting in an empty house for a murderer to call. This was the classic suspense-builder of films and Jennifer could picture the horror of sitting in a darkened room and the knob of the door slowly turning! She shook her head violently to snap herself out of such silly fantasies. Her shoulder-length hair danced across her face and Odhiambo was suddenly aware of her sensual quality: this was a woman whose exterior concealed great depths.

'You're on, Inspector. But I rely on you being hidden behind the sofa.' She laughed and to his surprise it was a genuine laugh; she had begun to see the comical side of being caught up in a murder hunt, but befriended by the detective in the case. This was too rich for words, she thought. Her thoughts went to her lover, in England – wait till I tell him about this.

They discussed details for a few more minutes and then Odhiambo brought his visit to a close.

'Are you going to resume your holiday? I mean, I can understand that given the circumstances . . .'

'No, Inspector, I was booked for two weeks in the Sailing Dhow at Malindi, but I've cancelled the remainder. I'll go home as soon as I can.'

Odhiambo said his goodbyes with assurances of seeing her again in the afternoon. Then he accelerated away, the spurt of gravel evidence of the urgency now spurring his actions.

His next stop was at the Livestock Centre. Shropshire's secretary, an Indian girl of stunning beauty, informed him that the Director had a visitor, but would soon be free. Odhiambo asked if he could use the telephone while he waited. He called his wife's office and was told she was in a meeting. He thought for a moment and then left a carefully worded message.

'I'm back in Nairobi. All is well, but I'm not going to the station as things are heating up. If you have any urgent news I am currently with Mr Shropshire at the Livestock Disease Control Centre. Later I'll be at the cemetery for George Albinger's funeral. See you this evening, but it may be late. Love, James.'

Peter Shropshire came through the door of his office, ushering his visitor out. He showed surprise when he saw the waiting policeman, but greeted him affably and waved him into his office.

'Good morning, Inspector. What can I do for you? Still involved in closing down the Hawk's Nest business? I thought, maybe, that was all settled now.'

Odhiambo sat in one chair as Shropshire sank into another at right-angles to it. A glass-topped coffee table lay between them.

'There are one or two loose ends, Mr Shropshire, one of which is connected with George Albinger.'

Shropshire passed his hand through his hair.

'George's funeral is this afternoon. I intend to go. Terrible,

terrible. Can't you people do something to get rid of these bloody panga-wielding gangs?'

'You told me you had seen Mr Albinger about his connection with Mrs Farwell in Lusaka. I think you raised his curiosity. A day or two later he's dead. Strange coincidence, don't you think?'

'Tragedies come in effing threes they say. Course it's a strange bloody coincidence, but what else can it be?'

'Nothing, I dare say. But now, George . . . Mr Albinger . . . is unable to tell me anything about the Lusaka end. I'm sure he and you know something I don't know, so I've come to you.'

'There's not much more than I already told you. He represented Diana in an insurance case in Lusaka – must be ten years ago. She was badly injured. Boyfriend dead. I knew of it because the boy was working with me. Bloody promising scientist, as I told you. What can that have to do with the goings-on here?'

'You were worried enough about it to check with Albinger, though. You said it was because of the insurance, but Albinger told me the amount was not large. Are you sure there wasn't some other point that was worrying you?'

'No, no. It was just what I told you. Wanted to check with Albinger that there was no need to mention it.'

Odhiambo watched and waited. Shropshire was clearly uncomfortable. It could be merely the discomfort of repeated police questioning, but Odhiambo was sure it was more.

'Look, Mr Shropshire. I don't want to put you on the spot, but you're concealing something from me. I think you're protecting someone. Time is running out on this business and I want everything you know now.'

Shropshire pulled at the fold of flesh under his chin. He gazed out of the window for what seemed a long time, before sighing and turning back to Odhiambo.

'All right, Inspector. But it's nothing, really. Don't want you chasing off after red herrings. Harling, that was Diana's boyfriend who was killed, had a sister. She made a fuss. Said Diana was driving the car at the time and that she was drunk. Killed her brother, that sort of allegation. Of course, Diana said Harling was driving and George Albinger won her case. But the sister was bitter. Swore she'd get Diana. Silly business. No doubt she forgot all about it quickly enough. The fact is that the sister is in Nairobi, she lives here, I mean. Naturally couldn't help wondering. Didn't see her at that damn lodge, but didn't see everybody. So I went to Albinger to ask him if he'd seen her. He was able to assure me she wasn't there, so she couldn't have anything to do with it.'

'What is the sister's name? I mean, is she married or is her name Harling too?'

'She's married. But, Inspector, she wasn't there. Neither Albinger nor I saw her and Albinger checked the guest list. So I don't intend to drag her into it. You'd be wasting your time.'

Odhiambo considered for a moment then decided to play along.

'OK. We'll leave the sister out of it for now. Two more questions, if I may. One, can you give me Mr Farwell's telephone number in England? Two, may I ask, where did you meet your wife?'

At the first question, Shropshire started to get up, to fetch his address card box on his desk. At the second question he turned back to Odhiambo, his brown face darker with the blood pressure caused by his anger.

'My wife? What the hell has that got to do with anything? You're just thrashing about at random. What's the matter with you? Your bosses say Causington did it: why are you still going after everyone else?'

Odhiambo gave a slight placatory gesture of head and hands.

'I'm sorry, Mr Shropshire. But I would like Mr Farwell's address.'

Shropshire found a card, called loudly, 'Sunni', which produced the Indian secretary, asked for a copy and stood obviously awaiting his visitor's departure. Odhiambo rose and crossed towards him.

'Thank you. You really have been helpful. Closing down loose ends is always useful, you know.'

Shropshire grunted, but relaxed a little. As Odhiambo reached the door Shropshire addressed his back.

'Fine. I'm sorry I was a bit abrupt. It's been a bad time you know. Busy enough at work and then one's guest getting herself killed, husband to look after, then Albinger, to say nothing of Causington. Nerves getting a bit ragged, to tell you the truth.'

Odhiambo continued on his way, picking up the Farwell

address and telephone number from the secretary *en route*. Shropshire's reaction, if not his words, suggested strongly that Helen Shropshire too had been in Lusaka. He thought it very probable that she had met her future husband there. Then there was the mysterious sister of the dead scientist. He wondered what Shropshire's reaction would have been if he had asked for his wife's maiden name.

As he drove away, Odhiambo considered his next move. The funeral of George Albinger was not for another two hours. Perhaps having tackled one Shropshire he should now accost the other. As he debated with himself he became aware of a car that had approached him from behind and was now easing out alongside. They were on a straight piece of road bordered by scrub and bush on both sides. He knew before the arm signal for him to pull over that his luck had run out. How did they know where he was? It had to have been the phone call to his wife's office. Either they were bugging Cari's line or someone in her office was an informer. This reminded him that Cari had herself been on Price-Allen's list. No sooner had the thought flashed into his mind than he shut it out, revolted by how close he had come to doubting his wife. Cari, forgive me, he thought as the two plain-clothes men approached his car. It was a few minutes later as he was driven away that he remembered Jennifer and his pledge to her. Involuntarily he tensed and started to come forward out of his seat, but arms gripped his and the handcuffs prevented him from resisting. Oh my God, he thought, what have I done?

The American reporter had been cursing his luck for some time but now it seemed his luck might be changing. He had just missed Odhiambo yesterday, approaching the house as Odhiambo pulled out and drove away. By the time he had turned to follow, Odhiambo's car was gone and his wife refused to divulge where. Now he was witnessing what was clearly a Security Unit arrest. He passed by as an African was bundled out of one car into another unmarked car with his hands handcuffed. It was the recognition of Odhiambo's car that grabbed his attention. He stopped a discreet distance further along and waited for the two cars to pass, Odhiambo's now being driven by another driver. He followed, keeping a considerable distance between himself and the other cars, and was able to observe their destination. It appeared to be an unobtrusive private house, close to the government office building set on a hill that had once housed the colonial East African secretariat, but the American knew better: he had heard it described as one of the hideaways used by the State Security people. He passed without stopping, thinking furiously as to the meaning of what he had just witnessed and what to do next.

21

Helen Shropshire sat staring at her own image in her dressing-table mirror. Her eyes were taking on a sunken appearance as if retreating from the images they were recording. She felt she was in a trap and that the jaws of the trap were closing. She had lied to the police and was no longer sure that her lie was believed. She had deceived her husband and Peter was now suspicious of her. Originally, she had acted as she had without questioning the need or the morality. It was the least that love and loyalty demanded. But her conscience was troubling her and the weight of guilt increased as the days passed. It was worse than merely feeling guilty. She had tried hard to keep at bay the fear that she refused to acknowledge; but now that fear was in the open, conscious part of her mind causing her to feel physically ill.

She turned away from her mirror and rose unsteadily as a wave of nausea overtook her. Don't be such a stupid bitch, she said to herself. Everything will turn out all right. Peter would be on his way to the lawyer's funeral. He had asked her to go, but she couldn't face it. Anyway, she hadn't known him: only of him. Then there was Odhiambo. As she thought of the policeman she could see him as he loomed over her at the airport in Mombasa. Now, as she examined all her emotions, guilt, fear, distaste, she knew what she felt towards Odhiambo – it was attraction. Damn it, she was sexually attracted to the large dark man with the serious expression. What was the matter with her? It had all started when Diana walked in her door, two, or was it three, weeks ago. Up to then her life was happy. Well, reasonably happy. Certainly it was placid. Look what a mess she was in now.

She found herself in the garden and tried to concentrate on instructions to give to the gardener. But pictures of Odhiambo kept forcing themselves into her mind: Odhiambo's face, brooding but silent. Speak, damn you, she cried to herself. Tell me what you suspect. But the image remained frozen. Finally, aloud, she cried out to that figure of her imagination.

'They hang murderers here, don't they?'

As he stood in the sun in the small cemetery attached to the Anglican church, Peter Shropshire was thinking of his wife. He was worried: Helen was behaving very strangely, frantically trying to convince him and herself that first Fulton and then Mallow was the true murderer rather than Causington. Her mental search for suspects was becoming obsessive and dangerous. There wasn't much he could do about it immediately, but, perhaps, if things got worse he should take her away; the Seychelles, that would be a good choice, Helen liked it there and they'd be out of the watchful eyes of the Nairobi crowd, to say nothing of that blasted policeman, Odhiambo, who wouldn't let well enough alone. Why on earth should he try to link Albinger's murder to Diana's case? The *modus operandi* was completely different and there were witnesses, for Christ's sake, that it was a gang of Africans who killed him.

The service was over, the coffin lowered, and Shropshire looked to make a quick escape. He had seen the Mallows, but didn't wish to get trapped into a conversation with them, even though Letty looked sober for once. If Helen was looking for suspects she could do worse than consider Letty Mallow. If Shropshire was any judge, she was a woman who would carry a grudge over the years. He watched the Mallows have a word with the young lady who seemed to be the only family mourner. She was with Albinger at Hawk's Nest, he remembered. A niece or something. He supposed he'd better pay his respects, so, waiting until the Mallows moved on, he made his way towards Jennifer.

The Mallows were now too wrapped up in their own thoughts to notice Shropshire. Letty could scarcely wait until they were a reasonable distance away from the others before accosting her husband.

'What did the little bitch mean by that? What could Albinger have known about it? And if he did know something and put it in a letter to whatever-her-name-is, what's it got to do with us?'

Her husband hardly heard his wife's expostulations. He was deep in thought, trying to remember the precise wording of the conversation just ended. He was so startled when Jennifer spoke that he did nothing but mouth inanities. He and Letty were expressing their condolences and were preparing to move on when suddenly the girl said in a quiet voice, 'I may need your advice on something, Mr Mallow. And Mrs Mallow, of course.'

'Anything, my dear,' Mallow remembered replying, thinking she was concerned over some financial aspect of her uncle's affairs. 'Do you want to come and see me at the bank? We didn't handle your uncle's account, but if I can be of any help . . .'

'No, it isn't that. You see, I've just received a letter from Uncle George. He must have written it the day he died. He writes that he'd found out something important about the murder at Hawk's Nest that points to the murderer. I didn't understand it myself the way he described it, as I don't know the people concerned. I thought I'd ask your advice before going to that nice policeman. He mentions you in the letter.'

The last sentence was said with a sweet smile, but Mallow was not deceived. It was scarcely credible, but this innocent-looking girl seemed to be acting like a blackmailer – putting the arm on him, as he believed the vernacular had it.

As he went to move on, spluttering 'of courses' and 'any times', Jennifer added, 'I'll be at Uncle George's tonight on my own. If you have a minute I'd be grateful if you would phone me there.'

The Mallows' departure in an obvious state of nervousness did not go unobserved. Cari Odhiambo was at the funeral, partly because she had been fond of George Albinger, even though he was only a slight acquaintance, but also because she wanted to contact her husband. Her worry over his well-being was increasing. She was puzzled at his non-appearance at the funeral; his absence did nothing to diminish her concern. She knew the Mallows by sight and noted their apparent discomfiture after speaking to the pleasant-looking young woman, who she assumed, from her husband's account of his evening at Hawk's Nest, was Albinger's niece.

On an impulse she approached Jennifer and hovered as a bulky, strong-looking man completed his conversation with her. She caught the last exchanges between them.

'I don't know what to make of his letter. I thought I'd ask if you can explain it before I go to that inspector who is investigating the murder. Can I ring you later?'

This was Jennifer, and Cari's interest was aroused. What on earth was the woman saying? She heard the man's reply.

'Don't worry, I'll phone you this evening. Where are you staying? At George's house. OK, I'll be in touch. Or do you want me to stop by?'

'I'll be home so if you call I can read the piece that mentions you. You'll probably have a simple explanation.'

The man reiterated his intention to be in touch and moved on. Cari seized her opportunity.

'Hello. I'm Cari Odhiambo. I think you know my husband, the police inspector. He was a friend of Mr Albinger's. He was hoping to come to the funeral. I'm sorry, something urgent must have come up.'

Jennifer's face changed from a serious, somewhat nervous cast to an open, bright smile.

'Oh, Mrs Odhiambo, how nice of you to come. Inspector Odhiambo was with me this morning. He said he hoped to come to the funeral. But he must be terribly busy. This dreadful business.'

'I hope you won't think me impertinent, Miss . . . er, I'm sorry, I don't know your surname. My husband referred to you as Jennifer. Are you an Albinger?'

'No. My mother is his sister. My name is Harris. But please call me Jennifer. I feel I know your husband now. He was with us at Hawk's Nest, you know. He's a lovely man.'

'Well, er, Jennifer, as I say, I don't wish to appear rude, but I couldn't help overhearing you just now. Are you sure it's wise to approach people like that if you've got a letter that may be evidence? Perhaps he's a close friend?'

The two women were standing near the gate of the cemetery. The mourners, particularly the suited men, were making haste to depart so that they could remove their overdressed bodies from the sun. Jennifer took Cari by the arm and drew her aside under the shade of a flamboyant tree.

'No, I hardly know him. In fact, I don't know him. But he was one of the guests at Hawk's Nest and a member of Mrs Farwell's party. Your husband asked me to contact people and say that Uncle George sent me a letter containing clues as to the identity of the murderer.'

'Good God.' Cari was startled and concerned. 'But is there such a letter?'

'No. The point is to see who reacts. It's like an Agatha Christie novel, really. Quite exciting.'

How could James do something so stupid, and, yes, dangerous for this girl, Cari thought. And then disappear!

'I don't think exciting is the word I would use. I don't understand how James could drag you into such a scheme.'

'Well, he didn't want me to do it, really. Not until I insisted. But he promised to be around this evening.'

Cari could scarcely believe her ears. James must have taken leave of his senses. She could guess why. He knew the time left to him was limited. Perhaps something had happened to convince him that time had almost run out. So he was trying anything to tempt the murderer to expose himself. However foolish.

'Do you know where he is now?' She could feel her voice rising and fought to keep it neutral in tone and pitch. 'When did he say he'd see you again?'

'Well, he was supposed to be here. But I'm sure he'll be in touch.'

For the first time there was a note of slight uncertainty in Jennifer's voice.

'Yes, of course.' Cari did not want to frighten the girl unduly. 'But until he does, who are you staying with?'

'Well, no one really. I had lunch with uncle's partner and he asked me to come back to his place, but I want to return to the bungalow because of, well, because of the plan. So he's given me the use of a car and driver.'

'OK. Until James gets in touch I'm staying with you. I've got my office car here so why don't you come with me? Tell your uncle's people you don't need a car. I'll wait for you at the gate here.'

'That's nice of you. But I don't want to be any bother.'

'No bother. And quite necessary. James had no right to . . . well, never mind that now. How many people are you supposed to give the message to?'

'Three. Well, five really, if you count the wives. The Mallows who were here, the Shropshires and a man called Fulton. Inspector Odhiambo said that all but Mr Fulton might be at the funeral. So I rang him at his hotel. He seemed outraged, actually. He hung up on me. Now, come to think of it, Mrs Shropshire wasn't here. I wonder if I should telephone her separately. Separately from her husband, I mean.'

'I should think you've caused enough alarm already. Anyway, let's talk about it in the car when you've finished your goodbyes.'

Jennifer moved away, leaving Cari under the tree. As she waited a voice she recognized suddenly spoke from behind her.

'Mrs Odhiambo. I guess we meet again.'

It was the blasted American reporter. Cari turned, ready to protest, but the American interrupted her.

'No. I'm not after you again. This time I may have something for you. Do you know where your husband is?'

'Why do you ask? He's on duty. I've told you several times – '

Again she was interrupted.

'Mrs Odhiambo, by coincidence, I saw your husband taken from his car on the Ngong Road a couple of hours ago. Taken by the police, I think. Well, you know what I mean – Security men.'

Cari felt the blood drain from her brain and clutched the tree as she felt herself swaying. The reporter continued.

'Look, lady, I'm doing you a favour and asking nothing. He's in the house called Ashdean, on Mustafa Road. I think it's used by the Security people.'

Oh no, Cari thought. My God, James is in one of their torture chambers. Somehow she forced a travesty of a smile.

'Thank you very much. I'll check it out.'

The reporter turned away, thinking, And the best of luck. He intended to keep a close eye on this dame and the other young woman who now rejoined her. Something queer was going on and he hoped to get the story. It seemed obvious that Odhiambo was inconveniently pursuing the Hawk's Nest murder and was now being put on ice. At least she owed him one now. He watched the two women leave the now deserted cemetery and cross the road to where Cari's office car and driver were waiting.

Further down the road, behind the wheel of a rented car, was Guy Fulton. He needed to know what Albinger's niece looked like. What sort of woman he was dealing with. He had hung up in a moment of anger and panic, before getting the girl's address. He thought of asking Mallow, but decided against it. Then he'd had the idea of ringing Albinger's law firm and asking for information on how to contact his niece. He was given Albinger's address. He wondered what the girl knew, or rather what Albinger knew and had passed on. Was there to be no end to this business?

Back in her office, Cari found herself fighting off incipient panic. A call to Masonga produced nothing. He was obviously in the dark and could only promise to contact Cari as soon as he knew more. He tried to reassure her, but Cari could tell that he was a very worried man. She had left Jennifer with her secretary in the outer office having a cup of tea. It would hardly do for the girl to realize that her protector from a possible murderer was in a detention cell. She dialled again, praying hard that Price-Allen would answer his private number. For once her prayer was answered.

'Price-Allen.'

'Mr Price-Allen. It's Cari Odhiambo. I'm trying to locate my husband.'

'Mrs Odhiambo, good afternoon. I'm afraid I don't understand you. I haven't spoken to your husband since Saturday. At that time he was at home, if I remember correctly.'

'But I'm told he's been detained. By your people. State Security. Using your house on Mustafa Road.'

There was a silence that seemed to Cari to extend for ever. She was about to speak again to determine whether Price-Allen was still there when he spoke.

'I have no information as to that. Certainly, if such is the case, it was not at my instigation: I can assure you of that. I will, however, find out what is happening. What is the source of your information?'

Cari knew better than to answer this.

'Never mind that. It's the fact he's in detention that's important. Apart from me, I mean. He's set a trap for the Hawk's Nest murderer, baited it with George Albinger's niece and then disappeared. He was rushing it because of you, so you've got to do something.'

'You interest me strangely, Mrs Odhiambo, to coin a phrase. And when is this . . . er . . . trap to be sprung?'

'This evening. Any time from now, in fact. I've got the girl with me at the moment, but she's supposed to go to Albinger's house and wait for the murderer to show up. And there'll be no James to protect her.'

'How melodramatic. Very well, leave it with me. I'll be in touch.'

'OK. I'll wait here. You've got my office number. And listen. I've told you the immediate cause for panic. But my real concern is James. You've got to help me. If necessary I'll promise to take him away, but you've got to stop him being locked away. You owe me that.'

'Calm down, my dear lady. Let's wait until I determine the facts. You may be concerning yourself unnecessarily. And, by the way, I strongly suggest you take the Albinger woman home. Let's not destroy your husband's plan. He wouldn't thank you for that. You go there and wait for me to contact you. You understand it's important to do as I say if you want me to help?'

With that the line went dead. The bastard, thought Cari. But unpleasant though it was, she was reliant on Price-Allen's goodwill. He could pull the necessary strings if he wanted to. So there was no option but to do as he said. She was under no illusion that his goodwill would be retained if she failed to do what he wanted. Price-Allen did nothing for anyone unless he saw an advantage to himself, immediate or postponed, in so doing. Her vision blurred as tears of frustration dampened her eyes. Damn it, she said to herself, you're not going to let these bastards get you down. She wiped her eyes, repaired the damage to her make-up and left her office.

'Jennifer, we're on our way. We'll just stop off at my place to pick up a little protection.'

22

As his car jolted over a stretch of pot-holed road on the way to Nairobi, Aramgu turned to his companion, a Member of Parliament with a loyal tribal following in the eastern districts of Kenya and currently Assistant Minister for Roads and Transport.

'Nlemi, my friend, it's time you allocated some funds for our roads here in Nyeri and Kiambu. You must have all the roads you need now in Machakos.' Aramgu laughed to indicate he was making a joke. You never knew with some of these politicians. 'We are suffering here, my friend.'

His companion grunted. He was a smaller man than Aramgu in all physical dimensions, but only slightly so. It was in other ways that he seemed dominated by his companion. He lacked Aramgu's force of personality and driving ambition. He liked to be led as long as the leader rewarded him well for his support.

'Never mind the roads, Aramgu,' he grumbled. 'What's worrying me is whether our joint venture is prospering. You've told me nothing lately.'

'Because I want to keep you away from any mischief that would hurt you.' Aramgu lowered his voice; although his driver was his nephew, it was wiser to speak with silent tongue as his father had been fond of saying. 'Everything goes well. But there is no hurry and haste may cause us to fail. By the end of this year we will be prepared. By then certain obstacles will have been removed.'

The minister looked closely at Aramgu, who was leaning back with his huge head against the head-rest fitted to the back seat of the Mercedes saloon. Aramgu, he thought, looked contented. Nlemi hoped Aramgu was not underestimating the President.

'How are your relations with the Big Man? Are you sure no one is poisoning his ear against you?'

Aramgu laughed again and slapped his hand down on the arm-rest between them.

'Have no fear, Mr Minister. Leave it to me. You are, in fact, right to ask about evil influences on the Big Man. I tell you who

I believe to be one of the obstacles. The white man. The Executioner Extraordinary.' He paused and spat on to the car carpet. 'Price-Allen. He does not like me. Or you. Or some of our friends.' Aramgu glanced at his companion, who was betraying signs of nervousness. 'But have no fear, my friend. I have the *juju* to deal with our *mzungu* friend. He is trying to reopen that Hawk's Nest business. God knows why. Maybe he wants to hang another *mzungu* as well as the one he stole from us. This could be embarrassing for Kenya, and the Big Man. But I have his man now and he will be persuaded to tell me about his friend Price-Allen. It is not good that a white man is so close to the Man. We are not colonials now.' Again the laugh rumbled around the car.

Odhiambo in his small cell was going mad. His predicament was hammering at his nerve ends. No one of any significance had visited him. His protestations and demands, the latter including the delivery of a message to Price-Allen, had been ignored. The room was windowless and his watch had been taken from him so he was not sure of the time, but the thought of Jennifer, at his instigation, sitting in Albinger's bungalow waiting for the murderer to pay a visit was putting him into a state where he had to restrain his impulse to pound the rough walls. How could he have been so stupid?

He doubted if Price-Allen was behind his arrest; there seemed nothing to be gained by Price-Allen in such a move. That left Aramgu as the likely cause: it would be easy for him to pass a request through the lower echelons of State House to the State Security Unit, bypassing Price-Allen who was not formally within the command structure of the unit. What Aramgu would do next, however, Odhiambo had not considered. The picture of Jennifer facing a deadly killer swamped such other concerns. He was now sure of the identity of the threat that Jennifer faced. The pieces of the puzzle had formed themselves into a picture that Odhiambo was convinced was the true one. Diana Farwell had been blackmailing her killer. It may not have been money, in Odhiambo's view. He believed he had come to understand the dead woman now. She used her knowledge as a constant threat hanging over the head of each victim. She would make sure that they knew that she knew and had the evidence to prove it, and then took pleasure in the sight and even the thought of their unease. He was sure, too, that the meeting of victim and killer had not been coincidental, but carefully arranged by the victim. Her miscalculation was her belief that she could taunt her victim face to face and not produce the murderous response that had occurred. So, Odhiambo could see clearly the face of the murderer looming over Jennifer, but how could he stop the events that he himself had put in train? In his agony he cried aloud in frustration. His control finally snapping, he did indeed begin to pound the wall with clenched fists until the blood started to trickle down the rough stone. So far gone was he in his despair that he did not hear the cell door open behind him.

In a room as dismal and dark as Odhiambo's cell, three men were drinking *changa'a*, or rather sucking *changa'a* through straws inserted in a jar. They spoke in Luganda, the language of the Baganda, the major tribe of the lake area of Uganda. All three had been members of Idi Amin's own murderous security force: they had escaped to Kenya when the Tanzanian army forced Amin to flee north, for the Baganda would have taken a dreadful revenge on members of their own tribe who had been renegade members of Amin's terror squads. Since then they had eked out a precarious existence in the crime underworld of Nairobi. The recent contract for a killing of a *mzungu* was a well-paid and welcome assignment. And now there was another commission from the same source. A little haggling had raised the price and in the future there was the possibility of blackmail. They had dealt through an intermediary but they had already traced a link between the intermediary and a certain *mzungu*. Their leader realized it was time to control the drinking: there was dangerous work to be done.

'Enough,' he said, putting down his straw and removing the others from the jar. 'Time enough for more *changa'a* after we finish the night's work.'

'I need some *changa'a* to keep my belly warm for the work,' protested one of his companions, reaching for his straw.

'To put courage in your heart, you mean.' The leader snatched the straw and crumpled it in his large hand. 'You need *changa'a* now to kill women, is that it? You are afraid of white women? And you,' turning to the third man, 'you are driving the car. We want no accidents.'

The third man grunted and spat.

'Driving is not the problem. Driving was not the problem last time. You ran in too much haste. Would have been better if you had killed the houseboy. This is still of much worry to me.'

'You are an old woman, like this one.' The leader gestured with his thumb at the second man. 'You worry like old women. Now you are sure that drink has not befuddled your brain? You drive up to gate. Blow horn. If there is watchman he will let you in or fetch the woman. You drive carefully and slowly. You make sure no one follows you. Then you stop where we are waiting. We finish job, take letter from her and get rid of body in dam. Stones and rope are in boot already.'

'I'm the one taking all the risk,' grumbled the driver. 'If there is trap only I am caught.'

'And if there had been problem last time,' said the second man, 'you would have driven off and left us. So don't cry that this time you must earn your share.'

'One thing more I have decided,' said the leader with a grin that revealed his startlingly white teeth. 'This time before we give up paper or letter, this time we make copy first. These papers that *mzungus* kill for, why, they must be worth as much as tusk of elephant.'

The others laughed. It was good that Charles was smart. Smarter than themselves, they knew. They liked that, but they also feared him. They killed because they were trained to and now they had to in order to live, but Charles killed because he liked it.

Guy Fulton drove carefully through the suburban roads to George Albinger's bungalow. He had waited until twilight before setting off and now it was nearly dark. He pondered as he drove how he would approach the girl. She had asked for his advice, but would be surprised to see him turn up without notice, particularly in view of his earlier manner. But that presupposed that her approach was innocent, and he didn't believe that. He tightened his grip on the wheel as his anger sought an outlet. Damn and blast the woman. He would have to play it by ear. First, find out if she was bluffing. There was the possibility that it was a trap set by that black bastard Odhiambo, but he had been assured that Odhiambo was off his back in view of the need for his co-operation on the loan. It might be wiser to stay out of the scene himself, but he was intrigued as to the motivation of the demure-looking Jennifer. As far as he could see there was little risk, given the back-up insurance provided by his protectors.

He slowed further as he entered the road he was seeking and found the gate into the Albinger driveway without overshooting. The gates were shut so he stopped in front of them. Where was the horn button on this car? These Japanese compacts were unfamiliar to him. As he looked at the knobs on his steering-wheel the door on his side was suddenly wrenched open. An African voice speaking English spoke in his ear.

'Do not move, Bwana. I am police. No disturbance, please. The *bwana mkubwa* wants a parley with you.'

Fulton cursed, but there seemed no option other than to obey. So it was a trap. But why? The other door opened and a second African slipped into the passenger seat. They were taking no chances. He cursed again as he got out of the car, but followed the man who had spoken to him along the hedge and into a narrow grassed path that bordered the property. A large car was parked in the path facing the road. Fulton's guide opened the back door and gestured for Fulton to get in. As he slid into the seat the inside light went on and he found himself closeted with a European unknown to him.

'Good evening – Mr Fulton, isn't it? My name is Price-Allen. What brings international bankers here at night?'

Fulton knew the name Price-Allen as that of the man with the power to ensure that he completed his negotiations without further hassle from the police. However, a little bluster seemed called for and, indeed, he was genuinely startled and frightened.

'What the hell is going on? I am making a call on an acquaintance. Why is it impossible to do anything in this bloody place without treading on policemen?'

'Ah, Mr Fulton, I'm afraid you are your own worst enemy. You were told to forget the Hawk's Nest affair and concentrate on your business, but still you allow yourself to be diverted.'

'How can I concentrate on business – '

He was interrupted by Price-Allen, who spoke in a voice suddenly cold and venomous.

'Enough. You are a fool as well as a pervert. You are now in the way. You have one last chance to get back to your hotel, wind up your business to everyone's mutual satisfaction and get out. Otherwise it will go hard on you. Have I made myself clear?'

Fulton was shaken. The events of the day were proving too much.

'All right. I am leaving. But do I have a guarantee that I have heard the last of the Farewell business?'

'If you mean the snaps and diary, you have been told that if your business is successful much can be achieved. I am beginning to regret even that generosity. Now go.'

After Fulton's car had disappeared back towards Nairobi, Price-Allen allowed himself a cigarette and sighed. It was as well he had posted men to watch Fulton so that he was warned of the fool's attempt to get to Albinger's niece. Although why Odhiambo had set her on to Fulton given the keep-off signs he had posted around him he did not know. Odhiambo was a stubborn man. He could be dangerous. But Odhiambo's future could be decided when this night's activities were concluded. Hardened though he was, Price-Allen felt the thrill of the chase as it nears its climax. The only remaining question was how the murder of the girl was to be accomplished. She had received a message that a car would pick her up to take her to a meeting. Price-Allen was sure that the job would be done *en route* by hired killers, probably the ones who disposed of Albinger. His first inclination was to let matters take their course, following the car until the attempt at killing the girl occurred. But the involvement of Odhiambo's wife made that course difficult. If anything went wrong it would be embarrassing. If, when the car arrived, the driver was alone his course of action was decided and known to his men.

He did not wait long. A car approached down the road, slowed and turned into the Albinger gateway. The driver hooted and one of Price-Allen's men emerged from the shadows inside and opened the gates. There was nothing suspicious to the driver's wary eye. The gate opener was clad in slightly shabby blue trousers and jacket – typical nightwatchman's attire. The driver proceeded to the front door and got out. As he did so two figures emerged from the shrubs, grabbed his arms, tripped his feet from under him and pressed his face into the gravel. The driver felt the dislocation of one of his shoulders as his body fell forward with his arm held rigid.

A minute went by that seemed much longer to the stricken driver, the pain in his shoulder rivalled by the discomfort of the gravel piercing the skin of his face. Then he was abruptly rolled over, causing him to cry in pain from the increased agony. He could see by the light from the verandah of the bungalow a *mzungu* looking down on him.

'I have no time to waste,' said Price-Allen in Swahili. 'I want to know where you are to take the woman. Where are you meeting your friends?'

The driver groaned with pain and muttered a cry for medical attention in Luganda.

'Ah. You are Ugandan. An Amin man, eh? Do not pretend you do not understand Swahili. Tell me now. Where do you go with woman?'

The man groaned, but finally gave the address of the destination. Price-Allen produced a revolver from his pocket and showed it to the prostrate driver.

'I warned you I have no time to waste. Where are your friends? You have five seconds only.'

The driver's protest that he was an official driver and was alone was interrupted by the noise of the shot. His other pains vanished in the shock of the new. He looked in terror at his leg. His knee seemed to have disintegrated. He started to scream, but a hand from behind him covered his mouth.

'I ask you one more time. The next shot will be higher, between your legs. Where is the meeting place? I want an answer not a scream.'

Price-Allen bent and pointed the revolver at the man's groin. He gestured and the hand over the driver's mouth was removed. The start of a scream issued uncontrollably from his mouth. Then he bit his lip until the blood spurted. Finally, he managed to blurt out the information Price-Allen was seeking.

'How many are waiting? Do not lie.'

'Two, Bwana. Now help me, for the sake of God. Help me.'

'Who hired you? Speak quickly. The sooner ended, the sooner your pain will be attended to.'

The pain from his knee was worsening if such a thing was possible. The driver felt faint and nauseous.

'I don't know. It is true. Only Charles knows. He is our leader. Charles is waiting.'

Price-Allen considered for a moment. He could recognize the truth from men in pain. There was nothing more needed from this wretch. He raised the gun and shot the man between the eyes. He watched the momentary convulsion and then rose and turned to the man beside him.

'You have the woman's wig?'

He received a nod.

'Tell your men to get rid of this trash. Have Tembo drive with you in the back with wig and two more crouching below the back seat. Your car to follow. Try and keep them alive. I may need the evidence of the boss man, Charles. Now I must see the women.'

Inside the bungalow, Cari and Jennifer were sitting in the lounge. One of Price-Allen's men was, they knew, inside in the passage leading to the front door. They heard only dimly the crunch of tyres on the gravel, but they heard clearly the two shots and the abruptly shortened sound of a scream.

'Oh, my God,' said Jennifer. 'What is happening?'

Cari could hazard a guess, knowing Price-Allen's reputation. She shivered, but managed to raise a thin uncertain smile.

'I expect one of them tried to run away or something. But they've got enough men out there to cope with anything.'

No further noise was audible until the front door and then the lounge door opened and Price-Allen walked in. He looked calm, in control, and pleased. Cari noticed some wet blotches on his slacks as if something had splattered on them. She shivered again.

'Ladies. Good news. All is well. We have the driver, who has revealed the plot. My men are on their way to apprehend the rest of the gang. Now, Miss Harris, and you too, Mrs Odhiambo, I think we should keep the appointment with what we might call the principal involved in this evening's events.'

Cari looked at him with a mixture of loathing and surprise.

'Why do we need a confrontation? Surely you have your evidence? And what about the man outside? We heard shots.'

Price-Allen looked apologetic.

'Unfortunately he was foolish and tried to run away. My men

had to fire.' He spread his hands palms up. It was the first expansive gesture Cari had seen him make, which convinced her of its falsity. 'Why should Miss Harris keep her appointment? Because the shock of seeing her may lead him to blurt out admissions that will ease somewhat the . . . er . . . interrogation phase. I guarantee Miss Harris's safety. Mrs Odhiambo, you may come with us and stay in the car, but I must ask you to give up the little gun you are carrying under your jacket. We don't want any accidents.'

Cari's hand went guiltily to her side. She had hoped that the gun in the inside pocket did not affect the fit of the jacket. She thought for a moment, shrugged and complied with Price-Allen's request.

'What about James?' she asked. 'You promised me news of him.'

'Yes indeed.' Price-Allen smiled. 'And good news it is. He should have been released from detention some short while ago. I have arranged for him to meet us. He should be in at the death, so to speak. Do you not think so?'

23

Odhiambo was waiting with growing impatience for Price-Allen to secure his release. When Price-Allen arrived in his cell Odhiambo, despite himself, was so relieved to see him that it took no urging for him to blurt out his deductions. Despite Odhiambo's protestations, Price-Allen was adamant that it would take some time to overturn the detention instructions; meanwhile the security of Jennifer and, as Price-Allen admitted, his wife was being taken care of.

'Despite your foolishness, Inspector,' Price-Allen said, 'not to say recklessness – despite this I assure you Miss Harris and her self-appointed guardian will be protected from any harm. However, if nothing happens at Albinger's house it will be necessary to bring matters to a head. I'll have a man and a car waiting for your release. You must go and get the necessary confession from the lady concerned. It shouldn't be too difficult a task. If she is not at home and alone, keep the house under surveillance until I get there.'

Odhiambo knew Price-Allen was keeping him away from the likeliest location for action and the spot where his wife would be. But he was in a very poor bargaining position. Price-Allen could keep him in detention until all was over. What Price-Allen's motive was he could only guess: presumably he regarded the presence of Odhiambo as likely to restrict his freedom of action.

'One more thing, Odhiambo. You are here, of course, courtesy of the estimable Regional Administrator in Nyeri. Apparently, he considers you have insulted his office. A serious offence that, Odhiambo. I am told he may be on his way to visit you. If so, do not be alarmed. These are my people here, not his. He sent the orders via his friend in State House, indicating that I need not be troubled. It was kind of him, that. I must remember the favour. When thwarted, however, he may try to use his friends again. I am protecting you, Odhiambo, so I want you to keep a good mental note of your encounter if it takes place. It would help if you indicated you knew something about his little games. See how he reacts.'

With that, Price-Allen left. His forecast was sound, for Odhiambo's cell door opened again within the hour. He was hustled to a room that seemed too small to contain the huge Administrator, to say nothing of the guards. Aramgu was sitting on the edge of a table. Once more, Odhiambo found himself listening to a reproof regarding his foolishness and, in this case, his insolence.

'So, my Luo friend, you are now facing a *shauri mkubwa*. You have shown great disrespect to the government and so to the President. You must absolve yourself of your sins by making gifts to the chiefs. Are you ready to show humility and make your gifts?'

Odhiambo spoke slowly. 'I am a loyal servant of the government and so am always ready to offer what I have and know. There are things I know that are close to you, Mr Aramgu. But perhaps we should speak of them between ourselves.'

Aramgu considered for a moment and then gestured to the guards.

'Wait outside the door.'

The guards withdrew, leaving the two large men staring

wordlessly at each other. Aramgu was the first to break the silence.

'Now is your chance. What I wish to hear is of your master Price-Allen. It is for him you have been putting your goats on other men's land. Why is he wanting more fuss over this white woman?'

'What I have done I have done for the good name of Kenya despite the deceit of you and Price-Allen. I know now you are both seeking your own gains. Not protecting the President and the country.'

Aramgu straightened slowly, raising his massive backside off the table. Suddenly his hands shot out and grabbed Odhiambo's arms. To his utter surprise he found himself, despite his resistance, levered upwards on to tiptoe by the enormous pressure until he found himself gazing into Aramgu's bloodshot, piggy eyes.

'Do not play games with me, you Luo donkey-shit.' The spittle on Aramgu's lips splattered into Odhiambo's face. 'I squash termites like you. Do not play games with me. You are small boy interfering with men's work. And licking the boots of *mzungus* like the colonialist slave you deserve to be. Now I give you one last chance. You co-operate with me and maybe I will forgive you your transgressions.'

Odhiambo was shaken despite himself. He regained his balance on to the balls of his feet and wiped his sleeve across his face.

'I am not playing games. Nor am I threatening you. I merely say I know what is going on. What I do next depends on who my friends are.'

Aramgu's face split into a smile, a snarl or, more likely, a combination of both.

'Well, it does no good to have *mzungu* friends, I'll tell you that. Your hope is to help me and, by helping me, the President. Tell the State House people how Price-Allen is trying to cause a big *shauri* to embarrass the government. This you will do, Odhiambo, if you wish to be a loyal Kenyan and not a white man's boy. You will tell how Price-Allen uses you as a messenger to his Ugandan friends. What this banker, Fulton, is doing for him. All this and more, Odhiambo.'

Odhiambo pretended to be frightened, but claimed to be equally frightened of Price-Allen. It didn't take very good acting, he thought, to be convincing in this role. Aramgu pronounced his plan.

'It is true that here is not safe from his influence. I will arrange for your removal to Nyeri. There you will write down all you know. If there are things you are doubtful of, I can help you.' At this the famous Aramgu laugh boomed around the room. 'For the moment, my Luo friend, it is back to your quarters.'

So now he waited, hoping that Price-Allen's plan worked before he found himself transported to Nyeri. When, finally, his cell door opened again, Odhiambo was relieved that it revealed an officer with a paper authorizing his release. He rushed through, waved aside the officer who was trying to make a formal affair of the event, and finally gained the courtyard where, true to Price-Allen's promise, a car and driver awaited. As he entered the car he was tempted to give the driver Albinger's address, but he realized that his arrival could upset Price-Allen's arrangements and so cause confusion and possibly danger to those involved, including Cari and Jennifer. In any case the matter was taken out of his hands. The driver thrust a sealed envelope at him and set off purposefully without waiting for instructions.

Odhiambo tore open the note and turned on the inside light which, luckily, and unusually in his experience of official cars, was working. He could just make out the distinctive script of Price-Allen. There was no salutation or signature, just the message.

> Reached Farwell on the phone. Checked and confirmed handwritten paper was amongst wife's effects. Assumed she kept it for sentimental reasons. Destroying all her 'unusual' mementoes, but I ordered him to keep paper. Important you follow instructions.

Odhiambo could not resist a feeling of triumph. He had worked his way slowly to the right conclusion. His mind conjured up the scene at the dinner table at Hawk's Nest. What a group! Virtually everybody there looking at Diana Farwell, trying to conceal hate and fear.

He pulled his mind back to the present as he realized the car was approaching his destination. The driver produced identification and spoke to the nightwatchman who proceeded to open the gates. Odhiambo got out of the car and told the driver to wait at the gates. Turning to the nightwatchman he asked who was at home.

'Memsahib hapa. Bwana kwenda.'

So, she was alone as he and Price-Allen had expected. He walked across the lawn, which was lit meagrely by a pale, half-sized moon. From the direction of the house he heard agitated barking: he remembered the ridgebacks he had seen during his last visit. He hoped they were under restraint. The house servant, alerted by the dogs, appeared from the kitchen side of the house. At first, as he saw the approaching large frame of a black man, he showed signs of concern, but when Odhiambo addressed him in their native tongue he recognized the policeman and went away to acquaint his mistress of Odhiambo's arrival and to secure the dogs. Odhiambo waited on the verandah, but not for long. The door opened and Helen Shropshire appeared, framed in the light from the hall. She had changed markedly since they last met. Gone was the humour and the sympathetic demeanour: now she was a badly worried and frightened woman nearing the end of her tether.

'Inspector! My goodness, what brings you here at this time of night? Is there something wrong?'

'Mrs Shropshire, good evening. I'm sorry to disturb you again, and at night. And I apologize for my appearance. I have been . . . er . . . in circumstances today where I have not been able to change and wash. But it is essential that I see you. May I come in?'

The woman hesitated and ran a hand through her already tousled hair. Finally she stood aside to allow her visitor to enter and then led him to the lounge. Odhiambo noticed a half-filled glass and a gin bottle on the small table beside her chair.

'Your husband is at the centre?'

'Yes, yes, he is. He is very busy at the moment. He has to spend most of his time there.'

Her voice was shaky and her eyes would not meet his.

'Mrs Shropshire, I think you have been lying to me. About what you saw when you were looking for your husband at Hawk's Nest just as Diana Farwell was being killed.' He paused. The woman swayed as if she was feeling faint and then collapsed into her chair. 'There have been too many deaths,

Mrs Shropshire. We have to end this matter now before there is another.'

Helen Shropshire looked up at him; her mouth opened but no words came. Suddenly tears welled up in her eyes and rolled unheeded down her face.

'You must tell me the truth. And now, before it's too late.' Odhiambo spoke in a quiet but insistent voice. 'I know why Diana had to die. And now we have the proof.'

Again the mouth opened with no sound emerging. Finally, the woman seemed to gather herself together and words emerged.

'No. It can't be. I don't believe it.'

But her tone belied her words. Odhiambo knew that she did believe it and that it was not a sudden revelation. All her anxious amateur probings were a subconscious effort to prevent her mind accepting the truth. He waited for the woman to find the strength to accept that her nightmare was reality. At last she wiped a finger casually under her eyes and started to speak.

'You see, he said he saw me in the corridor. He was behind me so it seemed harmless for me to say I saw him too. Saved unnecessary suspicion, I thought, but – '

The woman was interrupted by the sound of the telephone. Almost subconsciously she reached for it. As her hand grasped the receiver, Odhiambo shouted an urgent appeal.

'If that's your husband, you must say nothing. Do you – '

He, in turn, was cut off as Helen Shropshire spoke.

'Hello . . . Oh, Peter, it's you . . . Has anyone been?. . . Well . . .' She looked at the policeman who was frantically shaking his head. 'Er . . . no, no. Why? Are you coming home? No, there's nothing wrong. Do I? Well, it's just that things are getting on top of me . . . No, I'm all right. I'll wait for you.'

She replaced the telephone wearily and turned her face away from Odhiambo. He was already on his way to the door. Her tone in the conversation with her husband belied her words. He could guess what impression it had left on her listener. He paused as another concern hit him: if he left the woman here and somehow missed her husband *en route* there was a distinct danger involved.

'Come. Come with me quickly,' he said with urgent emphasis. 'Come on. You must come with me.'

The woman hesitated for a moment and then, as if sleep-walking, crossed the room towards him. He grabbed her hand and hustled her to the car. The house servant appeared as they reached the front door. Odhiambo ordered him, in Luo, to wait for further instructions. He almost pulled the woman along and bundled her into the car.

'The Livestock Disease Centre, and fast,' he said to the driver.

Odhiambo and Helen Shropshire sat in silence during the journey, each preoccupied with their thoughts. To Odhiambo the journey seemed agonizingly slow but the driver reached the centre within fifteen minutes. Odhiambo shouted at the watchman who was slow fumbling with the gates. Behind the gates he could see lights burning on the top floor of the main building. He remembered his last visit here as the car covered the final yards. He turned to Helen as he left the car.

'Stay here until I come back. Stay in the car.' And then to the driver, switching to Swahili, 'Park down there out of sight of the front here. And keep the woman with you.'

He entered the building and climbed the stairs at a run. As he neared the Director's office he slowed, caution belatedly exercising some restraint. As he hesitated a voice was raised high enough to be heard through the door.

'Come on in, Inspector. Somehow I thought it might be you.'

Odhiambo went in. Peter Shropshire was sitting at his desk, his hands in his lap. He seemed composed and gestured towards a chair on Odhiambo's side of the desk.

'I could tell, you see, that someone was with Helen. And that she knew. Then I rang Albinger's house. The servant answered. Said there'd been a big *shauri*. Policemen. Man shot. So I knew the game was up.'

Odhiambo walked across to the desk as Shropshire spoke, but remained standing.

'Mr Shropshire, I am taking you into custody for the murder – '

Shropshire brought his right hand up into sight from between his thighs. His hand held a revolver, now pointing at Odhiambo.

'No, you're not taking me in, Inspector. You think I'm going to go to one of your Kenyan cells? No way. And then be hanged by one of your fellows? He'd probably botch it.'

'You'll have a good lawyer. There's no certainty you'll be found guilty. You'll do yourself no – '

Once again he was interrupted, this time by the sound of car doors slamming. Peter Shropshire grinned and gestured with the revolver.

'Your friends have arrived. Open the window and tell them to hold off or they have a dead inspector to explain away. We have to talk.'

Odhiambo needed no urging. If Price-Allen's goons came hurtling in he was as liable to be shot as Shropshire. He opened the window and looked out. By the light of the headlights and the security lights in the compound he could see a cluster of figures amongst whom he could pick out Price-Allen and Helen Shropshire. She and his driver were apparently filling Price-Allen in on the current situation. He shouted down.

'Price-Allen, this is Odhiambo. I am here with Shropshire. He is armed. Please hold your men . . .' He stopped as he saw two more women and realized that Cari and Jennifer Harris were amongst the new arrivals.

Price-Allen looked up. Odhiambo could almost see the irritation on his face.

'Ah, Inspector. Once again you are inconveniently ahead of the rest of us, I see. How should we proceed?'

'What's my wife doing here? Cari, you've no business here – '

He was destined, it seemed, to be prevented from completing any statement. Price-Allen from below and Shropshire, behind him, were as one in interjecting that this was no time for domestic conversations. Cari herself started to shout to him, but stopped, realizing the impossibility of conducting a rational conversation in this bedlam of confusion. She restricted herself to an admonition to her husband to take care. It was a little late for that, Odhiambo thought. He returned his attention to Price-Allen.

'I suggest you hold off for a time, while I seek Mr Shropshire's co-operation. He is armed, as I say, and I am not.'

He felt the gun pressed against his spine as Shropshire, reassured perhaps by his statement that he was unarmed, got closer to him and shouted from the window.

'Anyone comes up here and the inspector will be killed. I am very serious. I will contact you after Odhiambo and I have worked something out.' Shropshire pulled back and continued to Odhiambo. 'Close the window and go over and lock the door.'

Odhiambo obeyed and returned to the desk. Shropshire was seated again and once more waved his hand towards a chair. This time Odhiambo accepted the invitation. Shropshire rested his gun hand on the desk. Odhiambo found it difficult to take his eyes away from the end of the barrel: it was the first time he had been threatened by a gun at close quarters. He looked up as Shropshire spoke.

'There's no way out, is there, Inspector? If I use you as a hostage to get out of here, where do I go? What have you to offer? And don't waste time with talk of going quietly. I've told you, no way.'

'I was trying to tell you. You may get off. Give yourself a chance.'

Shropshire shook his head.

'No. I'm not a fool. You must have got those Ugandans. We're too far down the road now. Tell me, Odhiambo, what led you to me?'

Odhiambo thought for a second and decided that to talk, even about the case, might calm Shropshire down, reduce his hair-trigger tension.

'It seemed unlikely that the men Diana Farwell had just met coincidentally would be driven to murder so quickly. True, the murderer seized an unexpected opportunity, but the impulse must have been in the mind for the chance to be taken without a second thought. And I knew Causington didn't do it.'

'And I suppose you had a hard job believing it was one of the women; the drunken Letty or the fair Helen.' For a moment Shropshire's voice quivered, but he regained control and continued in an even voice as if they were discussing a matter of abstract interest. 'But how did you get past suspicion? What mistake did I make?'

'You and George Albinger told me about the Lusaka connection. In a way that was a master-stroke. As you volunteered it to me as well as bringing it to Albinger's attention, how could there be any guilty motive? Why did you raise the Lusaka end?'

'Because I saw Albinger at Hawk's Nest and I knew he would eventually get around to Lusaka and the fact that Diana and I had a connection through Harling, who was killed. I wanted to know if he had any papers left over from the case or whether he knew that Harling and I were working closely together. I couldn't rest somehow without knowing whether he was likely to get suspicious. I don't know whether it was me who got him going. I think not. He said he'd remembered before I got in touch. He didn't seem suspicious. No hint he knew about the paper. But I heard later from someone still in Lusaka that he was making enquiries. So I thought it was too risky to let him go on. He'd referred to his old cases file when I spoke to him and I got those thugs to take it, but there was nothing relevant in it. So I ask again, how did you guess?'

'Albinger's death. It didn't seem like an ordinary burglary with violence. Then I found one of his files was missing. I had asked him to make enquiries about Morgan Farwell and he did. But it seemed clear he was looking into another lead too. And Farwell could scarcely have arranged for a local murder squad. It had to be someone local. And then there were the puzzling clues that in the end provided the key. George Albinger wrote two cryptic entries in his diary. "M 1 m", which I presume referred to Morgan Farwell's one million insurance policy on his wife's life – he had just discovered this. So this was his doodling way of formulating a murder motive. But under this was another entry, "H 1 p", and a question mark against both, so it seemed reasonable to suppose that he had another murder motive in mind. It came to mind much later that H might stand for Harling, your colleague and Mrs Farwell's boyfriend. Only today I confirmed that "1 p" stood for one paper, and Farwell has found a copy in his wife's effects. The other clue was that on Albinger's desk was one journal out of place with all the legal stuff: a veterinary journal with academic papers, several years old. One of the papers was yours: only it wasn't yours, was it? Your reputation and eminent position in this centre are due to a major work that was written by Harling. You took the opportunity offered by his death to steal his work. Only, unfortunately for you, Diana Farwell had a handwritten copy. What did you have – a typed version?'

As he spoke Odhiambo placed his own hands casually on to the desk, trying to hold Shropshire in eye-to-eye contact as he waited for a chance to grab the hand holding the gun. He was thwarted as Shropshire suddenly leaned back in his chair with the gun held above the chair-arm, pointing with hypnotic attraction at Odhiambo. When Shropshire spoke his voice had changed: it had the reflective, resigned tone of one who has seen his end and come to accept it.

'Yes, it was typed in the office. Also, his notebook was still there with early draft sections scribbled in it. I didn't know until later that he had a full longhand draft and that bloody bitch had it. Do you know what it's like, Inspector, to have your fate in the hands of a woman like that?' Shropshire laughed quietly to himself. 'Of all the women Harling could have been sleeping with, it had to be Diana.'

Odhiambo was interested, despite himself.

'But she didn't ask for money? She didn't blackmail you?'

Shropshire laughed again and for a moment the gun barrel wobbled, but too quickly the round blackness focused back on to Odhiambo's face.

'No, she wasn't the type to give up enjoyment for pecuniary gain. She got her kicks from keeping her victims in suspense for ever. Always the impending threat that one day she would lower the sword: the sword of Damocles. But I had nearly managed to forget her when, bugger me, she turns up married to Morgan Farwell. I tell you, Odhiambo, that was a shock and a half when she came through Customs on Farwell's arm. She got him to come, of course. She wanted to watch one of her victims squirm. Then she got a bonus, meeting some more wretches at that bloody tree place. What did she have on them, Inspector?' He paused, but Odhiambo remained silent, his thoughts on how he was to act when Shropshire finally ended the conversation. Shropshire grimaced and continued. 'Anyway, it doesn't matter now. I was out on the platform getting a bit of fresh air when she suddenly appeared: she saw me going out there, it seems. "Ah, Peter," she said, "I've been thinking. I think you should propose to your managing committee, or whatever, that your new laboratory should be named after poor Bob Harling; to recognize his pioneering work!" I laughed in her face, sort of calling her bluff. But she said she was serious; that the time had come for him to have the recognition he deserved and she was going to send the paper to the journal that published mine. Suddenly there was a rifle shot. "Oh, goody," she said, "he's done it. I must get to a good vantage point." But instead of going she leaned over the rail and then there was the noise of the elephants. It seemed my chance had come. After all, they were off to the coast a day or two later. It was now or never. And then I saw the axe.'

Odhiambo never knew why he asked such a trivial follow-up question. 'Where were they going to stay at the coast?'

'Oh, I don't know. Malindi. The new place, I think.'

Odhiambo heard a noise outside the door. Price-Allen, no doubt, was organizing his forces. Shropshire heard it too; his eyes flickered towards the door and back to Odhiambo.

'I think your friend Price-Allen is coming. Could it be he doesn't care if you get killed in the process?' Shropshire smiled and then added, 'Good luck, Odhiambo.'

The action was so sudden that Odhiambo was left thunderstruck in his chair. The gun was raised, the hand reversed, the barrel thrust into the mouth: the explosion. Odhiambo shut his eyes against the horror of the splattering of bone, tissue and brain. Behind him the door burst open as a boot crashed against the lock. The man with the machine-pistol released a few shots before he assimilated the scene. Odhiambo, who was not hit, was never sure whether the shots were warning ones or whether the policeman was a lousy marksman.

As Price-Allen entered, Odhiambo slipped away to find Cari. She was coming up the stairs, her face revealing the fears of what had transpired in Shropshire's office. When she saw her husband she leant against the wall to prevent herself from falling. He reached out for her and, as they embraced, it was James Odhiambo, tired, nerves stretched by a day of near-triumph, imprisonment, and now the bloody and traumatic denouement, who wept.

EPILOGUE

As he sat with his wife in the departure lounge of Nairobi's Jomo Kenyatta airport watching the British Airways jumbo manoeuvring to a stop, Chief Inspector Odhiambo knew that his feeling of discontent was hardly justified. He had been lucky. The wrath of a frustrated Regional Administrator had been thwarted by Price-Allen, who had used the unmasking of the true murderer to good effect in damaging the credibility of

Aramgu in the mind of the President. Aramgu had been named as Ambassador to Algeria, which should dispose of him, at least for the time being. Odhiambo was too seasoned in Kenyan politics to suppose that Aramgu's day might not yet come. His own promotion was announced to him by Masonga; his initial reaction was to decline.

'It's a bribe, isn't it?' he said to his patient superior. 'Keep quiet about Price-Allen and his methods. And the Fulton connection.'

Masonga sighed.

'Don't be a bigger fool than God made you, Odhiambo. Price-Allen doesn't fear you. Your promotion is overdue and, yes, thanks to his experiencing your work at close hand, Price-Allen was able to remove any stumbling blocks in State House. There's more than just the promotion. You've been selected to attend a Senior Officers' Management Course in England. At the Police College there. Six months, Odhiambo, a nice break. A place has become free, unexpectedly.'

So in the end he accepted the promotion and the gift-wrapped trip, plainly intended to get him, like Aramgu, out of the way. He was going because Cari threatened to leave him if he didn't and because he couldn't think of any other course of action that was feasible. But he didn't like the situation or himself.

The departure announcement echoed unintelligibly across the lounge. The passengers, many appearing sleepy as midnight had passed, rose to make their way down the passage to the plane.

Cari took her husband's arm.

'Come on, James. I'm going to settle you into your English college and then on to the States for my meetings. Forget Price-Allen, Hawk's Nest and all the *mzungus* involved. It's a new start.'

Odhiambo managed a grin, but he didn't believe it. Somehow he knew in his Luo bones that his destiny was here.

As they entered the plane and made their way to their seats, Odhiambo caught sight of a familiar face already seated on the other side of the plane. It was Helen Shropshire returning home after settling her affairs in Kenya. She did not see him and Odhiambo made no move to attract her attention. He had visited her a week after her husband's death. She had not seemed to welcome his visit and he quickly took his leave. And then, as he had reached his car, standing on the verandah she had said something that puzzled him.

'Goodbye, Inspector. I'll try to forget you, but it's not for the reason you think.' And then she was gone.

Odhiambo sighed and followed his wife further into the plane. His thoughts moved on to the other woman he had seen off at the airport. A nagging doubt had refused to leave him in the days that followed Shropshire's death. Finally he telephoned Albinger's solicitor friend. With a bit of persuasion and a lot of chat the enquiry he asked for was put in hand. The result sent a chill down his spine. He approached Jennifer Harris as she passed through the emigration channels.

'Good evening, Miss Harris.'

He admired her coolness. A perceptible start and then composure and a smile.

'Inspector. How lovely to see you. Is this coincidence? Are you on duty?'

'No, I'm not. But it's not a coincidence either. I wanted to ask you a question.'

The blue eyes gazed intently into his.

'Goodness. Whatever can it be, Inspector?'

'Why were you at Hawk's Nest? Were you hoping for an opportunity there, or were you waiting for your chance at the Sailing Dhow Hotel?'

Another pause.

'I think I must go, Inspector. I want to keep my happy memories of you. I was at Hawk's Nest with my uncle. You know that.'

She moved towards the narrow escalator that rose to the departure area. Odhiambo spoke to her back.

'You and your lover, Morgan Farwell, are lucky. Shropshire did for you what you were planning to do yourselves. Just remember this. When you are in the way, he may seek a similar solution again. And tell him from me that he should keep one eye open when sleeping with you. I hope the insurance money chokes the pair of you.'

As he eased into his seat next to Cari he could see now in his mind's eye the little smile he received as she briefly turned back to face him. Then she turned again and was gone.

High in the office tower one office was still occupied. The man saw the lights of the plane as it rose into the air and turned towards Mount Kenya. He checked his watch. Probably Airways, he thought, with a potential loose end nicely tie Odhiambo could have been dangerous. Actually, he could be useful one day, as long as he outgrew his ludicrous sense integrity. Ah well, sufficient for the day is the evil thereof. And he laughed.